Meet Me in the Parking Lot

Other works by Alexandra Leggat:

Fiction
Pull Gently, Tear Here

Poetry
This is me since yesterday

Meet Me in the Parking Lot

Alexandra Leggat

implosion
imprint

INSOMNIAC PRESS

Edited by Stephen Cain
Copy edited by Emily Schultz

National Library of Canada Cataloguing in Publication Data

Leggat, Alexandra
    Meet me in the parking lot / Alexandra Leggat.

ISBN 1-894663-61-6

I. Title.

PS8573.E461716M43 2004   C813'.54   C2003-907383-1

The publisher gratefully acknowledges the support of the Canada Council, the Ontario Arts Council and the Department of Canadian Heritage through the Book Publishing Industry Development Program. We acknowledge the support of the Government of Ontario through the Ontario Media Development Corporation's Ontario Book Initiative.

Printed and bound in Canada

Insomniac Press
192 Spadina Avenue, Suite 403
Toronto, Ontario, Canada, M5T 2C2
www.insomniacpress.com

THE CANADA COUNCIL | LE CONSEIL DES ARTS
FOR THE ARTS | DU CANADA
SINCE 1957 | DEPUIS 1957

ONTARIO ARTS COUNCIL
CONSEIL DES ARTS DE L'ONTARIO

Acknowledgements

I'd like to thank *America's Writer On-line* for publishing "The Car" and *Taddle Creek* for publishing "Sonny," "Good and Happy," and "A Time I Never Knew" — and *Esquire* for the thoughtful rejections.

I have Yves Lavigne, Hells Angels, *City Confidential*, Raider Nation and Johnny Dowd to thank for darkening my psyche.

A heartfelt thank you goes to my husband Salvatore for his invaluable advice and encouragement, and to my folks, as always, for their continuous support.

Last, but not least, I extend my gratitude to the Canada Council for the Arts for their assistance and to my editor Stephen Cain.

Thanks y'all.

for Samo

Table of Contents

Meet me in the parking lot
Up on level three
There's something I must show you
There's something you've just got to see

From "God Created Woman"
          by Johnny Dowd

THE CAR

I sleep in the car. The nondescript four-door. I love that car. Even though it stopped running a week ago.

"Get rid of the car," said Morley.

"I can't."

"Get rid of the car," he said.

I couldn't.

"Morley, just because it stopped running? If you stopped running, just stopped moving one day, I wouldn't get rid of you. I wouldn't get rid of you because you didn't move anymore. Not if you just didn't move. Not if I loved you as much as the car. Just because the car can't move, it's still a great car. It just can't do the things it used to. It's still a great car. It's simply changed its purpose. It has a new purpose. I love that car. It's serving a purpose."

Morley leaves the house at six. Rattles on the hood of the car when he passes. Just to be a jerk. It wakes me. I go back to sleep.

Melba, next door, says, "Get up when he goes to work, get up and go and sleep in the house. Why stay in the car?"

"I love the car," I tell her. "I sleep better out here. I sleep better in the back seat of the car than I ever did in bed with him. I'm fine, Melba. This is fine. I'm happy. I'm happier out here in the car. I love this car."

I've got a stack of books on the front seat. I have a reading light, runs on batteries, I read by it at night. I'm getting a lot of books read. It's good. I have a radio, runs on batteries. Just plays AM. I like AM. More talk, less music. It's the speaking I like. That and the jazz station. They do a lot of speaking on the jazz station — horn blowing. I bet Billie Holiday slept in cars.

The ashtray is overflowing. Friday I'll empty it. Open the door and dump it on Morley's shiny black driveway. It'll drive him crazy. I feel like puncturing the bottom of the car, creating an oil leak. Have oil ooze down his shiny black driveway. Oil slick. Morley'd go crazy. Couldn't do it to the car. Could never puncture the car. Would never hurt the car. I'm guessing there's more than fifty butts in the ashtray. More than fifty. I'm proud.

Morley said, get rid of the car. I refused. Told him what I told you, that I love the car, won't part with the car just because it stopped moving. So he said, "Fine take your goddamn love for that shitty piece of metal and live with it. Go and be with your godforsaken piece of metal trash and all the best to you. All the best to you both. You deserve each other."

And I said, "Fine. Fine and you're right, Morley. You are right. We do deserve each other. You are right. I love that car and that car has never done anything to hurt me."

"It broke down," he said, "broke down. How's that for reliable? How's that for dependable? Godforsaken piece of lemon shit. You and that piece of shit deserve to be demolished. You will be demolished," he said and threw me and the keys on the front lawn.

I got up and marched right back into the house and upstairs and grabbed my pillow and a blanket and my reading light and my radio and books and a sweater and warm socks and I marched right back down the stairs, out the door and into the car. Locked all the doors and went to sleep. Slept like a baby 'til Morley rattled on the hood when he passed. I opened my eyes just as his fat belly was brushing passed the windows.

And I went back to sleep and slept like a baby 'til Melba came knocking on the glass. Her round face peering into the car like into a fish bowl. Looking for what seemed like more than me.

"What do you want, Melba?"

"What are you doing in there?"

"Sleeping."

Melba doesn't understand but Melba doesn't matter.

I roll down the window. She hands me a loaf of her fresh baked bread. I eat it and go back to sleep. Morley comes home around four. Peers in. Wakes me when his face squishes up to the window and casts a shadow that rouses me. An ominous presence, enough to rouse me. His face pressed against the window like an astronaut against his helmet.

"What?"

"Unlock the door."

"Why?"

"I need something out of the car."

"Too bad."

"Open the car door," he says, like he's RoboCop.

"*Step away from the vehicle, sir*," I say, like I am too because I will not be outdone.

"What?" he says, then he does because he's that stupid.

I open my book. I read a few lines and stop because something's looming off to the side of me and it's distracting. Morley's standing there. Still standing a few feet away looking at the car. Just standing there, waiting for his next instruction.

"Go into the house, Morley."

"What?"

"Go into the house," I yell slowly, opening my mouth rounder with each word so he'll possibly read my lips and for backup, I point to the house. Point at the house hoping that if all else fails he will follow the direction my finger is pointing and move toward the building in which he lives and enter it, close the door and never come back out. Not until I tell him. Which I won't.

"No," he yells back. "I need something out of the car."

He storms up to the car, tries the door on the driver side. Storms around to the passenger side and screams. He's looking down and screaming.

It's Friday. I dumped the ashtray out the passenger seat door onto the shiny black driveway. Drained the bottles I've been peeing in over the butts, the ash. It's a wet, grey clump of vile-smelling filth.

SONNY

It's a small town. Everyone knows Sonny hit the guy. Everyone knows Sonny. He drives through red lights. He isn't colour-blind. He ran a red and hit a guy. The police came. Sonny was gone.

He pulls over on the side of the highway to think. Watches the eighteen-wheelers creep across the bridge past customs, and motor on. Sonny always wanted to be a truck driver. Thinks the trucks are beautiful. The way they move across the highway at night like monsters. Cabs as big as apartments. He likes the black ones — the phantoms. Once he tried to hitchhike across the country and only stuck out his thumb when he saw a black one, but the black ones don't stop.

He contemplates ditching the car, sticking out his thumb for a sleek eighteen-wheeler to deliver him from consequence. But he doesn't. He goes home. When Sonny gets home, the keys don't work in the locks. It's late. Puzzled, he walks to the back of the house. The bedroom light is on. He knocks on the window. A thin hand moves the curtain aside and a woman presses her face up against the glass. He bangs on it. She screams and jumps back.

"Jesus," he says, "what the hell's going on?" He bangs his fist against the window again and again.

"What do you want?" yells the woman. "What do you want? 'Cause I'm calling the police. I'll get Jim over here. Jim will be over here in a flash and that'll be it for you."

"Well, that's fine, because if you don't get the hell out of my house, I'll call the police and you'll be out on your ass so fast you won't know what hit you. So, if you're smart lady, you'll get the hell out of my house before Jim gets here."

Sonny picks up a rock and throws it at the window. It bounces off. Sonny isn't afraid of Jim. He's been dealing with him for years, for one reason or another. In fact, the last time Jim locked Sonny up, they played poker all night and Sonny whipped his ass. It turned out Sonny hadn't really broken into the Smith's house anyway. He just got confused on his way home from the bar and walked into the wrong house and ended up crawling into Amy Smith's bed. And Amy Smith screamed like any teenage girl would if some drunken man crawled into her bed at night. Bob Smith stuck the tip of his hunting rifle up Sonny's nose and hoisted him out of the bed. Sonny screamed and ran out of the house with Bob Smith chasing him and Jim waiting at the foot of the driveway with his men. Poor Sonny was so disoriented. Jim took him away in the cruiser and locked him up just to appease Bob Smith really. So Bob Smith wouldn't accuse Jim of not doing his job.

"What do you mean, 'Get out of your house'?"

Sonny turns around. A young woman in a yellow housecoat and yellow slippers approaches Sonny with a carving knife. Her red hair is piled on her head like a turban. Her redder lips flap at him in a way that reminds him of his mother.

"Jesus, lady, put that thing away. I'm not going to hurt you. I just want to go to sleep. I've been on the road. I'm tired. I just want to go to bed but turns out that some dame's already in it. And on any other night that would be the answer to my prayers but tonight I just wouldn't know what to do with a gift like that and I will thank whichever one of my friends was kind enough to give me such a thoughtful welcome home gift but..."

Sonny stops. He doesn't have any friends. He looks at the young woman. She looks at him and puts down the knife.

"Would you like to come in?" she asks.

"Yeah."

"I'm Amanda."

"I'm Sonny."

"Sonny what?"

"Sonny and warm. Ha, ha."

"That's not funny."

"Oh."

"Really, Sonny who?"

"Sonny James. What difference does it make?"

"Well, I'm not going to let you into my house if I don't know your last name. I mean, what kind of a girl do you think I am? God, you have to be so careful these days. You can't go inviting just anyone into your home. How do I know who you are? How do I know you're not some freak? I've never seen you before. I don't know where you're from. I don't know where you live."

"I live here."

Amanda stops on the porch and looks at him.

"This is my house, Amanda."

Amanda sits down on the porch. Sonny does too. She sighs, gets up and takes a deep breath.

"Maybe you better go," she says.

"Where?"

"Look, it's late. We can't do anything about this tonight. Let's talk in the morning."

Amanda goes inside. Sonny stands on the porch, watches her walk into his house, close the door, lock it and turn out the porch light. He turns and looks at the street. He watches the neighbour's cat cross the road and disappear into the backyard. He watches his breath.

"Jesus," he says.

He sits back down on the step. His heart sinks into his stomach. An emptiness comes over him he hasn't felt since his mother shoved him out of the car onto the side of the highway one afternoon and left him there, alone, in the heat. He was twelve. After a few hours another car came by. An old, white Chevy. He remembers because he thought it was sent from heaven. His legs were getting weak, his lips drier than chalk, his eyes rolling into the back of his head and he saw a light — *the* light. Through that light came a glimmering white automobile, in slow motion. Angelic voices sang in harmony amidst the cloud of dust. It pulled up to Sonny and stopped. The door slowly opened and he smelled something like home-baked bread and chocolate-chip cookies and he was sure he was saved.

Mrs. Nichols tells a different story. She was driving home from church. She decided to go and visit her mother and somehow got lost and ended up on Dragnet Highway, which is what all the young punks call it. They race cars there because nobody really drives on it. It has too much gravel and dust and it doesn't really lead to anywhere worthwhile. One of those mistakes a town makes attempting to improve things. Mrs. Nichols kept on driving when she thought she saw the silhouette of a child. At this point she thought she was hallucinating from the heat but the closer she got the clearer it became that there was a young boy standing on the side of the highway. She slowed down and as she got closer she could see that it was Sonny James. She slammed her foot on the brake and tried to turn around. It was too late. He'd already spotted her. She opened the door. He got in and closed the door.

"What are you doing out here, Sonny?"

"Waiting."

"Waiting for what?"

"My mom."

"Is she supposed to pick you up? Should I take you back? What were you doing out there? There doesn't look like there's too much to do out there."

Sonny stared out the windscreen.

"I didn't see your mom in church."

"Hmm."

"Was she supposed to pick you up after church?"

Sonny looked out the passenger-seat window at the dead-cow carcasses on the side of the road, the dormant tumbleweed — the dry earth.

"You'll be a little sunburnt tonight," said Mrs. Nichols.

She turned off the highway into town. Sonny's stomach churned as she turned down his street. His heart went limp when he saw his house — the empty driveway. He looked at Mrs. Nichols.

"Oh my, I'll feel so bad if your mom's out there on that highway looking for you. I should have left you there."

Sonny was angry. He wondered how Mrs. Nichols could be so thick. It was understandable that he would take a little longer to get it. That it wouldn't be obvious to him that his own mother would kick him out of the car and abandon him on an abandoned highway in mid-August at midday in the sweltering heat. Just leave him there to die, to burn, to dry up like the dead cows on the side of the road — to stop tumbling like the tumbleweeds. Why would a mother do that? But Mrs. Nichols should've been suspicious. She should know better.

"Well then, Sonny, you'll be safer here anyway. You're better off waiting here for her to come home."

"She's not coming home, Mrs. Nichols," Sonny said as he got out of the car.

Jim's police cruiser pulls around the corner with its high beams on, no flashing lights or sirens. Sonny takes a deep breath and walks down to the curb to meet it.

Jim rolls down the window and says, "Sonny James. Well, I never would have guessed you'd show your face in this town again."

"Jesus, Jim, you'd think I hit that guy on purpose or something. Dumb bastard had it coming to him."

"Let's go, kid."

Sonny looks at Jim, looks at his house. Jim puts the cruiser in reverse. Sonny gets in. They drive for a bit in silence.

"There's someone in my house, Jim."

"Look, kid, I got a call up on the hill, I'll let you off here, we'll talk later." Jim drops Sonny off at the bar. Just leaves him standing there staring with his mouth half-open. Jim throws him a few bucks and the key to his room at the motel. Jim has his own room at the motel. Says it's for police business. Sonny's too tired, too confused to question it. He just wants a beer, some sleep and morning.

He sits at the bar, eats peanuts and sucks on a cold bottle of beer. He orders another beer and looks around the bar. He doesn't recognize anyone. He thought he knew everyone in this town. The man a couple of seats down reading the paper munches peanuts and chuckles away to himself.

"What's so funny?" Sonny asks.

"The news," says the man.

"The news is funny?"

The man looks at Sonny and laughs. Sonny watches him. Watches and feels himself start to laugh. Feels his stomach tightening in the way a stomach tightens when you try and prevent it from laughing. Sonny can't stop it anymore and the two men are laughing their guts out at the bar. Slapping their knees, holding their stomachs, wiping their eyes.

"Oh, God," says the man. "God, I haven't laughed like that in years."

"Yeah," says Sonny. "I've never laughed like that."

The man laughs a little more.

"What's so funny?" asks Sonny.

"The news," says the man, shaking his paper.

"Oh, yeah," says Sonny, "the news. Huh."

Sonny looks down at the bar, looks at his hands, looks at his hands and feels tears welling up in his eyes. Not laughing tears, not the funny kind. Real tears. The bar is silent, as if everyone tiptoed out when he wasn't looking, are tiptoeing out now while they think he's not noticing, but he can feel them leaving. Can feel them vacating behind his back. He doesn't turn around.

"Do you want another beer, kid?"

The man moves closer to Sonny. Slides his beer along the bar with him and motions to the bartender to get them another.

"You know, you look familiar, kid. I don't know why. I just get that feeling. You know that feeling you get about people."

"No, I don't," says Sonny.

"Oh, come on, kid, you know."

Sonny looks at the guy. "No, I don't know."

"Funny, I had a friend once, swore we had been related in a past life. He was adamant. He'd tell people we used to be brothers. People'd get so confused. Used to be? Used to be? They'd say. And we'd laugh. How can you not be someone's brother anymore?"

Sonny stares at him.

"So, you from around here?" the man asks.

"Yeah."

"You live in the neighbourhood?"

"Sort of."

"Oh. Wife trouble?" He laughs.

"No."

"Oh, lucky. Man, have I got wife trouble."

"Look mister, it was fun laughing with you but I'm tired."

"Hey, it's okay. I understand." The man leans closer to Sonny and whispers, "I can help you."

"What?"

"I've been reading about it in the papers. I can help you. It's okay. I understand. I could read it on your face, could tell the second I saw you. I'll help. I'll do it."

"What are you talking about?"

"Oh come on, don't play dumb with me. Look at you. You're pale, sweaty. Look at your hands. They haven't stopped shaking. Look at all the napkins you're destroying. You're a wreck. Look at you."

"I'm fine. There's nothing wrong with me. I'm tired. I come home and someone else is living in my house. I just need a good night's sleep. I need to get my house back, my clothes, my TV. I just need to be home. I need my home. That's all, mister."

"It's okay. I know we all think we can look after things on our own. That reaching out for help isn't very manly. But it's okay. I understand. I cry. Man, if I told my wife. But I cry. I do, and you know what? It's okay."

The man pats Sonny on the back. Sonny stands up, knocks over the stool. Picks up his empty beer bottle.

"Easy there, kid. Look, I'm just trying to help you. I offered to help you. I've been reading about all those assisted suicide doctors and people like that and I understand. I understand that it's not so easy to put a gun in your own mouth or jump off a bridge.

You know, you need someone there to pull the trigger, to push you. Think how much easier that would be — less pressure, faster."

"What are you talking about? I don't want to die. I don't want to kill myself. I don't want you to kill me. I don't even know you. "

"What's going on here, Sonny?" says Jim as he enters the bar. "Can't I leave you alone for a second without causing some kind of trouble?"

"Officer," says the man. He nods at Jim, sits back down on his stool, spins around and reads his paper.

Jim puts a set of handcuffs around Sonny's wrists and escorts him out of the bar toward a waiting ambulance.

"What's going on here, Jim? I'm not sick. I'm not sick."

"Oh, yes you are, Sonny."

GOOD AND HAPPY

I'm at my regular seat at the bar. A tall man in jeans and a ratty green T-shirt walks in and sits down next to me. I say hi. He sets his eyes on me. He's not from around here. I've seen every pair of eyes in this town and these are unfamiliar. He rubs his thighs, rubs his hands together like he's just come in from the cold. It's August. I look at him and smile. He orders a rye, throws it down his throat and shivers. I imagine it flowing through his sleek insides. He puts his elbows on the bar and rubs the back of his neck. The skin around his fingernails is stained. It looks like rust. Maybe he works with cars, builds fences. He orders another rye, lifts it to his mouth.

Bottoms up, I say. He raises the glass to me, swallows its contents in a gulp. He wipes his mouth, looks over at me and chuckles. He asks for my name. I tell him. He repeats it. Luanne, Luanne, Luanne. I like the way he says my name, the quiver in his voice. He brushes his ratty black curls off his forehead and tells me he's tired, been driving awhile. I tell him, relax you're in good hands. He raises his eyebrows, sighs and tells me he likes me.

We have a few drinks. Talk about the long, hard summer. The dry heat. He tells me this has been a summer to end all summers. I tell him mine has been like every other one that came before it. It rains on the same days. He complains about his car, the broken air conditioning, the condition of the interstate. I tell him I've never been on the interstate but I've fallen into every pothole on RR1. He looks at me, but not at me. I jostle his knee. His jeans are damp and discoloured, like he spilled his coffee on them earlier. He raises my chin with his chapped hand and says he could take me away from all this. I give him my hand. Take me away from it, I say, whatever it is.

We stumble across the parking lot to his motel. Enter room 29. He throws the keys on the table, himself on the bed. He holds his head and mumbles something about the booze, the drive. I lie down next to him. He strokes the hair out of my eyes. His breath is warm against my face, his arm tightly bound around my waist. He snores. It figures. I lie still for a moment staring at the ceiling. I move his arm. He doesn't budge. I get up and tiptoe around the room, look over my shoulder every few seconds to make sure he's still sleeping. He has a side to him. I sensed it at the bar. He would not be pleased if he caught me fingering his belongings. And I don't want to make this man mad. I want to make him happy — good and happy.

Today's paper is on the desk. The crossword is incomplete and lying next to unfinished coffees, old milk coagulating. Clothes are strewn across the chair. A black T-shirt, jeans, underwear, briefs — a bra. A bra? Strange. He's strange. A bra? I look at him. The bra is small, too small for him. Too small for him — well, of course. I laugh at myself; at the crazy notion that for a moment I thought it was his. Then whose? Now it's not so funny. It's odd. It's more than odd. This bra. This tiny bra. 32A, exactly. Must be a young girl's, a teenager's, a thin teenager, a thin woman, a thin older woman — an anorexic. He turns over, mutters something about another drink, something "bitch," something, and another drink. I drop the bra, look around, then plop myself into the chair. I sit and watch him sputter in his sleep. I sit here and wonder why I'm sitting here in this drunken man's motel room. A skinny girlfriend on her way back for her bra any minute.

It's long gone 3 a.m.and I'm still sitting here. He's cute, but he's not that cute. I'm tired. I guess that's it. Too tired to get up and find my way home.

The bathroom door's shut. I'm assuming it's the bathroom door. Maybe I'll have a bath. No. A bath's too noisy. And what would he think of me coming back to his motel room and helping myself to a bath. But a bath would be nice. Hot, bubbly. Would he care? He might like it, might join me.

With an eye on him, I get up and go to the bathroom door. I open it slowly and back into the bathroom. I close the door, lock it, lean on it with my eyes closed and sigh. Sigh like I'm safe, like I've escaped him. Escaped him successfully and now I'm locked in the bathroom. It smells. Smells like rot, like sickness. I feel around the wall for the light. I flick the light switch and nothing happens. It's too dark to see where anything is.

My eyes aren't adjusting to the darkness like they should. They're not seeing outlines of anything — not the mirror, the toilet, the tub. The tub must be close. I shuffle my feet around. Hit something. I can't breathe. I look up. A speck of something gleams in the corner. Gleams in the corner like a small window covered. A bit of it not covered, letting light in from somewhere — the parking lot, the pool.

I find the toilet, put its lid down, stand on it and reach for the speck. I grab what feels like cardboard. I dig my nails into it and rip it down. Light. I can breathe. I can breathe and I can feel the sweat drying on my brow and I shake my head at this lunacy. Shake my head, jump down from the toilet and drop to my knees. I hold my stomach and vomit on the floor.

There's a woman in the tub. She's screaming with her eyes. Her mouth is bound, her arms and legs bound. Her hair is oily dreads. Her body's thin, naked, blue. She is breathing. She is blinking and she is trying to say something.

"Jesus Christ," I whisper. "Don't make a sound, Please, please be quiet."

Let me think. I can't think. Let me try to think. Oh, God. Dear God, don't let him wake up. Let him die, die in his sleep. Dear God, dear God, dear God, let this not be true. Let this not be true. I'm hallucinating. I must be hallucinating. I'm sick. This is sick. Okay, okay, okay. Take a deep breath. Get me out of here. God, please get me out of here. The window is too small — barely big enough for a voice to get through. It doesn't look like it opens. If I yell he'll hear me. He'll burst through the locked door and kill us both. Let me think. I climb up on the toilet and study the window. It opens, pushes out, pushes out but I can't see. I'm too short. I can reach it but I can't see through it. I could dangle something out of it. I'll dangle what? The bloody towel. That's it. I grab the towel.

The handle of the door turns. It turns and the whole door starts rattling. Jesus Christ. She's screaming with her eyes again, moaning. I'm searching for razors, poison. He bursts through the door. We're caught. I slump down on the toilet. He wipes his mouth. His face is red. He walks back into the room. I hear the click of a cigarette lighter. The smoke wafts into the bathroom. It makes me sick. I vomit on the bathroom floor again. She closes her eyes. He comes back to the door with the cigarette and a drink in his hand. I cover the vomit with my feet.

"Well, looks like I made a big mistake," he says. "I should have known better than to get drunk in a shit-hole tavern and pick up a local girl and bring her back to my motel room. I should have known better than to think I could fall asleep without her prowling around my business. Should have known better than to think a pretty, little small-town girl wouldn't mind her own fucking business. I should have known better. Drink?"

"No. Thanks."

"Cigarette?"

"No."

"Uh, what's your name again?"

"Lou. Luanne."

"Luanne. Hmm. This is Abby."

"Abby? Hello, Abby," I say. I try to smile. I tell myself, just be normal. Just act normal, like this is completely normal. A tied and bound and beaten girl named Abby in the bathtub of some motel, a man and me — normal, perfectly normal.

He pulls the chair into the doorway of the bathroom. Abby strains her neck to see him, to watch him. I look at her and try to send a signal. Some look in code that he won't pick up on. She's not looking at me.

"You okay?" he asks.

"Me?" I ask. "Yeah, I'm okay. I'm good. I'm fine. Sure. Me? Yeah, no problem. I'm good. Good and happy. Sure, everything's okay. You?"

"Yeah, I'm a little tired. My head's sore. I guess I drank too much. But, Jesus, I just couldn't take it anymore. I woke up and the whole world was sitting on top of me. I thought, my God, where did I go wrong? I tried my best for my wife and our beautiful new child. I did my fucking best. I've got debts. But I work hard. Everything was under control I thought. Tables were turning I thought. But Abby lost it. She just up and fucking lost it. I tried to help her. I did. I did everything I could. I told her we needed to step back and think. I tried to keep myself together. I tried. But as soon as I parked the goddamn car, opened the door to this quiet, little room where I just wanted to lie down for a couple of hours in peace, rest my head and think about what the hell we were going to do, she started on me. And you know I feel bad for her I do. But I can't let it go. I cannot forgive her...."

I look at Abby. She's looking at me and I'm thinking of everything. Where's the child? He said a wife and child? Where the hell is the child? But I'm afraid to ask. I'm afraid in general. I can't feel my limbs, my body. My body has disappeared. I'm a trembling mind on a toilet seat, in a rundown motel, in a small town in America. I'm insignificant, soon to be non-existent. That I can feel.

"I have to lie down," he mumbles. He gets up and goes into the room. I don't believe he's going to lie down. I can't see him. I can't move. I don't want to move. I look at Abby. She's looking at her toes. It seems like she's looking at her toes. Her eyes are pooling. She's staring at her toes, tears oozing down her defeated face.

"Abby," I whisper, "be strong."

I can't hear anything. I don't believe he's sleeping. I bet he's waiting outside the bathroom with a sawed-off shotgun for me to run out and make my way to the door. He's waiting for me to make a stupid move. He'll have to wait forever. But Abby can't wait forever. I get up and slowly walk into the room. He's lying on the bed, staring at the ceiling.

He looks over at me and moans, "Will you help me?"

"Me? Uh, yeah, yes of course, I'll help you. What would you like me to do?"

"Kill Abby."

"What?"

"It won't be that hard. She's half gone. She's like a fly been trapped inside a house too long. One swipe and she's done. Then we can go, go and start fresh, you and me. I like you. You've got a good head on your shoulders. We can go, go and find my boy. Go and find my boy. Find out what part of the lake she dumped him in."

ATHENA FROM LOBO

Athena arrives at work, stops at the refurbished entrance and stares at the outlandish door. The latest in the Castles-of-Europe series. The wood is stripped, treated and accented with decorative, wrought-iron handles. She shakes her head, shoves the heavy-leaded key in the lock. The door creaks when it opens and closes.

Inside, it's muggy and smells of yesterday's cigarettes. She puts her purse in her desk drawer and grabs the air freshener. A mix of rose petals and ammonia drifts through the room. She opens Chad's office door, waves the still air with her hand and a spray or two from the can. She passes the coffeemaker, pushes the power button.

The phone rings. Chad's wife Delores doesn't say hello to Athena, just demands to speak to Chad. Chad has asked Athena to lie when she calls this early and say he won't be in until the afternoon. He has house calls. Delores hangs up. Athena hangs up. She stares at the phone. It's cold and rigid. One call and the entire office loses its calm. She lights a cigarette, takes the phone off the hook and goes outside. She knocks on the window of her mother's hair salon. Her mother joins Athena for a cigarette.

"Delores called, " says Athena.

"The curse of Chad's Custom Doors strikes at the crack of dawn? What a nightmare," says her mother.

"I can't deal with it every goddamn morning, Jesus Christ. I wake up, get dressed, have a relaxing cup of coffee on the porch. I smoke a cigarette, pet the dog. Take a pleasant walk to work along Main, inhale the Wilson's rose garden and *boom,* the second I reach the office that screeching bitch torpedoes my ear and blows the day to shit."

"Oh, honey."

"And Chad is losing his mind. Look at the new door to the office. How far back in time does he want to go? He mutters to himself, slams things around and smokes at least two packs of Winstons at work. His blood pressure must be at breaking point. One day he'll have a heart attack at my feet and I won't know what the hell to do. I'm caught in the middle. It's ridiculous. Can't she leave him alone for a second? I have to deal with her the minute I walk through the door and somehow keep her at bay for the rest of the day. It's not fair."

"Look, honey, why don't you find another job? Something a little less stressful, somewhere you might meet a nice man. Why don't I talk to Albert over at The Co-operators? Insurance might be the way to go and Albert's got a nice wife."

"Ma, I like my job. I like Chad. I worry about him."

"Well, honey, I don't know what to say. If that's the way you feel you'll have to accept that Delores comes with the territory. I know what'll make you feel better, let me do something with your hair."

"What?"

Athena butts out her cigarette and returns to the office. She goes into the bathroom, pulls her straight, dirty blonde hair off her face and splashes cold water on it. Water drips down her beige skirt. She studies herself in the mirror. Her limp hair falls to her shoulders without a bounce. Back at her desk, she puts the phone on the hook.

There are four messages, two from Delores, one from a client regarding his new doors, and one from Athena to remind herself to mail the cheques. Athena turns up the volume and replays her message. She rolls her eyes at her droning voice.

Chad walks into the office. His face is grey. His unwashed hair's glued to his scalp. He hangs onto the handle of the new door.

"It's nice, isn't it? Good grip, good weight," he says.

"Yes, it must have looked great in eighteenth century France," she says.

"You look lovely this morning, Athena," he says.

He goes into his office and closes the door. Athena touches her crinkled white blouse she'd retrieved from the dirty laundry pile. She glances at her chewed nails, touches her unpainted lips. She puts her hair behind her ears and reaches into her purse for the pocket mirror. Nothing's changed. She calls her mother.

"I think there's something wrong with Chad."

"What?"

"Well, I'm not sure. He looks ill and he sounded odd. I think he's snapped."

"Honey, you're over-sensitive. Get a grip. He's a middle-aged man. They go through phases. Humour him. Tell him he should take some time off. You can look after things for a week."

"What?"

"Honey, I've gotta go. Take it in stride. He's trying to deal with a wife that would drive anyone crazy."

Athena stares at his office door, at the shape of the palm tree formed by the natural grain of wood. Every door in the office is different. The door to the warehouse has a porthole. The one to the bathroom is chrome with a matte black handle in the shape of a tap. Athena wants the one with handles shaped like revolvers for her bedroom door. Danny's strip joint off the highway bought one for the men's bathroom and the handle to the ladies room is a stiletto. Chad goes for the natural wood models. The closet door is an overwhelmingly welcoming, warm mahogany that makes you want to hang yourself behind it. She wonders why a man obsessed with doors finds himself in a situation with no way out. A man with a hundred doors at his fingertips and not a single one to escape through.

She calls him. He doesn't answer. She knocks on his door. He doesn't answer. She pushes on the palm tree. He's lying on his couch, one arm above his head, the other across his chest. His tie's loose around his neck and he's breathing heavily.

"Are you okay?"

"I'll be fine. No calls."

"Your wife called."

"No calls."

Athena backs out of the office and closes the door. She picks up the *Vogue* her mother brought over attempting to inspire her. Athena doesn't wear make-up or bother with fashion. She only goes out to walk to and from work. At night, she sits at home and watches TV. There's not a single man in Lobo she wants to impress. Other than her dad, Chad is the only man she's even really liked. He's been a friend of her dad's for years. When Athena left high school, Chad offered her a job and she took it. If she hadn't, she'd be sitting on the couch all day watching other people's lives on TV. In her dreams she's on the back of a motorbike with a guy in a muscle shirt. She calls the dream guy Cody and he calls her doll. She sits at her desk and looks at the six-foot high women with velvet faces, skeletal bodies, tans and large, perfectly round breasts and knows that doesn't matter in Lobo. She throws the magazine back on the coffee table and sucks in her stomach.

Chad bursts into the room, his belly hanging over the top of his pale green trousers, his chubby cheeks flushed and damp.

"Athena, let's get out of here. I need you to come for a drive with me."

"What?"

He grabs her arm. She grabs her purse. They leave out the back door and get into Chad's new aquamarine BMW. Chad rolls down his window and lights a cigarette.

"Would you like a cigarette?" he asks.

"Sure," she says. "Where are we going?"

"Away."

"Away? Where? I have to be home by dinner."

"I don't think you'll make dinner."

"Well then, I'll have to call my mother."

"Not now."

"If I don't make dinner, she'll worry."

Chad turns off the main street onto an unpaved side road. Mailboxes stand at the end of long dirt driveways waiting for news, houses are hidden by woods. Sparse trees whiz by, scraggly and sinister. The air is grimy for the country, like city air that got lost.

"These aren't exactly friendly parts, are they?" she asks.

"Don't worry, I won't let anything happen to you."

Athena closes her eyes and leans her head against the seat.

"I've never left Lobo," she says, "not even for a minute. Except once when I was a kid, I walked to the county line and put my toe over it. If that counts for leaving, well, I guess I have once. Like you, I was born and raised here. My dad's always owned the grocery store and my ma's always owned the hair salon. I left school and you came over for dinner one night and asked me if I wanted a job. When I said sure, Dad gave me my first beer. That's it."

She slaps her hands against her knees.

"Well, maybe it's time to take you somewhere you've never been," he says.

Athena opens her eyes. She looks at the road in front of her. Nothing but a streak of brown, lined with lifeless foliage and a sky devoid of anything encouraging — a bird, sunshine. Her hair flies around her face and her blouse flaps against her chest like another beating heart.

"Maybe you're right," she says. "Damn, I should have let my mother do something with my hair."

Chad's face is blank, his forehead dripping. White knuckles grip the steering wheel. He turns off the side road onto a newly paved one that leads them to the highway. He's quiet, all but completely disappeared. The radio blares. Athena doesn't like the music. A mash of jangling pianos and whining saxophones. It agitates the fillings in her teeth, makes her skin crawl. She turns it off. Chad doesn't notice.

Eighteen-wheelers storm past, swaying the car. Athena rolls up her window. Chad glances at her, slows down and pulls onto the shoulder.

"What's wrong?" she asks.

His body shakes. He cries. Athena puts her hand on his shoulder, tries to look into his face. He covers it with his hands.

"My God, Chad. It's okay. It's okay."

"I can't take it anymore, Athena. I can't."

"I'll flag down a car. We should go back. I'll drive. I'll drive you back."

"No, my God, no," he says.

He starts the car. Lurches onto the road. A pickup truck swerves into the other lane blasting its horn.

"Please, Chad. Let's go somewhere and talk about this, a coffee shop, the truck stop. Next exit, come on let's take the next exit."

Chad drives faster. Athena grips the passenger door. She doesn't know what to say. She's never had to save anyone before. Her arms ache. Her mouth is dry. Chad's eyes pierce the windshield.

"Are you trying to kill us?" she says. "What good would that do? Why give Delores the satisfaction? Jesus, Chad, pull yourself together. Listen to me. You're a really good guy, handsome, successful. Look what you've done for our town. What a difference a door makes, right? That's what you always say. It's true. It's true, Chad. Look at the good things, please. You can get out of this situation. You don't have to stay with your wife. People do it all the time. It's okay. Everything will be okay, Chad. Chad?"

Chad releases the gas pedal. Athena exhales and wipes her face. The whites of her eyes brighten the car. He flicks on his indicator and moves into the slow lane. A Corvette rides their tail.

"It's following us," says Chad.

Athena looks over her shoulder at the traffic behind them. Chad shoves his foot on the gas and swerves onto the passing exit ramp.

"There's no one following us," says Athena. "You're just tired. You're under a lot of stress. Chad, please can we just go back? Come on."

He drives for awhile along an empty road. They don't say a word. Athena stares out the window at the elongated evergreens, all alike, row after row after row. She rubs her lips together and wonders what it takes to make a difference. Chad lurches the car to a halt and gets out.

"Jesus, Chad. Chad?"

Athena punches the dashboard. She grabs a cigarette and gets out of the car clutching tightly to her purse.

Chad's sitting on the side of the road, legs crossed like an Indian.

"I can't go on," he says.

"Chad, please, we can't leave the car in the middle of the road. Give me the keys. I'll pull it over. Someone's going to hit it."

"I can't go on."

"Chad, please give me the keys."

Chad reaches into his pocket and throws the keys into the bushes.

"Holy shit," says Athena and runs after them. The sun's going down. She trips over an old tire and cuts her knee on a rusted pop can. Her pantyhose tear. She digs for the keys through a mess of weeds, fast food bags, faded cigarette packs and stones. It smells like urine and rotting plants. She feels her stomach reaching her throat and blindly plunges her hand into another group of bushes. She cuts her finger on a shard of glass. Mosquitoes buzz around her ears and land on her white shirt.

"Fuck you," she screams and swats them. Blood seeps into the cotton. "Fuck you," she screams again and storms over to Chad. "What are we going to do?"

"It's okay," he says.

"It's not okay. It's getting dark. There's nobody out here. Where are we? Who the hell knows where we are? My God, I've never been away from home and this is my first trip? Some road in the middle of fucking nowhere? I live on some road in the middle of fucking nowhere. What are you doing? What is this accomplishing?"

She sits down next to Chad. Her hair in tangles, shirt bloodstained and torn. She wraps her arm around her cut knee. The air is dense, no breeze. She lights a cigarette, lights another and gives it to Chad. His hair, usually swept up off his face, hangs limply across his forehead. He looks too young to be sitting on the side of a road waiting to die.

"Where does it all go wrong?" she says. "Why is it we're born so keen and one day it all turns for the worst. My girlfriends always say they wish they could go back and do things over again knowing what they know now. None of them would have got married or pregnant. They all got married and pregnant, or pregnant and married. Carm got pregnant at fifteen. Imagine. Most of the girls in our town were knocked up before they were twenty, all married by twenty. What else is there to do in Lobo? I used to think I was damned or had the plague because nobody wanted me. Nobody wanted to sleep with me. Goddamn it no one even wanted to rape me. But now I realize there was nothing wrong me. I was the goddamn lucky one."

"You are lucky."

"Was Delores pregnant? Did you love each other? Does anyone around here get married because they actually love each other? Or is it just the next step after high school. It's what you do quickly before all the single people get taken, you get too old, or you get your first goddamn girlfriend pregnant."

"I didn't get her pregnant. I loved her. I was in love with her. She got pregnant after we got married. Then she changed. Everything changed. I worked my ass off so I could give her everything. So we could give our kids everything."

Two nighthawks swoop down from the trees, then ascend separately into the greying sky. Athena throws a handful of gravel after them, desperately hoping they'll let someone know they're out here. With the heel of her shoe she etches her name in the dirt.

"Why don't you leave Delores, Chad?" she asks. "Is it that hard to leave a wife? My dad told me once it's expensive but it's not like you don't have the money. Is it because it's a small town, you'd always bump into her? Is it the kids? I suppose it always comes down to the kids."

"I don't really think the kids would care," he said. "They're not that fond of me anymore. She's turned them against me. Their daddy's never home. He works too much. I work too much for them. Besides, I think she has a lover. He takes them places."

"What? How do you know? Did the kids say something? Kids don't hide something like that. How does your wife hide something like that?"

"Wives hide it all the time."

"In Lobo? There's only so many men and fewer places to go with them. There's bored neighbours attached to telephones living for something new to gossip about. My mother's a hairdresser, I know."

"Hmm."

"Why does she harass you then? Why doesn't she just let you go if there's someone else?"

"I won't let her go."

"What?"

"It's my brother. She's fucking my brother."

"David?"

"It all looks so normal. The kids go places with their uncle. What a great uncle. My wife goes with the kids. Her husband works too much. Now her husband works so much because he can't stand his wife. But I can't stand the humiliation of losing my wife to my brother. I can't live with it."

"My God, and your brother lives in Bath so it's easier to hide. That's how she's getting away with it. It's not under everyone's nose and no one in Lobo gives a shit about what goes on in Bath."

Chad grabs her hand. A universe of cicadas buzz in unison. She stiffens. His hand is soft. She glances at it holding hers. He stares into space and she relaxes. It isn't uncomfortable. She pictures Delores, her skinny hands. The bones protruding through her over-tanned skin. They'd probably snap if he held them like this.

"Athena, what would you do if you could go back knowing what you know now?"

"I don't know anything."

A neon green grasshopper leaps onto the road in front of them. It rubs its arms together. Athena feels like prey. Chad stares at it enviously. It glows against the sepia veil of dusk.

"Chad, let's walk to the highway. I'm cold. We can work this out. I can help you. But I have to go home. My mother will be so worried. I'm never not there."

Chad moves in front of her. He touches her face.

"I can't," he says.

She throws her arms in the air and gets up.

"Chad, all these years you've been really good to me. I care about you a lot, but I can't sit here all night. I can't. I'm going to the highway. It can't be any less safe walking there than sitting here with your goddamn car stuck in the middle of the road. I'm going to get help. We're going home, Chad. You have to deal with this. Look at you. Is this where you thought you'd be one day? Let me help you. I can help you. I want to be useful."

Athena runs. Something her legs haven't done since public school. She's possessed by an overwhelming sense of purpose. This is it she thinks. This is what she was meant to be — Chad's salvation.

In the distance, she sees the darting specks of highway traffic. The asphalt stretches. Her spirit deflates. Out of breath and aching, she's standing in the middle of the same road. She sighs and looks at the infinite sky. The hands she wants to hold hers now don't descend from it. She thinks of the aquamarine BMW stranded on a road that will never know enough to appreciate it, and Chad. She looks behind her at the tunnel of black and pictures him mired deep within it. An owl hoots. And it hits her: for the first time in months he's free of Delores. He's beyond her reach, completely hidden.

A car horn sounds. She hadn't noticed its headlights illuminating her feet. She stands aside. A woman leans her head out of the window.

"Honey, are you alright? Get in the car. Are you alright?"

Without thinking, Athena gets in the car. The man and woman turn around to look at her.

"Wait a minute are you that missing girl?" says the man. "There was news on the radio about a young woman gone missing. From Lawrence, Elana?"

"Athena? I'm Athena, from Lobo. It must be me. Oh my God, the police are looking for me? Oh, my mother must be so worried."

"Jesus girl," says the woman. "You have got to be careful. What happened to you? Look at you, did your car break down, were you in an accident?"

"No, I...I...," She looks out the car window at the tranquil dark, the flaring burnt orange of the fireflies. "Please, just take me home," she says.

The couple shrug. They turn the car around and head for the highway. Athena looks at her hand, feels the ghost of Chad's palm clinging to it. From behind, she hears a noise like a door slamming.

CRADLE ME

Panties, bras, slips, stockings and a mohair sweater cover the carpet. May is on her knees. Her hair pulled back in a fist. Red faced. She's sweating, moaning. Every drawer is emptied on the bedroom floor and still no key. The entire apartment is turned upside down and still there's no key. May panics. She tries to remember what she did when she got home. The same thing she does every night she gets home from a bar. Comes into the house, locks the door. Goes to the kitchen, pours herself a glass of water. Takes two aspirin. Lies down. Gets up. Goes to the bathroom. Splashes her face with water. Looks in the mirror. Shakes her head. Holds her head. Goes back to bed. Spins.

The key should be on the kitchen table, the coffee table, the bedside table, the back of the toilet, in a pocket of her blazer or a pocket of her purse. All the tables are bare. The blazer and purse have been turned inside out, only an outdated *Cosmopolitan* rests on the back of the toilet. The carpet has been combed. The floor swept.

The phone rings. May looks at it. She grabs it.

"Hello, May?"

"Yes."

"Hi. This is Bev."

"Bev?"

"Yes. Hi, how are you?"

"Bev who?"

"Bev Saunders. We met last night at the bar, at The Whiskey. It was late. I was tired. Well we were talking and..."

"Were we sitting at a table?"

"No. We were at the bar. We met at the bar. You were by yourself having a drink and I came in by myself for a drink and we started talking."

"Hmm."

"I'd had a big fight with my husband. I'd been crying. You noticed and asked if I was okay and we started talking."

"I gave you my number?"

"No. But you told me your last name, the name of your street, your birthday. You're a Libra. You'll be forty-six this year and you're having an affair with your boss."

"Was."

"Oh. You were so kind to me. You told me to leave my husband. You said I was crazy. An attractive woman like myself shouldn't put up with his bullshit. You said, get out. Get out now, while you're still young and relatively thin."

"Oh."

"So, I did, May. I did it. I left him. I left him and I am free. A new woman already and I owe it all to you."

"What did you say your name is?"

"Bev."

"Bev, I'm happy for you. I think that's great. You don't owe me anything. Honest. Don't mention it. Good luck with everything. Thanks for calling."

"Wait, wait. I was so excited, I left without thanking you for your advice. I want to take you out to express my gratitude."

"Oh, thanks, but I really can't go anywhere right now."

"Oh."

May hangs up the phone and stares at it. She puts her finger in her mouth, chews the fingernail.

She opens a window, feels a little short of breath, claustrophobic. She's down on all fours crawling around the rust-coloured shag carpet. Scraping her gnawed fingernails through it. She sits in the middle of the floor, cross-legged. Closes her eyes. Pictures yesterday, retraces her steps. She gets up from her desk, adjusts her skirt. Says goodbye to Jack, her boss. The man she was in love with once. He barely looks up, mumbles something.

May's been his secretary for six months. By the second month they were having an affair. Jack told her he had never met anyone like her. Told her this while he was unbuttoning her blouse in his office. She was in love, she thought. He was going to leave his wife, she thought. He had sex with her at lunchtime in his office with the curtains drawn and the phones on hold. He said all the right things at all the right times. She swore she would wait for him until the kids grew up and left home because that is what he said she would have to do one afternoon after sex when she asked him when he thought he might be leaving his wife.

"Well, I'm going to have to wait just a few more years, honey, you know, once the kids have grown up and left college and have wives and kids of their own," he said while pulling up his pants and straightening his hair.

"Oh, so another ten or twelve years?" said May.

"Umm, yeah, roughly," he said.

She got dressed, straightened her hair, and went back to work. This happened for a couple of months and poor May just couldn't take it. So she told Jack that's it, that's it Jack, I just can't take this anymore. I'm leaving. I'm leaving. Then she stopped crying, stopped talking, looked down at the ground, left his office, went back to her desk, sat down and thought, what am I leaving? So, as of that day, they didn't have sex in his office anymore and the whole thing was over. Whatever it was in the first place.

She kept a flask of bourbon in her desk drawer. She saw Shirley MacLaine do it in a movie. She always wanted to be Shirley MacLaine. She took a swig in the morning when she got to work. A swig at lunchtime because lunchtime brought bad memories. Then she downed a mouthful at the stroke of five. She'd leave and go to the bar across the street from the fitness club where Jack worked out.

Yesterday, she didn't go to that bar. She went to a new bar, one with a nicer decor. The one with carpet on the ground and fancy little lights that hang from the ceiling by one wire and have blue and red and yellow pointy light bulbs. She saw it advertised in the weekly newsletter that comes around the office.

It's the kind of bar with drinks that match the light bulbs. Martinis that glow in the dark, get you hammered with a sip and cost you a month's rent. She felt out of place. Felt more alone than she was. Her face wasn't smooth anymore like the young female executives curving around the tables. Her legs had lost their ankles.

"Can I get you anything, ma'am?" asked the bartender.

May turned to the bartender, she looked up at him, shook her head a little.

"Aren't you on TV?" she asked.

He laughed and served the next person.

"I'll have a red one of those," she said but he didn't hear.

She turned back around and watched the women smoking cigarettes and laughing. Tossing their silky hair back and forth, laughing. Sipping their multi-coloured drinks with multi-coloured lips and fingernails that could poke eyes out.

"What do you want, ma'am?" asked the bartender.

"One of those," she said, pointing to the women.

"Yeah, me too," said the bartender.

May slowly got up and walked out. Walked to the tavern across from Jack's fitness club. The bartender poured her the usual. Poured her the usual until the bottle ran dry and the room was spinning.

"Do you want anything else, May?" he asked as he wiped down the counter and raised the house lights.

May looked at the bartender, slapped too much money on the bar and said, "I want long legs that touch my armpits. I want hair that curls and falls over my shoulders like gold yarn. I want clothes with a label on them that people recognize. I want a face like the porcelain china my grandmother kept behind glass. I want a man that looks like he's on television to pick me up after work in his 12-digit automobile and take me to our 20-digit home. I want to be beautiful. I want to be adored."

The bartender looked at her. She got up and left. She felt warm, sweaty. She leaned on the side of the building, saw a man get out of a blurry red thing. Watched his mouth opening and closing and opening and closing. His fuzzy arms stretched toward her. His fuzzy hands grasped her before she hit the cold concrete.

"May, are you all right, May?" he said.

"Spring has arrived," she mumbled. "The spring is here.

She woke up in her own bed, looked around her room without moving her head. Eyes darting from one side to the other. Not moving in case she was broken. In case she might break. That was her first thought, don't move. She felt cold. She was naked, naked and cold, cold and stiff. But she knew she wasn't dead. She thought she wasn't dead. She called out, *hello, hello*. Nobody answered. When she got up she was dizzy, looked around the room again. She heard what sounded like the door closing. Closing and locking.

She went to the door. Looked through the peephole. There was nobody there. She tried the lone door. It was locked, double locked. She went to get her key to unlock the deadbolt. The key wasn't in her purse. She got down on all fours, dragged her gnawed fingernails through the rust-coloured shag carpet.

It's a beautiful morning. Jack drives with the top down. The wind ruffles his thinning hair. The sea air bites against his unshaven skin. He pulls off the road. Gets out of the car and stands at the edge looking down upon the restless ocean crashing against the jagged rocks. He pulls a single key from his pocket, throws it into the insatiable mouth of the Atlantic. He returns to the car, avoids the glare of the pale redhead sitting next to him. He places an unsteady hand on her quivering thigh.

"Bev," he says. "I never meant to hurt you."

WHISKEY DOG

Hal shot out from between his mother's legs like a bullet from a gun into the obstetrician's gut and knocked her unconscious. Hal's mother was sorry for the doctor but overjoyed by her son's spunk. She just wished it had been her husband standing there.

Hal was an active boy. Spent most of his time in the field at the back of his house playing with guns. Just before his dad walked out on his mother, he taught Hal how to shoot. He didn't really have to teach Hal how to shoot. Hal had helped himself to his dad's guns long before his dad would have let him. When his dad left, Hal took photos of him, nailed them to trees, and shot at them. His mother would hoot and holler in the background encouraging him.

"Shoot the head off the old bastard," she'd yell.

Hal revved up and shot a round of bullets into the photos. Then his mom and him would roast hot dogs on the barbecue. Hal was too young to understand why his dad left. When he got a bit older his mother tried to explain to him that it was because his dad was a stupid, good-for-nothing sewer rat. Hal thought that sounded like a good reason for a man to leave. So, he stopped shooting at his photos.

Hal used to sleep with his dad's old rifle. His mom would wake him up for school and he'd have his arms wrapped around it. The first time his mother caught him doing this, she screamed and pulled the rifle from his arms.

"Jesus, Hal, what if that went off in the night?" she screeched. "What would you do if you accidentally shot yourself? What would I do? You're all I have, boy. You're all I have."

Hal removed the bullets, said he wouldn't need them until he was older. He wasn't sleeping with the rifle for protection. He slept with it because he loved it, because it felt good — cold and sleek against his skin.

The high school principal called his mother at least twice a week. Told her, Hal has to keep his guns at home. He can't have Hal pulling out his Smith & Wesson .357 Magnum every time the teacher tells him to do something he doesn't like. He can't run around the playground firing shots into the sky, threatening to kill every boy that doesn't give him a ball or his lunch candy. Hal's mother would apologize and say he's just having fun — let a kid be a kid. But he's not a normal kid, the principal would say. Hal's mother thought it was perfectly normal for boys to play with guns and she told the principal this. Toy guns, the principal would say, toy guns are acceptable.

Hal didn't have to be drafted into the army. He was waiting on the doorstep of the military base the day they declared war. He was sixteen. His mother was petrified to let her boy go to war. Hal believed he could win the war single-handedly. He knew he could handle it the day he accidentally shot and killed the dog and didn't feel anything. His mother gasped. The dog gasped. Hal put another bullet in it to make sure he'd done the job right. He knew if he could kill a dog, his own dog, he could a kill a man — any man.

The army was unsuccessful at keeping Hal away from the artillery. It's one thing to want to fight for your country, they told him, but it is an entirely different thing to want to shoot everything that moves — especially members of your own platoon. Hal wasn't liked. Nobody wanted to sleep near him, share a bunk with him. He missed his mother. Every week she received letters from the barracks, the jungle, the brothel. One night he was accidentally shot by one of the hookers when she showed him her new semi-automatic. It went off and clipped his shin. They shipped him home for a few weeks to recuperate. He was bored. He visited the local bar and told the bartender stories of fighting in the Nai Pai jungle. He could recreate the sound of a machine gun like nothing the bartender had ever heard. When he got shipped out again he took his own rifle with him for company.

His mother stopped receiving letters. There was no correspondence for months. The six o'clock news and the newspapers reported on the devastation, the hundreds killed, wounded, lost — the inevitability of defeat. Hal's mother couldn't sleep at night. Checked her mailbox three times a day even though the mail only gets delivered once. One morning she got a call from the infirmary, said Hal was back and she should come and see him. She dressed quickly, shaking, expecting bad things. Why hadn't he called? Why didn't they tell her what was wrong? What was wrong? She grabbed the new gun she'd bought for him and was saving for his return, a BFR .45-70, and left.

Hal's mother arrived at the infirmary and waited in the waiting room. No one appeared. Nurses walked by her. They didn't acknowledge her existence. She got fed up and decided to search for Hal on her own. She wandered down the hall past groaning men, screaming and crying men. She felt ill. She found the TV room, looked around and saw what looked like Hal attached to a wheelchair, arms strapped behind his back, his shaved head bobbing up and down.

She walked up to him. "Hal?"

Hal bobbed his head, made exploding noises.

"Hal?"

The room swarmed with war casualties; men with missing arms and legs, burns, bandaged heads. Hal's mother grabbed her stomach, cried out. Hal ceased bobbing, turned his head as far around as he could and said, "Mama? Mama, is that you? Oh, God, Mama, please shoot me."

Hal's mother shoved the gift-wrapped BFR .45-70 she'd been holding into her large purse. Grabbed the back of Hal's wheelchair and pushed him down the hall past the questioning eyes of patients. Past busy nurses. Nobody stopped her. The nurses weren't bothered. They let her go. They just let it go. That night Hal's mother packed some things and Hal into the station wagon and drove north. She drove and drove until Hal spoke. Then she pulled over and listened.

"There was a dog in the village of Mao Lee," said Hal, laughing a little. "It drank whiskey. One of the fisherman, Gai Pan, said he'd sit up at night by the ships in the harbor with the dog and tell it his sorrows. It sat close to him. Gazed at Gai Pan with his wise dog-eyes, comforting him. They'd drink whiskey 'til Gai Pan could barely stand and the dog would guide him home, then disappear. In the morning, Gai Pan rose feeling renewed. Whenever he felt despair, he'd walk to the harbour and open a bottle of whiskey. The dog always showed up, to kick back a few and listen."

Hal's mother put the car in gear and drove to the nearest town. The motel had its lights on so she pulled into the parking lot and told Hal to wait in the car, made him promise not to move. She got a room at the back with two double beds and a TV. She returned to the car with one set of keys and two extra towels the lady at the front desk had given her. She got in the car. Hal was gone.

"Oh, God," she said.

She put down the towels and took a deep breath. She leapt out of the car and spun in circles looking for Hal. She called out his name. It came back to her. He couldn't be too far. It was dark. It was dark and cold. She ran onto the road, looked up and down. It was barren. She dropped her head into her hands and wept. Off to the side, she heard a car approaching. She watched it pull into the tavern across the road from the motel. A large guy got out of the car and when he opened the door to the tavern it was like the whole town came alive for a second with the murmur of voices, laughter, pool balls breaking, glasses clinking, then silence.

Her heart sank. She stood there, numb, transfixed on the green light blinking against the road in front of her. Her eyes rolled up above the tavern and met the flashing neon sign. It said The Whiskey Dog. The Whiskey Dog beat against her face like the heat of the rising sun.

ABERDEEN

The last of the campers left the campground. Aberdeen closed the gate for another season. Leaves crunched beneath her feet as she walked down the laneway toward the house. A cool breeze blew across her face. She shivered. A car approached. Its headlights blinding. She squinted and stood aside. The car stopped and someone got out.

"Evening ma'am," said a man. "Is this Aberdeen Campground?"

"Yeah, but we're closed for the season," said Aberdeen.

"Is there an Aberdeen Bruce here, ma'am?" he asked

"Well, that's me, but I'm not Bruce anymore," she said.

The man laughed and walked out of the dark into Aberdeen's view. He was dressed in black pants, a black shirt and a long dark trench coat. He flashed Aberdeen a badge.

"Are you a sheriff?" she asked. "You look kind of young to be a sheriff."

"No, I work for the sheriff," he said. "I'm a dick. A private investigator."

She studied his face, his sloping shoulders. He looked more like he was running from the law than working for it. He moved closer to her. She looked into his blank eyes. His skin was pale and drawn like a vegetarian's. He held out his hand and smiled. His yellow teeth hung like old bones from his colourless gums.

"I'm Lenny McMichael," he said, "Lenny. I'm investigating a missing person's report."

"Well, I'm not missing," said Aberdeen and stepped away from him.

"No, your mother is," he said.

"My mother? My God, she's been missing for years."

Lenny asked Aberdeen if there was somewhere they could go and talk. He told her it was a formality. She pointed back at the campground and led him to the office. She went into its little kitchen and put the kettle on the stove.

"You live here alone, ma'am."

"No, I live with my husband, Hogarth. We run this campground together. We've been running it successfully for years. Listen," she said, "I don't want you nosing around here causing trouble. I don't want you sniffing around town stirring up rumors. I am very well-respected in this town and a hundred others. Campers travel from all over to come to our campground. We've never had any trouble here. I haven't seen or heard from my mother since she left when I was six. And if this is some godforsaken ploy of hers to get back into my life because she's broke, or lonely, or just wants a goddamn free campsite for a night, she's out of luck. It's too late to come crawling back into my life attempting to say she's goddamn sorry. I am a grown woman. I had a hard time getting here. I grew up with a dad and two mongrels. You don't learn a hell of a lot about how to be a woman from a dad and two mongrels and I don't need you to remind me why."

Aberdeen clenched her fists and stared at Lenny.

"Maybe we should talk tomorrow, Mrs. Bruce," he said.

"Trent. I've been Mrs. Trent for years. My mother is Mrs. Bruce."

Lenny looked around the tidy office, at the photos on the walls. "Campers?" he said.

"Yes," she said. "They're like family. We take care of our campers. We're one big happy family. "

"Who's that?" said Lenny pointing to a picture of a tall man with a wide smile.

"That's my father," she said. "He passed away last year."

"I'm sorry to hear that. Where's your husband Mrs. Trent?"

"He's cleaning things up."

"It's awfully dark out there."

"It gets like that in these parts."

They looked at each other. Lenny nodded to Aberdeen, took another glance around the place and told her he'd come back in the morning. She shrugged. He left. The kettle whistled. A chill pierced Aberdeen. She put on the jacket draped over the back of a chair. She walked into the little kitchen, removed the kettle and turned off the element. She looked out of the window into her own reflection. She looked tired, she thought, older, like a grandmother. The office phone rang. Aberdeen stared at it for a minute before picking it up.

"Hello," she said.

"Mrs. Trent, I didn't mean to alarm you. I should have been a little more sympathetic," said Lenny.

"How did you get this number?" she asked.

"It's on your brochure, Mrs. Trent. I have all that information. I'm a private investigator. That's the easy stuff." He laughed then caught himself.

"Mr. McMichael, this is not an enjoyable thing for me. I don't find it the least bit funny."

"I'm sorry. You know, when I was a kid, I loved camping," he said.

"What?"

"Oh, nothing. I'll talk to you tomorrow, Mrs. Trent. Sleep well."

Aberdeen hung up the phone and looked around the office. She turned off the lights and left. She ran. All around her echoed the sound of cracking branches, leaves, owls and her own breath. When she reached the house she was shaking. Hogarth was putting wood on the fire. He jumped up when she came through the door and dropped the wood he was holding.

"What is it?" he said. "Are you all right? You look petrified. Jesus."

He grabbed the blanket from the corner of the couch and wrapped it around her.

He sat her down and stroked her head. Her hair was damp and pasted across her forehead. She was still shaking, gazing at the floor, trying to catch her breath.

This isn't fair, she thought, after all this time. She rubbed her brow and peeked over her hand at Hogarth. He was gawking at her.

"Hogarth," she said. "It's not that bad."

He got up and closed the fire screen. He was a big man. His shadow filled the room. He grabbed his pipe from his shirt pocket and hit it on the mantelpiece, stuck it in his mouth and lit it. Aberdeen tried to regain her composure and told him not to worry. She asked if all the latches were tied down on the woodsheds, if the hookups were closed and the electricity turned off. Hogarth walked over to the couch and loomed over her.

"What aren't you telling me?" he said.

"Nothing," she said. "I got a scare on my way back from the office. I got a little scared in the dark. It happens sometimes. You hear something, a creak, a snapping branch. It's unnerving. And I got a visit from a private investigator. Turns out my mother's missing."

Hogarth sat down.

"That's not nothing," he said.

"No, actually, it was quite something. What do you do? I can't tell him to get lost. Can I?"

"What did you tell him?"

"That she's been missing for years. What took them so long?"

"What do you have to do with this?"

"Well, I don't know. Guilty by association, I guess."

Hogarth stood up and walked to the door. He grabbed his coat and put on his shoes.

"Where are you going?" she asked.

"To find the bastard. Who the hell does he think he is approaching you out of the blue with no explanation and scaring you half to death? Why the hell didn't he call first? Doesn't he know you haven't seen your mother in years? You wouldn't know her if you tripped over her. She could have been camping here a thousand times, how the hell would we know?"

"Instinct?" she said.

Hogarth took his hand off the doorknob. He removed his jacket, his shoes, and resumed his place beside her. He put his hand on her knee.

"He'll be back tomorrow," she said. "Then you can deal with him"

Hogarth ran Aberdeen a hot bath and made down the bed. She couldn't sleep. She heard things and imagined Lenny's face peering through the window. She got up and drew the curtains. How did he find me? she asked herself. She wondered if her dad had reported her missing when she ran off the first time. She never thought to ask. But her dad knew she'd left with his business partner, so he probably didn't want to find her. And now, forty years later, Aberdeen lay sleepless beside her tranquil husband wondering why she had never asked anything about her mother. She was just gone one day and Aberdeen carried on. What else could she do at the age of six? She adjusted and didn't question things. It was as though her mother had died. And that's what she would tell people when they asked where her mother was. She'd say, she died.

Aberdeen awoke to the smell of bacon. The room was cold. She got up and peeked out the window. Two squirrels darted down the fir tree and chased each other across the grass. She thought to herself, some things are put on this earth to cause trouble and Lenny McMichael was one of those things. She got dressed and went downstairs.

When she walked into the kitchen Hogarth gave her a kiss on the forehead and handed her a cup of coffee. She flipped through the mail. He put a plate full of bacon, pancakes and eggs in front of her. She picked at it.

Aberdeen heard tires on the gravel. She put down her fork. Hogarth stood up abruptly and went outside. Aberdeen peered out the kitchen window, watched Lenny lope toward the house.

"You must be Hogarth," she heard him say.

Lenny held out his hand, separated his stiff lips and bared his decrepit teeth. Hogarth grimaced.

"And you must be the PI," he said.

Lenny walked to the foot of the porch and stopped. Hogarth lorded over him. Take another step and I'll kill you, was what Lenny read from his stance, like when a dog bristles the hair on its back. Lenny knew dogs.

"I'm Lenny McMichael," he said.

He put his hands in his pockets and looked around. "Nice property you got here. If you hadn't just closed up I might have stayed and camped for a few days." Lenny bit his lip. Aberdeen walked onto the porch and nodded to him.

"Morning, ma'am," he said.

"Morning. Would you like a coffee?"

Hogarth frowned. She shrugged and walked back into the kitchen. Hogarth stepped aside and told Lenny to come in. Lenny scratched his head. He walked into the house and removed his black leather cowboy boots. Aberdeen stared at them. They were tiny. Hogarth sat down and lit his pipe.

"I suppose you take your coffee black. Am I right?" said Aberdeen. She handed him a coffee and pointed to the living room.

Lenny took the cup from her and sat down in the rocking chair.

"Well, what did you find in the night?" said Aberdeen. "Any traces of Mrs. Houdini?"

"Houdini was an escape artist," said Hogarth. "He didn't have a disappearing act."

"I don't have a lot to go on," said Lenny.

"Who filed this report?" Aberdeen asked.

"Her daughter."

"Her daughter?"

Hogarth shook his head and said, "Well, I suppose she could have had a hundred daughters in forty years."

Aberdeen was horrified. The thought never crossed her mind. Her skin tightened. Hogarth got up and went into the kitchen. He poured himself some coffee and stared out the window. Aberdeen felt his discomfort. She knew that despite her husband's gallantry he was too kind to tell Lenny to get lost. From the corner of her eye, she watched him slip out to the front porch.

"What kind of a name is Aberdeen, Mrs. Trent?" Lenny asked.

"Unusual," said Aberdeen.

Lenny laughed.

"You certainly haven't done your homework have you, Mr. McMichael? It's where my mother was born — Scotland. That much I know. What is her other daughter's name?"

"Tess."

"Tess? Tess?"

She thought, Tess is the kind of name you give to a child you love. It's a loving name, a name full of adoration. She imagined her mother giving birth, looking down at her brand new baby girl and whispering Tess, baby Tess. Tess is the name of a child you don't leave.

"God," she said. "Have you met Tess?"

Lenny removed his fingers from his lips. "Well, yes, briefly. We had to meet. I needed background, photographs. I had to know where your mother was last seen, her state of mind. You know like, had she been depressed, had she had a fight with her husband, with Tess, routine questions."

"And had she had a fight with her husband? Who the hell is her husband? She already had a husband."

Lenny put his hand into his coat pocket. He pulled out a handful of photographs. Aberdeen sat forward in her seat, picked her glasses off the table and put them on.

Lenny passed her the photos. She braced herself. Her hands were shaking. Lenny moved over to the couch beside her.

"That's your mother," he said.

She stared at the photo. She brought it close to her eyes. Her mother was wearing shorts and a T-shirt. Her legs were thin, her skin like rice paper. It was lined with red and purple veins and small brown blotches. Her hair was white and sparse.

"She's so old," said Aberdeen, "so small. Is she ill? Maybe she just crawled into the woods like an ailing cat and died."

"No, she's not ill. Tess would have told me."

"I guess her past caught up with her then. That's what happens when you abandon your family. She looks like she should for what she's done."

Aberdeen flipped to the next photo. Lenny told her that was her mother with Tess. Aberdeen held the photo away from her, stared at it from a distance. Tess was tall, long fair hair, beautiful smile. Her mother had her arms around her and they were laughing. They were standing in front of a red brick mansion. Yellow and white rose bushes lined its front and a black Town Car was parked off to the side.

"What is that?" said Aberdeen pointing to the house.

"That's their home," said Lenny.

Aberdeen put down the photos.

"I can't help you," she said. "I've never seen these people before in my life."

"Tess thought maybe she came here looking for you. She only just told Tess about you and had been quite upset about it. When she went missing you were the first person Tess thought of."

"She hasn't been here. Women like that don't camp."

Aberdeen got up and walked to the door. She held it open and stared at Lenny.

"If anything occurs Mrs. Trent, please call me." He picked up his photos and handed Aberdeen his card. She took it.

Lenny nodded to Hogarth as he passed him on the steps. Hogarth went inside. Aberdeen was sitting on the couch, fisted hands gripping her hair. He removed his pipe from his shirt pocket and walked over to lean on the mantelpiece. Aberdeen leapt up and grabbed her purse. She whisked out the door and into the van.

Hogarth ran after her but she was already too far gone to stop. When she reached the road she saw the back of Lenny's Buick. She went the other way. She turned on the radio, drove fast through the falling leaves. She screamed as hard as she could and burst into tears. She pulled into the cemetery and parked the van. She grabbed some remaining wild flowers from the woods and ran to her dad's grave. She placed the flowers against the granite headstone and sat down on the bench a family had placed there in memory of the deceased. The air was cool. The smell of burning leaves drifted by.

"Dad, she left you for money," she said. "Maybe now you can rest in peace knowing it was nothing you did. Being a farmer was an honorable job. Being the farmer's lawyer was simply more profitable."

Her dad probably knew all along that she was that kind of woman. He must have worked as hard as he did attempting to keep her happy. But love and food aren't enough for some people. Aberdeen felt grateful that it had been enough for her and — despite the fact that her dad wasn't very adept at being a mother — he had been a loving father. She got up to leave. She turned back around and rearranged the wildflowers.

"Dad," she said, "in case you were wondering, she doesn't look very good. She looks like a woman who's been paying for her sins."

Aberdeen walked across the graves to the van. She looked back and up at the clouding sky. Another season was moving in. Summer takes care of itself; in the winter things need nailing down. She drove through town to the hardware store and grabbed some supplies for Hogarth.

She walked across the street past Betty's Diner. Inside looked warm and inviting. She decided to pop in for the comfort of a hot cup of coffee and a warm piece of pie. The bell chimed when she walked through the door. Betty looked up from her magazine and smiled. Aberdeen smiled back. There were a few people in for lunch. Some truck drivers at the counter. They were always too large for the stools, yet they insisted on sitting there. She looked around for a quiet table by the window. In the corner booth she spotted Lenny's stringy black hair and hunched back. Her initial reaction was to leave before he spotted her but she didn't. She walked over to him.

"Well, imagine finding you here," she said. "Maybe I should have been a private investigator, except the last thing I wanted was to find you."

Lenny grunted. Aberdeen sat down. They sat in silence. Aberdeen felt sorry for him. She didn't know why.

"You know," she said softly, "when I was old enough to think about what I was called, I hated my name. I thought it sounded like a plant you'd find in a swamp, or a type of wool. You know, thick, heavy things. When I found out it was my mother's birthplace, I felt special. I felt proud that I was named after somewhere faraway. When my mother left, my name was a burden. I felt trapped in a strange place. Then one day it didn't matter anymore."

"Have you ever been there?" said Lenny.

"God, no. I had no desire. I had hard feelings. What if that's where she was?"

"Didn't you ever want to find your mother?"

"I didn't lose her, Lenny, not like Tess. She left me. And if she's looking for me now, she's too late. Imagine leaving your child at six and thinking forty years later that maybe it's time to reunite. I think that's even worse than the initial leaving. I mean, what would you do?"

Lenny twiddled his spoon between his tattered fingers. He kept his face down. "I don't know," he said. "It doesn't matter what I think, does it? Not a goddamn bit."

Aberdeen looked at the knuckles piercing through his skin, the scars. She took a deep breath and scoured the place. She was looking for strangers, little old ladies with red and purple-veined legs. Lenny was the only stranger in the place and a few truckers. But the truckers don't count. Truckers are familiar regardless if they're different each time.

"Would you like more coffee?" she asked Lenny.

"I think I'd be okay with it," he said. "I think I'd allow my mother to come back and tell me why she left. I'd want to know. I believe she owed it to me and to herself. People shouldn't die without resolution, without some kind of redemption. It's not right. People are not bad by birth. They become that way. Some change and it's important for them to face what they have done."

Lenny looked at Aberdeen with his sweating black eyes.

"You don't have a mother either, do you?" she said.

"I've had a few."

Aberdeen squinted. Lenny waved Betty over and asked for more coffee. She gave Aberdeen a look like, who is this guy? and refilled their cups.

"You know," said Aberdeen, "the other day I watched a robin feeding one of her babies on a spindly branch. The mother would fly away and the baby hopped up and down in one spot chirping. Then it would stop and look around. The longer the mother was gone, the more nervous I became. Then the mother would return and the baby fluttered its wings, opened its beak and the mother fed it. She'd leave again and each time she left, it seemed to me that she was taking longer to return. I feared for the baby. I watched for other birds, meddling squirrels, prowling cats. The baby bird stopped chirping. It sat quietly, vulnerably on the branch waiting and waiting. And you know what, Lenny? The mother didn't come back."

Lenny looked up at her. His eyes softened. "Did it get eaten? Did it fall off the branch? Sometimes they fall off the branch."

"I don't know. I just prayed it flew away and began its life."

Lenny darkened. "What are you trying to tell me Aberdeen, that I should get lost, that I should fly away and stop intruding on your life?"

"I'm not your mother, Lenny. What are you looking for, my mother or a mother?"

They both looked down again. Aberdeen closed her eyes. Lenny drank more coffee. He looked at her clenched face shrouded by her mousy brown hair. She was younger than she looked and older than she ever thought she'd be.

"Why did you give up your child, Aberdeen?"

She froze. Lenny wiped the sweat off his forehead with a serviette. Aberdeen opened her eyes.

"What exactly are you up to Lenny? Where did you come from? Is the rest of your body as scratched up as your hands? Do you have handmade tattoos on your biceps? Look at you. How many twelve-step programs have you begun and failed on account of the fact that one, you probably can't even count to twelve, and two, you probably never finish anything that you begin. What the hell do you want from me? Who are you? Who the hell are you?"

The truckers spun around on their stools.

She lowered her voice and leaned into the table inches from Lenny's face. She whispered, "You told me you knew hardly anything about my mother, that you hadn't done your research. You didn't even know where bloody Aberdeen was. But you know this about me. What the hell are you really looking for?"

Lenny slid out of the booth and walked out of the place.

"Wait," yelled Aberdeen.

She threw some money down on the table and ran after him.

He got into his rusting white Buick and rolled down the window. Aberdeen ran up to the car and grabbed the door.

"I didn't abandon my child," she said. "I did what was best. I was too young. My dad decided it wouldn't have been right. I'm sure that baby had a better life and I wouldn't try to get back into its life now and if you get a call from some kid looking for their mother and you think it might be me, don't you come back around. Do you understand?"

She let go of the car. Lenny leaned out of the window and grabbed her arm.

"When I was a kid my adoptive mother used to take me camping," he said. "We'd set up the tent and head to the lake and we'd swim and swim. My mother swam so beautifully. I used to think she was a mermaid. But one day this funny thing happened. My mother woke up later than usual. She wasn't herself. She was listless and pale. We walked to the beach in silence. My mother gripped my hand so tightly it hurt. I waded in the water. She dove in like she always did but she never came up, Aberdeen. I sat on that beach for hours, waiting like that bird on the branch I guess, just waiting. Except my mother wasn't teaching me how to fly away and be on my own. I believe that she had every intention of coming back. I spent years in and out of homes, mother after mother after mother. I realize some things can never be found, Aberdeen, once they're truly gone."

Aberdeen pulled her arm from his grip. Lenny put the car in reverse, raced down the road and headed for the highway. Aberdeen straightened her hair. Betty and the truckers were staring out the window. She ignored them and got into the van. She drove too fast. Drove with the windows down. She pulled into the campground and screeched to a stop. Hogarth was waiting on the front porch. He ran down to meet her.

"Jesus, Aberdeen, I've been so worried. Where the hell have you been? What's going on?"

Aberdeen gazed at Hogarth and felt her heart warm.

GALLOWAY

Galloway signed along the dotted line. He took off his glasses and rubbed the bridge of his nose. Barnes was flipping through his next client's file.

"Do you think they'll miss me when I'm gone?" said Galloway. "My kids?"

"For a while," said Barnes.

Galloway stood up and held out his hand. Barnes grabbed onto it.

"I'll miss you when you're gone, Gal, but you're not gone yet."

Barnes placed a copy of Galloway's will into an envelope.

"Shall I seal it, or do you want the honour?" he said.

Galloway nodded.

Outside the sun had barely set. The moon was pushing its way in. The streets were full of nine-to-fivers anxiously exiting buildings, scurrying toward subways and bus stands, arms flying up for cabs. Galloway felt a sense of melancholy for his past. For the days he spent hunched over a desk, people's life savings spread out before him in an office with a 100-watt bulb in a shadeless desk lamp keeping him warm, a telephone and a radio he never turned off.

He grasped his will with both hands and crossed the

street. What if I die now, he thought, out here on the road? And so what?

He walked the three blocks to Midge's Deli. The wind chilled his old bones. Midge's was full. He looked around the place for Annabelle. She wasn't there. He sat at the counter and Midge greeted him with a hot coffee.

"Nice to see you, my friend. Everything okay?" he said and patted Galloway on the shoulder.

Galloway smirked. "You seen Annabelle?" he said.

Midge furrowed his brow and shook his head. He placed his hands on the counter.

"I lost at the races for the tenth time, Gal. You're killing me. People like you don't retire. Once a bookie always a bookie. You want to change your ways now? You can't convince me you don't dream about blue ribbons, tickets flying, fists full of dough falling into your best friends' hands, into your hands. Don't tell me you're not watering at the mouth with the onset of the Superbowl. Come on. What's got into you? You're being selfish, Gal. Look around the place. Look at us. Your pigeons are lost. Throw us some scraps at least, give us some tips."

Galloway rubbed his face. Men who'd kept him in business were seated all around him hunched over newspapers, their ballpoint pens skimming the standings.

"Ten to one you'll be back," Midge said. "A hundred to one."

Galloway shrugged.

"I miss the horses sometimes," he said, "but I don't miss the fights, Midgey. They don't make boxers like they used to. Lewis is no Kid Gavilan, no Basilio. The stakes are mediocre at best. And the football... football's changed. Jesus, it takes four hours to play Monday night football. Seems like soccer's the only game where the players don't have to pause for commercials. Try making a buck on that kind of football in this country."

Midge nodded his head, half in agreement. He poured Galloway another coffee and leaned closer to him.

"Look Gal, what's really going on? What's got into you?"

"I gotta tell you, Midge, I'm almost seventy. And you know when it hit me that I was that old? It was a Monday night, fourth quarter of the Raiders/Seahawks game, two-minute warning. Raiders were up by six. Seahawks were three-point dogs. Looked like I had it in the bag. Everybody had bet on the dog. I mean Seattle, the Seahawks. I should have cleaned house. Raiders were up by six, Midgey. Seattle had the ball: but it was fourth and long. Fourth and long. Hasselbeck stepped up to the line of scrimmage, checked the formation, threw his hands out and changed the play. Jesus, Midge, Seattle's kid quarterback changed the play. I felt a thud in my stomach like I'd been shot. From that point on everything was slow motion. Hasselbeck lifted the ball like he was going to throw a screen pass to Alexander. But he faked, tucked the ball away, slid through an opening in the Raiders' defence and ran twenty for a touchdown. He strode into the end zone like a born-again Montana. The camera zoomed through his face guard and on that pretty face of his was the future of football, Midge, and I knew then that the Raiders were finished, that I was finished."

Galloway took off his hat. The bald circle atop his head was red and beading with sweat. He wiped it with a napkin and replaced the hat. He took a sip of his coffee. Midge unclenched his fists to shake the hand of a new customer. Galloway put fifty cents on the counter and nodded to him on his way out. Midge stopped him by the cash register.

"Just tell me one thing, Gal, don't you want to hang in there for the love of sport?"

Galloway took a cigarette from his pack and stuck it in the corner of his mouth. He put his large spotted hand on Midge's shoulder.

"I never did it for the love of sport, Midgey. I did it for the vigorish."

He lit his cigarette and walked out the door. The wind had picked up. Snow buried the streets. Galloway pulled his collar up around his neck and dropped his head. He trudged through the weather. Traffic crawled at the same pace. He turned down Ferry and headed for the train station. He could hear his heart beating in his head. His breathing quickened. A wave of fear washed the colour from his face. He stopped. A woman bumped into him. He grabbed her arm.

"I've lost my will," he said. "My God, I've lost my will."

She pulled her arm from his hand, scowled and rushed away. Galloway panicked. He looked down at his feet, then behind him. The snow had covered his tracks, everyone's tracks. He spun around, looked up and down the roads. There was nothing but white — a whirling spectacle of white. He was short of breath, hot. A young man in a houndstooth blazer stopped and asked him if he was all right.

"I've lost my will," he said. "I've lost my way, god-damn it. Look at it. I don't know which way I came from. I don't know where the hell I am."

The young man guided Galloway into the station. He brushed the snow off his coat, sat him down and asked if he wanted some water. Galloway shook his head and closed his eyes. The young man left. Galloway's mind drifted.

A train pulled into the station sounding its whistle. It screeched to a stop. Annabelle stepped off the train. Galloway waved. She smiled and it warmed every inch of him. The melting snow dripped off his hat and down the back of his neck. He shivered and opened his eyes. There was no train. An old man dressed in army fatigues was sitting across from him staring. He was smoking a hand-rolled cigarette. Galloway squinted and looked around. The station was flooded with bedraggled com-muters. All around him they moved in a muted drone. He focused on the old man and attempted to get up.

"Sit down, sit down," the old man said. "They'll see you. Do you want to get yourself killed? Guess you've never been to the front before, eh, boy?"

Galloway sat back down. Jesus, he thought. The old man reached into his bag of tobacco, rolled another cigarette and offered it to Galloway. He declined.

"See that cloud of smoke over there?" said the old man. Galloway followed his crooked finger.

"Sure," he whispered.

"Kamikaze."

"Oh, yeah."

"Japanese, barely twenty."

"You knew him?"

The old man raised his eyebrows.

"Why'd you sign up, boy? No choice? Why don't you go home while you still got a pair of strong arms and good legs? Get out while you can, boy. You don't belong here. I can tell by the lily-white of your eyes."

The old man lit his cigarette and leaned back on the blue plastic chair. A train rumbled overhead. Galloway felt defeated. He thought about the days when he helped his dad shovel stalls at the track, every day waiting for the trainers to heist him up on one of their horses and walk him around. His favourite was a filly named Watergate, a lanky chestnut, fast but not strong enough. She broke her leg days before heading to Suffolk Downs.

"You ever watch the horses?" Galloway asked the man. "You ever bet everything you ever had on four legs and a tail?"

"What do I look like to you?"

Galloway wondered.

"Ah, Cigar was a beaut," said a grubby man in a long tweed overcoat, lying on the bench behind him. "I used to stand close as I could get to the fence when that horse raced in town. Jesus, what a beaut."

Galloway turned around to face him.

"Cigar was good but he didn't have the size or the finishing speed of the ponies that came before him." What he had, thought Galloway, was an affinity for dirt.

The grubby man got up and sat down beside him. "Those damn ponies put me in the gutter, mister."

"That's not uncommon," said Galloway. He stood up slowly and tipped his hat to the men. He went outside. The snow was still falling. He hailed a cab. He told the cabby he wasn't going far but couldn't walk in the snow. He said he wanted Midge's Deli on Pine.

"No problem," said the cabby. "I played ball with him in college, you know. What a shiester. He was tight end — a hell of a tight end."

The cabby laughed.

"Is that the Philly/KC game?" asked Galloway.

The cabby turned up the radio.

"Yeah, yeah, first quarter. The Eagles are gonna kill 'em."

"Never count out KC at home," said Galloway.

The cab pulled to a stop in front of Midge's. Galloway gave the cabby a ten.

"Thanks, man," he said. "Say hi to Midgey for me. Tell him to put the coffee on early. I'm back on the road at six."

"Sure."

Galloway got out of the cab. Midge's was dark except for a stream of light coming from the back room. He knew the boys played cards back there every

Thursday night. He knocked hard on the glass, pressed his face against it and looked around in the dark for his envelope. He spotted it by the cash register. He banged harder on the glass until the back door opened and Midge stuck his head out to see what the noise was. He saw Galloway's face pressed up against the window.

"What the hell?" he said.

"What's up?" said a couple of the guys.

Marty James stuck his head out the door.

"Is that Galloway?"

Midge nodded.

"What the hell's he doing here? I thought he got locked up."

"No," said Midge. "Jesus, he just kind of disappeared for a while."

"That man robbed me of every cent I had. It doesn't pay to bet on animals."

"It paid Galloway," said Midge. "He has a knack that one. He really has a knack."

"Yeah, well I'm better off with a hand of cards."

"You're just a bad bettor, Marty."

Midge walked into the deli and closed the door behind him. Galloway saw him and moved away from the window. Midge unlocked the front door and went outside.

"What's wrong, Gal?"

"Nothing, nothing Midge. I'm sorry to be a pain but I left that envelope there by your cash register when I was here earlier and I didn't realize it until I'd been sitting around in the train station for a while."

"What were you doing in the train station?"

"Well, I don't know Midge. I don't remember."

"Hold on, Gal." Midge went back into the deli and grabbed the envelope.

"Thanks Midge, sorry to break up the game. Say hi to the guys for me."

"Sure Gal, are you sure you're all right. You want me to call you a cab?"

"No, no, in this weather? No, I'll be fine, Midge. Thanks." Galloway clutched the envelope close to his chest.

"Oh. Midge, you didn't see Annabelle at all tonight did you?"

Midge dropped his head and rubbed his eyes. He looked back up at Galloway.

"No, I haven't seen Annabelle for some time."

Galloway nodded and walked across the street. Midge stood in the snow and watched him until he disappeared. He walked for blocks. His toes were numb. The snow had silenced everything. He stopped at a pay phone, reached into his pocket and pulled out his phone book. He slid a quarter into the phone and dialed.

"Hello."

"Kenny?"

"Dad?"

"It's your father."

"Dad, where the heck are you?"

Galloway looked around.

"Ah, I'm in a phone booth son, somewhere. Hold on."

Galloway stuck his head out of the phone booth and looked up and down the roads.

"I'm at Bleeker and Pine, pretty much. There's a donut store on the corner. A tuxedo shop across the street."

"Listen, Dad, go into the donut shop. I'll come and get you."

"In this weather?"

"Just wait in the donut shop for me, Dad."

Galloway hung up the phone. He walked over to the donut shop and stomped the snow off his shoes before going in. The Asian man behind the counter was already holding up the coffee pot.

"You want coffee?" he asked.

Galloway nodded. "Double cream."

A scruffy young man was sitting at the counter doing the crossword, smoking.

"Some night, eh?" he said.

"Some night," said Galloway.

He took his coffee and sat by the window. He put the wet envelope on the table. Benny Goodman was on the radio. The roads were unmarked. Galloway wondered if it was snowing in Pittsburgh. If it snowed in Pittsburgh on Monday Gannon would be useless. The Raiders didn't stand a chance in the snow.

"You want more coffee," asked the shop owner.

"He just wants you to stick around," said the guy at the counter.

Galloway held out his mug.

"Donut?"

"No, thank you. This is terrific. I'm just waiting for my wife."

"Jesus, your wife is coming to meet you here in this weather?" said the guy at the counter.

"What?" said Galloway.

He looked down at the envelope. He wondered what was in that envelope that his sons didn't already have. There was nothing he could leave them that they didn't already have. And what did he have, he wondered?

He got up, reached into his pocket and put a dollar on the table. He nodded to the two men as he left.

He walked back to the phone booth and called Midge's. Midge answered.

"Hey Midgey, what are you thinking for Monday's game?"

"Huh? The Raiders, Gal, of course. Why, what's going on?"

"Look outside, Midge. A hundred to one Pittsburgh's getting or going to get the same weather. Everyone's betting on the Raiders for this game. The line's inflated. Take the points, Midgey. Bet on the Steelers. The Raiders don't have a chance in hell at winning in this weather. Gannon's gonna get cold hands. He's no Plunkett, Midgey. Meet me at the Whiskey and listen for the weather forecast."

Galloway walked into the snow.

Kenny pulled up in front of the donut shop and went in. The shop owner held up the coffee pot.

"Coffee?"

"No, no, thank you. I'm looking for my father."

The guy at the counter looked up from his cross-word.

"Big guy, gruff voice, looks like Vince Lombardi?" he said.

"You look kind of young to remember Vince Lombardi," said Kenny.

"Everyone knows Lombardi," said the guy.

"He was sitting there," said the shop owner. "Left 10 minutes ago."

He pointed to the table then pointed to the door.

"Forgot this."

He handed Kenny the envelope.

"He said he was waiting for his wife," said the guy at the counter.

Kenny sat down.

"I'll take a coffee," he said, "regular, to go."

He stared at the envelope.

"His wife, my mother, died a few weeks ago," he said. "His wife is dead."

Kenny rubbed his eyes and grabbed the hot cup of coffee.

Galloway trudged through the snow. He caught sight of the flashing neon sign with a green beer bottle and two naked pink ladies wrapped around it. He walked into the bar and headed deep into the dark, smoky room. Nick, the bartender, lit up when he saw him.

"Galloway, Jesus, it's good to see you," he said. "Look, I'm sorry about the news. The boys and I chipped in and bought you a little gift, something to offer our condolences. I've been hoping you'd come in. We've been keeping it here for you."

Nick handed Galloway a box. He set it on the counter and took off his hat. The room spun. He looked up.

"Nick, do you remember when Annabelle used to sing at that jazz club down the street. What was it called again?"

"The Velvet Room."

"Yeah, the Velvet Room. God, remember I told you the scariest bet I ever made was betting I'd spend the rest of my life with that woman."

"I remember, Gal."

"And remember when my boys were born I swore I'd never go back to the track, that I'd change my ways and get a proper job. Annabelle gave up what she loved to do. Goddamn it, I would too. But I didn't, Nick. And look at my boys. Grown up with boys of their own. Good jobs. Jesus, Kenny's a top gun at some software company. Charlie's a sports doctor. Some funny name I can't even pronounce. And they don't seem to be angry with me, Nick."

"No one was ever angry with you, Gal. You did your job. You never let your family down."

Kenny walked through the door and smiled at Nick. He sat down next to his dad.

"Kenny, Jesus, what a coincidence, son."

He grabbed him in his arms.

Midge came through the door with Marty James and a couple of the guys from the poker game.

"Well, if this doesn't seem like old times," said Nick.

He poured them all a drink. Galloway picked his up and stared at it. He was pale. The guys jabbered about the Kansas City game and debated the upcoming battle between the Raiders and Steelers. Midge pumped the Raiders and winked at Galloway. Galloway looked right through him like he was watching someone behind him.

Nick hit Kenny on the shoulder.

"Take him home," he said.

Kenny looked at his dad. He patted him on the back. Galloway turned to look at his son. He saw his lips moving. Everyone's lips were moving. But no one was saying anything.

ON THE FARM

Lester's chopping wood by the barn. He's been chopping for hours. The dull thud beats against my head relentlessly. I want to go outside and tell him to stop. But if he stops he'll be puttering around in here, asking me if I'm okay, if I need anything, if I'm warm enough, hungry. Hungry? I want to say, look at me Lester, I'm encompassing a chair that could fit four of you. Do I look hungry? I must look cold. He's been chopping firewood all morning, this hot August morning. Sweat's running between my breasts, my thighs. I want to assure him, I am not cold.

I turn up the volume on the television set. Lester comes in. Touches my forehead. Tells me I'm not hot. Checks my pulse. Tells me I'm not dead. He sniggers. I want to tell him to sit down. He goes into the kitchen, runs the tap. He's drinking water. He's hot.

I spend my days in front of the TV in my housecoat and slippers. I watch sitcoms. Wait for one to make me laugh. The laugh track howls without me. In the kitchen, Lester titters along with it. The phone rings. It's my daughter. I can tell by Lester's voice. He tells her I'm not well. He pauses then says he doesn't know. He hangs up. We don't speak. Lester comes into the living room, steps in front of me, blocks the TV. Tells me he's going to the barn to feed the chickens. I nod. He leaves. I lift myself from the chair and go into the pantry. Grab myself a shot of bourbon. It slides down my throat. Warms almost every inch of me. I pour another shot into my coffee mug. I walk into the dining room, glance out the window.

Lester's moving around in the barn, a few chickens at his feet. He loves those chickens. I light a cigarette, blow the smoke out the window. I feel my skin sag. Lester comes out of the barn and sits on a tree stump. He wipes his brow, lights a cigarette and stares at the sky. He looks as young as the day we married. Do chickens keep you young? I want to tell him, I'm sorry I'm not the woman I used to be.

He puts out his cigarette and goes back into the barn. A blue pickup truck pulls up in front of it. Jerry Smith gets out. He buys eggs from us. Lester comes out to greet him. They shake hands. Lester smiles. I have to sit down. They laugh and the sky lights up. Lester stops laughing. He looks at Jerry. They both look at the house. I hide my face behind the curtain. Lester looks down and shakes his head. Jerry puts his hand on his shoulder. When Lester looks up, his face is pale. Clouds move across the sun. I shiver. They go into the barn. I go to the pantry, fill my coffee mug and resume my place in front of the TV.

I hear the engine of the pickup truck. It drives away. Lester comes in. Tells me Jerry's going to buy more eggs. His business is expanding. Tells me Jerry says he should think of branching out into cows. There's big business in cows. I want to tell him that's good. Cows are good. Lester stands there for a minute, then goes upstairs. I hear the tap running in the bathroom. The toilet flushes. The tap stops running. Lester comes back downstairs. He's standing behind me. I flick channels.

I want to ask him what he's doing. I can't turn my head around without moving my whole body. I hear him walk into the kitchen and open the fridge. He opens a can, probably a beer. I think he's saying my name under his breath — Lisa, Lisa, Lisa. But maybe he's saying Jesus, Jesus, Jesus.

He comes back into the living room. I can feel his eyes on the back of my head. I pull myself out of the chair to face him. I want to say, Lester, is something bothering you? He looks at me. I look down. He tells me he's going to meet Jerry. He walks out the door. He starts his red Camaro. Why not the pickup truck? Jerry lives on a farm with a long gravel driveway. Lester doesn't like to drive the Camaro on gravel. I want to call after him and say Lester...and I'm sure there was something else.

I go into the pantry, fill my coffee mug with bourbon. I turn on the lights, listen to the newly awakened crickets. I walk onto the front porch. It's been a long time since I've been out here. It smells like chickens. I go back inside, sit down. I turn off the television, listen to my breathing. I hear my daughter's voice, her laughter, her feet running across the hardwood floor. She was my life, the reason for getting up in the morning. She filled me with purpose. She grew up, found a man. Men take our daughters and there goes everything.

I light a cigarette, listen to time ticking. We don't have a clock that ticks. One hour, two hours, three hours. The phone rings. It rings and it rings. It stops. I look out the window. It's dark. I want to call out for Lester. I open my mouth. It shuts. I walk onto the front porch, down the steps and begin walking to the barn. The phone rings again. I turn around. I get up the steps and into the house. It stops. I sit down and take deep breaths.

The chickens are squawking. He'll be back for the chickens. They only care about chickens, the men around here.

I get up and walk into the kitchen. I sit on the stool by the phone and wait for it to ring again. It rings. I pick it up. Silence. Then, mother? Mother, is that you? Where's dad? Mom, go and get dad. Mother? Mother? I hang up. I hear the Camaro. It stops in front of the house. Lester walks into the kitchen. I want to tell him I went outside. I turned off the television and went outside. He checks my forehead, grabs his jacket and goes to the barn. I pull myself off the stool. My back aches. I sit down on the chair in the living room and turn on the TV, flick channels and fall asleep.

I'm woken by the sound of a car coming up the driveway. The sun's up and it's nippy. Must still be early. The car's not from around here. It purrs. Only city cars purr. It makes me nervous. I think it's my mother. Lester must have called my mother. I hear two doors close. My mother calls my name. She should know better.

I hear Lester calling her from the barn. I don't hear my father. He doesn't speak either. It's not hereditary, different circumstances. My mother does the talking. My father is fine with that.

They come into the living room. Lester points at me like, well, there she is. I feel my face turning red. Oh, Lisa, my mother says. Her eyes water. I feel sick. My father nods. I nod back. Oh, Lisa, my mother says again and I can't go anywhere. I can't leap up and run away, like the lithe child I used to be. I can't escape their eyes. All three of them staring at me. I want to scream at them to stop looking at me. What can I do? It's the way it is. It happened. I lost faith. I lost faith in everything. I can't control it. I have no control of anything. I got bigger, quieter. I stopped talking. There's nothing left to talk about. What's there to talk about out here? Chickens? I want to laugh and tell them, oh to be a chicken. You should see how he treats the chickens.

My mother comes over, puts the back of her hand against my forehead. She's not hot, she tells Lester. Lester shrugs. I wonder what it is, says my mother, something she ate? Lester laughs. My mother looks at me and tells me she didn't mean it like that. I look down. My dad sits in the chair next to me. He puts his hand on mine. It's warm. My eyes fill with tears. They run down my face. I can't move. My mother and Lester go into the kitchen. I hear my mother's voice but I don't know what she's saying; her words drowned out by my beating heart. I want to tell my dad I went outside yesterday. I want to tell him there's hope.

Lester comes into the living room and motions to my dad to join him. They go into the kitchen. Lester whispers. I only hear bits and pieces. I can't stand it anymore. I pull myself out of the chair and lumber into the kitchen. My presence silences them. I open my mouth. My mother gasps. The phone rings. It's my daughter, I can tell by Lester's voice. My mother looks at me. It's your daughter, she says, I can tell by Lester's voice. I roll my eyes. I close my mouth. My father looks at me and chuckles. My cheeks tingle. I laugh. Lester drops the phone. My mother grabs my arms. Lisa, Lisa, she squeals.

She beams. I can't stop laughing. My mother laughs. My dad laughs. Lester stands there looking at us. It's not funny, he says, she'll hurt herself. I open my mouth and howl with laughter. I clutch my stomach. Lester storms outside into the barn. My mother watches him. My dad grabs his keys from the counter. He looks at my mother, she nods. I panic. I want to tell them not to leave me. It's not that simple. I'm not suddenly cured. I look into my mother's eyes. She clutches my hand in hers and leads me to the car. My dad starts the engine. It purrs. I can feel Lester watching us from the door-way of the barn. I can't turn my head around without moving my whole body. I want to tell my mother and father to stop. I feel sad. But something changes. I don't feel Lester's eyes on the back of my head. I don't feel his stare. We're not even out of the driveway and he's gone back to the chickens.

BONE KEY

A backyard isn't just a backyard when the wind is moving, leaves cavorting to piano music. Piano music cloaking my backyard with a haunting grace. It emanates from the house that backs onto mine. The house is big but barely visible through the wide, old oak trees. Even leafless, they obscure it. All I see are fragments of painted pink brick. The front isn't hidden. It has a huge "apartments for rent" sign in the window of the glassed in front porch. It has all the makings of a boarding house without the likes of a boarding house traipsing in and out, drinking beer on the front steps and blaring heavy metal day and night. If not for the lights that come on at night, I'd think no one lived there. If not for the piano music, the house is still.

When I get home from work, I let my dog out in the backyard, sit on one of the garden chairs and ungrit my teeth. The dog relieves himself on the barbecue, the picnic table. At this point in his life the trees have become mundane. He lies in the bed of leaves and digs up yesterday's bone. I watch him. On the way home, I look forward to watching him. A few minutes after I sit down the piano music begins and I feel my shoulders release their tension. My ears swoon. It's not a sound that's easy to describe. I feel it. It has a texture but what I don't know, something softer than silk, lighter than velvet, heavier than a cotton ball.

The phone rings and I heave myself from the chair, from the music. I took a taxi to the lawyer's office today, I tell my mother over the phone, as I pour myself a gin and tonic and take off my shoes. She asks me why I did that — cabs aren't cheap. I tell her, it's the way I felt. I tell her I couldn't bear sitting on a bus at three in the afternoon. The bus is too busy then and I didn't want to be jabbed. I didn't want to accidentally glance into the wrong person's eyes and be looked at with disdain, or sit amongst bitter middle-aged women who've already been through what I was on my way to execute. I will be middle-aged, divorced and bitter too soon and I don't want to sit next to what I am about to become. My mother asks me if the cab driver took me the long way. I tell her I brought the papers home with me. There are clauses I don't understand. He's asked for more than I am willing to part with and why am I surprised. That's why I'm leaving him, why I'm spent. My mother says she tried to flag down a cab the other night and even the ones with their lights on didn't stop. I tell her I'll call her later.

The house is colder than the air outside and my back tenses up in the cold. I hear something and wonder if I had left the radio on upstairs. I go upstairs. My bedroom's dark and cool. The radio's not on but the window's slightly open and the piano music is filtering in with the night air. I keep the room dark and push back my curtains. All I can see are slices of light between the trees. Behind drawn curtains, shadows. I lie down on my bed and listen. She stops occasionally. She, he? I don't know. Maybe it's wrong but I think it's a woman, something about the playing — its fluidity. I do know it's not a recording. I've been listening carefully. She stops, starts again differently. I think it must be a large piano, but the house is broken into apartments and I assume they are not large.

I've looked at the front of the house many times, tried to judge how big each room is, tried to fathom how on earth a piano fit through any of its doors. I walk my dog by that house almost everyday and I've never seen anyone moving in or out. But the piano and its player have only just moved in, no longer than a month ago. The music only began seeping into my backyard as the summer was ending, as my marriage was ending.

My mother calls back and asks me how things went at the lawyer's today. I tell her what I'd told her and she says it doesn't surprise her. She says I'm not to give up the house or the dog or any of my furniture and heir-looms. She tells me she's not going to let me go through the same thing my grandmother went through. She's not going to sit back and watch me leave with nothing. Her mother was left with nothing, had to rebuild every-thing at sixty. What a shame, she says, what a shame. I tell her not to worry. He can't take the house, I bought it, and he didn't like the dog anyway. Another reason why I want the divorce, how can I live with a man who doesn't like dogs? You married a man who doesn't like dogs, my mother says. It takes a long time to get to know someone, she tells me. Yes, I say, I know. Well next time you'll be more careful, she says. There won't be a next time, I tell her. I don't have the time it takes to get to know someone that well.

I go downstairs to the kitchen and stare at the sides of the boxes piled neatly in the freezer. Italian meatballs, fettuccine Alfredo, lasagna, honey chicken stirfry, meatloaf and mashed potatoes. I grab the meatloaf. It takes five minutes. A little longer than the rest but it's more filling. I stick it in the microwave. I take the envelope marked "final" out of my briefcase. The document is five pages, small print — a page for every year of my marriage.

I met my husband in the small town where I was born. We weren't childhood sweethearts. My family moved before I started high school. We didn't meet until I went back to the small town I was born in for my uncle Charlie's funeral. We met at the cemetery. After they lowered my uncle into his grave, I remained there until the rest of my family left. My mother called for me but I ignored her. I'd loved my uncle deeply. Probably deeper than the love I felt for anyone. He was a kind, empathetic man — a masterpiece.

"Most people don't like to watch the grave being filled in, miss," a guy said behind me.

I stared at the top of the casket, handfuls of dirt scattered across it.

"It's not so much the filling in that bothers me," I said, "but the sod."

"The sod?" he said.

I turned around slowly, bitterly. I wanted time alone with my uncle, here at dusk, just him and me and his casket and the handfuls of dirt — all his farewell gifts.

"What do you mean, the sod?" the guy asked.

He was as thin as the shovel he was holding in his gloved hands. His grey coveralls hung off him. Neither the name stitched onto them or the coveralls fit like they were his.

"Is that your real name?" I asked.

"Yes."

"Abel?"

"Abe. My friends call me Abe."

I turned back around. He began shoveling the dirt into my uncle's grave.

I didn't really know what it was about Abe. We only exchanged a few words. I didn't even look into his eyes for the entire exchange but I couldn't get his eyes out of my head. They were identical to my uncle's. On the way back to my aunt's I envisioned laughing with him, holding his hands, and kissing him.

My mother was waiting for me on the front porch. "You have no consideration for anyone but yourself. Where have you been?" she said.

"With Charles, mother. With your dead brother-in-law," I said and went into the house. My mother sniping at me from behind.

That night I dreamt about Abe, his eyes. On my way out of town I stopped at the cemetery. I'd brought stones to place on my uncle's grave that I'd gathered while walking that morning with my aunt. In Paris they put stones on graves. Flowers die. Stones were never alive. The dead can learn from them. I walked to the grave. Abe and another guy were down on their knees laying sod over my uncle's grave — sealing him in.

I stopped a few feet away from them. My eyes filled with tears. Abe turned around. He stood up when he saw me. He had a look on his face like a child caught. I dropped the stones and ran to my rental car. When I felt a hand grab my arm, I crumbled. Abe knelt beside me, went to wipe my tears with his gloves — his dirty gravedigger's gloves.

He asked me to wait until he was finished, then took me out for lunch to the pizza place in town. I told him how I'd had my first date here. I was thirteen. I told him the guy I went out with died in a car crash two weeks later. If Abe had been here, he might have buried him. Abe told me he just moved here last year. He came with his mother after she divorced. Abe told me the I'm-never-getting-married story. He told me he's seen too many good relationships fall apart as soon as the couple got married. It's a curse, he said, a trap. But for some reason people keep falling into it.

"Like graves," I said.

I told him about my uncle. How he'd been so good to me, listened to me, understood me when I spent most of my days in solitude. My mother thinking I was strange. She didn't want me to grow up to be one of those creative types. Uncle Charlie gave me confidence. He understood. He was a pianist — a child prodigy. His fingers the length of oars. He was struck with arthritis in his teens. It crippled him. The doctors told him there was hope, that young people often outgrow arthritis. He didn't. His fingers buckled, knotted, bent like aging branches. He was riddled with pain, couldn't play the piano. He was devastated. He fell for his pretty nurse. After many years they married. He taught music theory from home. He pined for his piano — the playing. He withered, was as thin as fingers. My aunt found him draped over his baby grand with a self-inflicted bullet hole through his heart. The keys were stained red — all 52 of them. My aunt burned the piano. As it went up in flames she swore she heard it playing Chopin's Nocturne opus no. 9.

I worked at the *Daily News*. I wrote about local events. Car crashes mostly, and missing animals. Abe moved to the city just after we met and got a job at the packing plant. He decided to join me here after he had nightmares that the dead were coming out of their graves after him. I asked him why he thought they would do that? Because of what you said about sealing them in, he said. Ever since he buried my uncle, he didn't feel right. I think Abe asked me to marry him so he wouldn't have to sleep alone.

When I married Abe I didn't shed a tear. I stood frozen at the altar. I heard my mother weeping behind me. I asked my father not to walk me down the aisle. He was offended but I didn't feel right being given away. I love my father, I just didn't feel like I was ever his. He was never home. He was a pilot. Flew the international flights. I always told my mother she should have married someone like my uncle. She said, but he was disabled. I never forgot that. It's not that I wasn't thrilled to be marrying Abe. I loved him dearly at first. He was quiet, never had much to say, but I thought in the beginning he was at least listening.

He started drinking. He worked from 6 A.M. 'til 4 P.M. then went to the bar with his buddies and spent all his wages. By the time he came home for dinner, dinner was hard. I was usually sleeping or walking the dog looking for him. This went on for a few years. Nothing happened between us.

Abe lost his job when he yelled at the foreman for yelling at him when he came to work late, hung over and stinking of booze. I got another job at Betty's Diner. I worked 9–5 at the paper and 6–11 at Betty's. Abe sat in front of the television drinking beer. He rarely slept. He was afraid of the dark. He thought he heard things, saw shadows out of the corner of his eyes. He told me he'd get a job as soon as he could put his finger on what it was he should do. I kept working, paying the bills, putting food on the table, and attempting to put a finger on what it was I should do. My mother phoned me too much asking me if the situation had changed. When he flew through town, my father phoned asking if there was anything I needed and had the situation changed. I assured them both that Abe was going through a transitional period and everything would be fine soon. My mother showed up with groceries. My father sent over a car. Abe got in the car one day and drove to the coast with all the tips I'd been saving in a shoebox at the bottom of my hope chest. He blew the whole lot in the casino and pawned the car to get home.

I sat in the backyard crying like I had never cried before. Harder than when my junior-high sweetheart died, harder than when my uncle died. The dog lay at my feet looking up at me with the what-have-I-done-now look that dogs get when they figure the reason you're upset must be because of them. I drank my umpteenth gin and tonic and swore I heard piano music. I shook my head and went inside. Abe was sitting on the couch with his hands shoved deep into his empty pockets.

"Get out, Abe," I said.

"What?"

"Get out, Abe. Get out."

Abe left. I fell asleep on the couch. That night I woke in a cold sweat. My ears were ringing with the sound of Chopin's Nocturne opus no. 9. I dreamt I was slouched over the remains of a burnt piano. My hands part of the keyboard. My fingers ten bloodstained ivory keys.

When Abe phoned the next morning I told him I wanted a divorce. I told him to never come back to the house. I'd send his clothes over to the motel. He told me he wasn't staying at the motel. In the background I heard what sounded like a woman giggling. The next day I quit my diner job. The paper promoted me to head correspondent for the entertainment section. I decorated the house. I landscaped the backyard.

I put the papers back in the envelope, finish the meat-loaf. I take a sip of my gin and tonic and walk into the backyard. The piano music meanders through it. It lulls the dog to sleep. I put down my drink and walk out to the street and around the corner. The front of the house is dark. No porch light. I walk up to the door and knock. I knock again, nothing. I turn the handle and the door opens. I follow the music. The hall creaks and my heart pounds through my neck into my throat. I'm sweating but I'm cold. I stop at the door at the end of the hall. The music stops with me. I knock and for a moment I want to run, but I can't run. I think of Abe. The door opens. A man stands there. I freeze. He disappears. I walk slowly into the room. A baby grand piano is wedged into the corner by the window. The man reappears at the piano and begins playing Chopin. He looks over at me, and smiles. My heart overflows. I reach out my hand, my words barely audible, "Uncle Charlie?"

A woman walks out of the kitchen. In broken English she asks me what I want. Asks me who the hell I think I am walking into a stranger's apartment without knocking. She shakes her dishcloth at me. I shake my head, regain focus. Suddenly, I notice the blaring television, two children sitting in front of it, heads tilted toward me assessing the commotion. The music has subsided. I look for the piano. The room is sparse. There is a plaid couch in the corner by the window. There is nothing but a plaid couch in the corner by the window.

A TIME I NEVER KNEW

In the lobby of the Falcon Motel a young Spanish woman leans on the front desk snapping her bubble gum. Her dirt-brown hair rolls with curls. An orange-and-red scarf keeps it off her face. Squeezed into a lilac tube top, her breasts are full like her hips and she bares her bellybutton without shame. She paints her fingernails gold. I clear my throat. She looks up, then down. I tell her there are people spying on us from the rooftops. They're wasted, I tell her, desperate. A hundred eyes leering through our window.

She says, "Close the curtains, señora, turn off the lights. People on rooftops."

A stocky, ebony-skinned man comes in from the outside. Looks at me through the corner of his eye and sneers. He mutters something to the young Spanish woman. She giggles and snaps her gum. I shiver from standing barefoot on the cold clay floor. A gecko scurries by, missing my toes by a hair.

Back in the room, I study the window. The people have taken a rest. Returned to their families, their jobs. The rooftop is barren but for a single clothesline, one white sheet floating in the wind. I had ripped down the curtains to make a new dress. I neglected to consider the consequences. I wanted a new dress. The heavy fabric laden in daffodils and baby's breath promised warmth and comfort, some style. I had yearned for a change. Sickened by my unwashed Everlast sweat pants and your Fruit of the Loom undershirt. There was a time I was so pretty.

I walk across the stained beige carpet to the bed. The man on the TV yaps about Cuba. He smokes a fat cigar. I light a cigarette and reach into the night-table drawer. Remove the blue velvet bag, unwrap it and arrange the apparatus before me. Ever since I was a child, needles haven't frightened me. The nurses would say, look away. The blood burst from my vein. My eyes widened in amazement. There it was — my blood, flooding into the vial like scarlet rapids. I'd yip with excitement. The nurses looked at me in disgust. I think it was disgust. To think it flows beneath my skin like a river and I never feel it, running and running and running without a sound.

I stick the needle in my neck. Blood turns to cream. Cool and thick, covering my entire body like strawberries. My head bobs, eyelids become weighty. My mouth dries. Wind gusts through the room. The window is shut. The bed sways. I am captain of my own ship.

I hear footsteps. You run across the room, cease to make noise, then clomp hard like you mean business. Reluctantly, I open my eyes. You're in a soldier's uniform. There has not been war here for years. You were never a soldier — nor your father. You weren't even born when the bombs blew your ancestry to pieces.

"What disguise is this?" I ask. "What vision?"

"I died. I will fight and die again," you say.

"Who are you?"

"The bombs drop and they drop and they drop," you say.

"Nothing changes. I agree with you," I say.

I look back out the window at the smoke-filled streets. Hear screaming babies, running feet, howls.

"What trick is this?" I ask you. "What nightmare?"

You kiss my cheek. A leaving-soldier's kiss. My stomach tightens, turns, a new sickness. I'm riddled with the dread of you going, never returning, falling bullet-ridden onto strange ground. I fall to my knees, grab your ankles. You drag me a few inches then shake me loose. You don't turn around. I'm lying on a crusty motel-room floor in a time I never knew.

I call the lobby. The young Spanish woman answers the phone.

"I need a new room," I tell her, "one with curtains. I need curtains now that I'm alone."

"You're alone now, señora?" she says.

"Yes, I lost the only love I ever had."

"Where did he go?" she asks.

"To war," I say.

"What war?"

"Well, that's the question. What war?"

"I have the key, señora."

"The key?"

"To your new room, señora."

"The one without windows?"

"The one with curtains. You said you wanted curtains."

"Oh, yes. Do you have one without a door? No door, so no one can leave me again?"

Sheers don't keep the light out. But I don't think the voyeurs can see in. I don't think they will return, maybe the occasional drifter. What is there for them to see now? I am faceless, bodiless. I just sit here and that's not worth watching. No.

Are you there? Are you there? You are not. Were you ever really there? I go to the window, peek through the curtains. Are they there? They are not. Did they follow you? Your army. Was it you they watched? No, it was us. It was because it was us. Apart we are nothing, to them or to each other.

It must be true that heat rises. This room is too warm. The young Spanish woman moved me up and, though I'm afraid of heights, I feel like I'm making progress. I get up. Walk to the sink. In the mirror looms a grey replica of myself, hair stringy and painted to my scalp. I run the cold water, stick my wrists under it. My mother told me it's a coolant. This is the desert, a murdering heat. I dry my arms. You warned me there'd be down times.

There's a knock at the door.

"Your paper, señora, your milk," says the young Spanish woman.

She knocks and she knocks. Can't she tell by the old news piling up on the outside that I have no interest in the paper; by the sour milk, no interest in nourishment? Yesterday's news sits outside my room and she thinks today will be any different. Is she really so concerned and yet not concerned enough to use her house key to come in and see what is what. It's that almost-concern that is more hurtful than helpful — that apathy.

Are you there? Are you there? Were you ever there? Were you ever here? I believe that you were. I have scars to prove it. I'll turn myself inside out and bare the damage. I'll strip this window of its curtains and bare it all. I pace the room. The chair is losing a leg. The desk light burnt out days ago. The mice keep their distance.

I flop down on the bed. What now? Let me see what I can pull from the ceiling. What cobweb remains?

I call the front desk.

"I need a new room."

"What room?" asks the young Spanish woman.

"What's left?"

"The honeymoon suite."

"The honeymoon suite?"

"Yes, but you haven't paid for your other rooms. I can't keep you. I cannot let you stay."

"You can't turn me loose. Where will I go? Not yet, soon, soon. He will bring money when he comes back and he will buy the whole motel, buy it all before he leaves again."

"He will leave again?" she says.

"They always leave again," I say.

"When he is coming back?"

"He's on his way."

"You've talked to him?"

"Sort of."

"Ah. I have the key."

"The key!"

"To the suite, señora. Do you want champagne? You will want to celebrate, no?"

"Yeah, two bottles of champagne. Two bottles and two glasses, yeah."

The honeymoon suite is big, bright, distastefully decorated. It's red, pink and frilly. Smells of baby powder and aftershave. Who consummates marriage in such a room? Who sleeps here? Who can? I see something out of the corner of my eye. You are lying on the heart-shaped bed like a newborn child. You are two steps ahead. I knew you would come.

"Are you safe?" I say. "Are you in pain?"

"It is not safe here," you whisper.

"No, it isn't. I know," I say. "Did you fight for this?"

"What? "

"Did you lose? Did you win? Have you won?"

"Won what?"

"The war?"

"There is no winning."

"You lost?"

"You can only lose."

"You came here to tell me that?"

I walk to the window. You raise your voice louder and louder.

"I'm talking to you," you scream.

"No you're not. You are listening to yourself. Listening to your own voice and why I do not know. Why you don't get tired of your own excuses amazes me. You have been saying the same thing for years. Go to sleep.

Sleep and be silent for both of us. Sleep and be silent or come up with something new. Where did you go?"

"Go?"

"When you left. Where was it you went? Did you not learn anything there?"

"I didn't go anywhere."

"You left. Left me alone."

"I was here."

"But I was alone."

You sit on the edge of the bed looking at me like I'm mad — like I am mad. You, feigning ignorance, suddenly amnesia-ridden. Have you forgotten the dramatic exit, the inexplicable leaving lines? All I had was the draught blowing through the closed window, across the room, straight through me and out the door. Then back through the door, across the room, straight through me and back out the window I didn't want. In and out and in and out, draught after draught after draught. And you wonder what I'm talking about?

We stare at each other, then out the window. Your mouth drops. I grab my things and leave.

"I need a new room," you tell the young Spanish woman behind the desk. "One with a new wife then I'll need the old room back."

"I thought you had a wife," she says.

"She left."

"Oh, when did she leave?"

"Recently."

The young Spanish woman snaps her gum.

"I'm sorry," she says. "Here's the key."

"To?"

"Your new room, señor."

"Does it have a wife?"

"No, señor, but it has a phone and a phone book. You can look one up."

The phone rings. It's you. You tell me you're lost without me. You never leave your room, where do you get lost? Surely, not in your room. In your head? I watch it ring sometimes, the phone. I sit carefully on the three-legged chair and watch it ring. It stops and sometimes I regret not picking it up, but I know it will ring again. Why you call is beyond me.

You tell me you speak to other women. I know it's a big phone book, lots of women to get to know. And that you talk to God. I wonder how you talk to God. You can't afford long distance.

I never see you, and my eyes long to, I must admit. I hear you and hear you and my ears are sick of you. My head hurts. You don't ask to meet me. You don't leave your room. You are satisfied where you are. I forget to ask why you call. Why do you call? I forget to ask myself why I answer. I'd draw the curtains but there are no windows here.

The phone rings. You tell me you met another woman. She's young, and it won't lead to anything, but you had to keep in with the young to keep up with what's going on out there. You said she calls and she calls.

"Why are you telling me this?" I ask.

"It's news," you say.

"It's nothing," I say.

"Exactly."

"It's something to me. It's nothing in general. News would be you've turned the corner. Had an epiphany. Can't live without me. Made plans for the future and I figure prominently in them. You've seen the light and you are coming to pick me up by it."

"I can't help you," you say. "Atlas carried the world on his shoulders, but there are no more men like that."

The phone disappears.

The young Spanish woman warns me that if I throw one more phone down the hole I made in the floor they will throw me out on the street. I say, if they keep replacing the phones, I'll throw myself down the hole I made in the floor and I'll be harder to pick up. I pace the room. There are traces of intruders, hairs, a merciless scent of sweat. How they get in, I don't know. I thought I locked everything up from the inside. Still, they manage to weasel their way in. I want no one here. And that phone, that link. That one vein I cannot puncture and drain dry. An umbilical cord that links me to you. The telephone cord. A telephone cord.

I call you. Another man answers.

"He isn't here," he says.

"What do you mean, he isn't here? Who are you?"

"I live here," he says.

"You didn't live there yesterday."

"And that means what?"

"That means that you only live there as of today and that someone else lived there yesterday and you probably know who and why he is not there now."

"No, I don't know. The room was empty."

"Except for a phone?"

"Yes."

"And a phonebook?"

"I don't know."

"Look."

"No."

"No what?"

"No, there is nothing else."

"Did you look everywhere?"

"There is nowhere else to look."

"I see."

The young Spanish woman cleans the lobby windows. Her jeans grip her hips awkwardly. Etched into her lower back is a fire-breathing dragon. I gasp, startling her. She shifts her hips, folds her arms across her chest and hisses at me. I shuffle back to my room and peer out the window. My hands ache. The skin is cracked, rubbed to the bone.

You walk through the door with two coffees. A brown paper bag protrudes from the pocket of your red velvet blazer. You're unshaven, hair in clumps. Your skin's ruddy but not like sunburn. You tell me it's a beautiful morning. The sun's on fire, not a cloud in the sky. The off-licence on the corner is closed. You had to walk over to Harvey's convenience, then meet Frank for the goods. I throw myself on the bed. You stroke my head, tell me I'm sweating.

Your face changes, eyes roll and widen. You stand up, turn in circles, ask why the bed covers and clothes are strewn across the room, the phone ripped from the wall, desk and chair upturned. You storm over to the window.

"What the hell have you done to the curtains?" you say. "I leave you alone for five fucking minutes and this is what happens?"

IMPALA

Joan bursts through the door. Doug jumps. Leans forward in the tartan reclining chair. He runs a weary hand over his weathered brow. She stands in front of him quivering. Eyes bugged, face tight and drawn, mouth half its original size. Averse to that look, Doug picks the pen off the coffee table, grips it in his fist and waits.

"I cannot look at the Impala anymore, Doug," says Joan. "It's been sitting in our driveway for one month. I cannot stand the sight of its peeling grey body. Its bulk. I'm putting it in the garage."

Doug looks at the hardwood floor, swallows.

"You can't drive it," he says. "The temporary licence ran out two days ago."

"I can drive it five feet into my garage," she says. "I cannot look at it anymore. I sit in my backyard on a nice sunny day and stare at a succession of automobiles. We have three in our driveway, Doug. More automobiles than kids. It's got to go."

"I'll call again," he says.

Last month the professor called from the city. Asked if Doug and Joan could do her a favor. The professor has been helpful to them in the past. As much as they dislike doing favours they agreed. For her they agreed.

"I need you to drive across the border and pick up a car from my brother," she said. "Keep it at your place for a week. Then when I get back from vacation you can drive it into town and I'll make you a brilliant dinner for all your trouble."

Joan took the call originally. She was quiet at first. It's not so simple to drive someone else's vehicle across the border, she thought. Not in these troubled times. She said she couldn't do it. She's not a citizen of either country. It's hard enough getting herself across the border and Doug has a record. Driving someone else's car from one country to another by a landed immigrant and an ex-con will not fly she told the professor. The professor said it was a long story but she needed to get the car over the border. She said she'd call back.

She called back. Doug and Joan were adamant about not driving across the border for the vehicle. It wasn't worth the risk. The professor said her brother would drive the car to a local motel. Then he'd take a cab to the airport and fly home. If Doug and Joan could pick the vehicle up at the motel, keep it until she returned from vacation then drive it to her, she would be forever indebted to them.

Joan and Doug agreed. Primarily driven by a nagging sense of guilt. They agreed to retrieve the car from the motel and keep it for one week until she got back from vacation. What badgered the staid couple most was the professor's assumption that it was nothing to drive it to her. Doug and Joan rarely leave the rural setting for a reason. Westbound highway driving has become a nightmare. And once in the city, traffic is a typhoon of rage and nonsensical maneuvers, not to mention the unpleasant smells hanging in the yellow air, and the parvenus.

The day came. Doug was conveniently summoned to work. The brother called. In a throaty drawl he said he was at the Sandman motel. He'd leave the keys at the front desk. He was about to hang up and Joan jumped in to ask what the car looked liked.

"How will I know what one it is?" she said.

"It's an Impala," said the brother. "A light blue Impala."

He said thank you and hung up.

Joan knew of the motel. It was one of a few to make the headlines of the local paper on a regular basis: shootings, stabbings, child-porn rings. Doug had just left. She considered leaving the professor's car at the motel until Doug returned to take her there. Then decided she didn't want to drive a strange vehicle home in the dark. So she had a cup of coffee, watered the backyard plants and drove to the Sandman in her Monte Carlo. She was exhausted. This was her only day off. She'd had plans. Perturbed by the inconvenience, she grumbled the entire way. She pulled into the motel. Parked the car by the little in-ground pool. A beer-bellied man in a red Speedo sat on its edge, a can of Canadian in his fat hand. From the pool a thin woman in a turquoise bathing cap stroked his puffy knee.

Joan looked over her shoulder for the Impala. When scanning the array of vehicles she realized she didn't know what an Impala looked like. A Mercedes, a Stingray even a variation of Honda she could pick out of a mish-mash of makes but an Impala? In the fifties they were muscle cars. The nineties rounded them out. She decided to get the keys first. A withered, bony lady sat behind the front desk smoking a cigarillo. She lowered her square lilac sunglasses as Joan walked through the door.

"I'm here for the Impala," said Joan.

The old lady nodded, handed her a set of keys and pointed to her left.

"I'll have to leave my own car for a few hours," said Joan. "Until my husband gets home from work. Will that be a problem?"

The woman shook her head, shrugged her shoulders. Must be nice to not give a damn, thought Joan. Or maybe she's too old to speak.

The man was in the pool. The woman sat on the edge rubbing his shoulders. His eyes were closed. A half-smile occupied his rumpled face. Joan walked around the parking lot. It didn't take her long to find it. The car was large, all body, more grey than light blue. At one time it probably was a light blue. It'd aged, lost its pastel chic. She assumed it was an '80s model. She got in, put the keys in the ignition. It wouldn't start. She thumped the steering wheel. It started. Sluggishly the two made it home. She pulled it close to the garage to make room for the other cars. She got out, locked the door. That was four weeks ago.

Doug picks up the phone. Joan stands by. He rolls his eyes, tells Joan it's the professor's answering machine. Doug leaves a message. Says, we can't keep the car anymore. It's taking up space. The licence ran out. We can't drive it. You'll have to come and get it. Doug hangs up. Joan leaves the room.

The phone rings. Doug answers it. It's the professor.

"I'm sorry," she says. "I'm sorting things out."

"You need to come and get it," says Doug.

"Well, I can't. I can't personally. I don't drive. I don't have anywhere to park it and it's not insured. I'm working on it."

Doug doesn't say anything at first. "You don't drive," he says.

"No,"

"Why did you get the car?" he asks.

"It's a long story," she says. "Let me work something out this week and I'll get back to you."

Doug hangs up the phone. He hears a car engine coughing. He goes outside. Joan's running the Impala. The garage door is open. She gets out, acknowledges Doug and proceeds to clear space in the garage. She shoves boxes, a lawn mower, bikes and garden tools aside. She gets back into the Impala, revs the engine and drives it into the garage. Closes the door, grabs a beer from the cooler and sits down on a garden chair.

"Look," she says. "Now I can see the lilies."

Doug goes into the garage and stares at the abandoned automobile. He juggles the irrationality of the situation: this woman who doesn't drive purchases a car from her father, has it driven halfway to her home by her brother and leaves it at a friend's house? This has no end, he thinks.

He comes out of the garage. "We overestimate academics," he says.

"I've looked at that car longer and harder than I've looked at myself," says Joan.

Doug frowns. He grabs a beer from the cooler. Through the crack in the side door of the garage he can see the passenger window of the car. Like a sad eye, it stares at the wall. Doug wonders why the professor's father wanted her to have it. He wonders how the car feels, stranded in a stranger's garage far from home, not really wanted by anyone. What must it be like not to be wanted?

"You know it looks like an impala," says Doug. "Except for the colour of course. Something about the way it's sitting in the garage like that just staring at the wall. That's how I imagine an impala in captivity would look, sorry for itself, dreaming of life outside in the woods, foraging for food, free. There's something terribly timid about those creatures and yet they carry around those lyre-shaped horns like they were Q-tips, able to move with enormous leaps if disturbed. One day that car might just up and leap out of that garage."

"What are you talking about Doug?" asks Joan.

"Impalas, Joan. I'm talking about an antelope, *Aepyceros melampus*, hailing from southern and eastern Africa, whose name is of Zulu origin — the impala."

Doug picks the portable phone out of Joan's frozen hand. Her gaping mouth exposes the damage that's been done since childhood. He calls his friend Brandon. Brandon asks if he got rid of the Impala yet. He laughs.

"Craziest thing I ever heard," he says.

"Well, it gets crazier yet. Turns out she doesn't even drive," says Doug.

Brandon laughs harder, hoots. Doug shakes his head. "I should see if she wants to get rid of it for few hundred bones. It's gonna cost way too much to insure. Who insures a woman who doesn't drive?"

Joan's shocked. "She doesn't drive?" she says. "What the hell? You didn't tell me that."

"I was afraid to."

Brandon says he might buy it. If not, his friend Bill is shopping for another car. Bill has six kids. Needs a vehicle to scurry around town in from the arena to the ballpark, Dairy Queen and dance rehearsal. Just needs an extra kick-around car.

"Six kids?" says Doug.

"Does it handle the road well?" asks Brandon.

"It doesn't look like it could handle anything at the moment. Poor thing looks like it'd appreciate a hug more than a highway."

Joan shakes her head.

"Yeah," says Doug. "Give Bill a call."

Doug calls the professor. Gets her answering machine. He says he's got a plan that will relieve her of the diabolical mess she's got them all into. He doesn't use those words exactly. Says he knows a guy who can take it off her hands for a few bones.

She calls back immediately, says she can't sell it. Her ex-boyfriend has agreed to be co-owner. He'll sort out the insurance, even come and pick it up. Doug tells this to Joan and Joan can't believe it. Who purchases a car with a man you no longer have relations with?

"It's like divorced parents deciding to have another kid," says Joan.

"No it's not," says Doug. "But it's odd."

Joan closes the side door of the garage. Picks a few leaves off the grass. All summer leaves have been falling. It's not a good sign. Joan tells Doug her mother had a friend who harboured a car for a friend of a friend of his. Turns out the car was used in a crime and her mother's friend was fined $10,000 when the police discovered the car on his property. Joan looks at the garage; wonders if there is something attached to this car? A murder, bank robbery, kidnapping.

"We never looked in the trunk," says Joan.

"Your mother has too much time on her hands," says Doug.

Brandon calls back. Tells Doug Bill's interested in the car. Doug tells Brandon the professor can't sell it. She says she's coming for it next week. But if it isn't out of here by the beginning of the month Bill can have it — for free. Joan smiles at her husband, at his authoritative tone. She loves it when he takes control. Doug wants his garage back. He likes to escape there, pace back and forth, smoke and kick things around. He's partial to that space, and he's particular about sheltering the Malibu when it rains.

The professor calls. She invites Doug and Joan for dinner. Joan says she has to check with Doug. She thinks he's working. She holds her hand over the receiver, "It's the professor. She's inviting us for dinner next Saturday. She's avoiding the car, I can tell."

"Tell her we'd love too but we can't."

"You tell her."

"No."

Doug leaves the house. Joan gets back on the phone. Tells the professor they'd love to come for dinner but they can't. Silence. "Is it because of the Impala?" asks the professor.

"No," says Joan. "Don't be silly."

"Oh, good. I wouldn't want a thing like that to come between us."

Joan runs outside. The driveway is empty. The garage door open. It's empty. She runs to the road. The Malibu and the Monte Carlo are parked in front of the house. It's dark. She runs down the road a way to the creek. Wonders if Doug's driven it in there. The creek is still. From the trees cicadas muster a piercing aria. The roads are quiet. She makes her way home. Doug sits on the garden chair, smoking. He smiles at his wife. The garage door is closed. She rushes through the side door. The Impala's engine creaks like an old cottage.

"What's going on?" asks Joan.

"I thought I'd take it for a spin down the side road. Figured it needed to run a little, get some fresh air."

"It's not a retired racehorse, Doug."

The professor calls, says her ex-boyfriend will take the bus in the morning to collect the car. Joan says she'll pass the message on to Doug and thanks her. Joan tells Doug.

"That's it," she says. "It's over. Someone's finally coming for it. Goddamn it, Doug, we can get our garage back, lose the burden and get back on track. We're free."

Doug grabs a beer from the cooler, wanders into the garage. Joan sits down on the garden chair, brushes leaves off the table. She peeks at Doug through the open side door. His hand rests on the roof of the Impala. He's never been the same since the kids left home.

THE PARKING LOT

Leo pulls his sleek white '86 Monte Carlo into the parking lot. He parks at the back, lights a cigarette. He rolls down the window and waits. Frank pulls up beside him in his brand new black Cadillac. Leo's cellphone rings. It's Frank. Leo looks over at his car, at its dark tinted windows.

"What is it, Frank?" says Leo. "You got a problem? You can't get out of your car?"

"I want you to come into my car today, Leo."

"What's wrong with my car, Frank? We always meet in my car."

Frank hangs up. Leo hangs up. He puts out his cigarette, straightens his hair in the rear-view mirror. He looks over at Frank's car, calls him back.

"Yeah," says Frank.

"You alone?'

"Yeah, Leo. Yeah, I'm alone. What do you think?"

Leo gets out of his car, straightens his trousers, looks around. He knocks on the passenger window of Frank's car. Frank opens the window.

"Jesus, Leo, what's got into you? What the hell are you knocking for? It's a new car, Leo, not a new fucking condominium. Get in the fucking car."

Leo gets in the car.

"It's nice," he says.

Frank looks at him. Leo looks out the window at his Monte Carlo. They always do business in his car. They meet in the parking lot. Frank would get out of his old Pontiac and get into the Monte Carlo without question and he would never phone. Things will change. Leo knows it. He's losing the upper hand. Power is shifting. Leo could have bought a hundred Cadillacs. He could have bought a Rolls-Royce but he didn't. You can't run weed in a small town from a car like that. You can't.

"You're a sitting duck, Frank."

"What?" Frank shifts in his seat to look at Leo. Leo's staring out of the windscreen at the back of a burnt-out K-car.

A red pickup truck pulls up beside the Monte Carlo. Leo's cellphone rings. He answers it.

"Hey," he says.

"Leo?"

"Yeah. Brute?"

"Yeah. Where are you man?"

"I'm in the Cadillac."

Brutus looks over at the Cadillac, squints his eyes.

"Tell him to come in here, Leo. Tell him we're meeting in my car today." Frank slams his fist on the steering wheel. Then wipes it with his sleeve. Leo gives him a look from the corner of his eye.

Brutus gets out of his truck, hoists up his jeans and wipes his nose. He walks over to the Cadillac, knocks on the window.

"Jesus," says Frank.

Leo reaches over his seat and opens the back door. Brutus sticks his head in, looks around.

"Nice. This yours, Frank?" he says.

"Get in, Brutus," says Frank.

Leo feels his face burning. He opens his door.

"Where are you going, Leo?" says Frank.

"I need a smoke."

"You can't smoke in here, Frank?" says Brutus. "Hey Leo, wait for me, man. I'll grab a smoke with you, bud."

Leo gets into his Monte Carlo, rolls down his window and lights a smoke. Brutus leaps in the passenger side, rolls down his window. Leo gives him a smoke. Leo stares out the windscreen. His phone rings. He looks at the Cadillac. "Jesus," he says. He answers his phone.

"What do you want, Frank?"

"Well, in a couple of months I won't care if you smoke in here. But I just got the car, Leo. Lucy hasn't even ridden in it yet. You know, it's my new car, Leo."

Leo hangs up. Brutus looks at Leo and smiles. Brutus reaches into his pocket and pulls out a joint.

"You want a reefer, Leo?"

"Nah, thanks. I got a trunk full of the shit. I'm sick of it."

"You got a run today? You driving out to Moby's?"

"Not in that fucking Cadillac."

"Why'd ya have to go in the Cadillac?"

"Because Al Capone over there will have a fucking tantrum if I don't."

A bright orange Trans Am pulls up by the pickup truck. Brutus and Leo stiffen in their seats.

"It's Jim," says Brutus.

"I know," says Leo.

Leo looks over at the Cadillac then back at the Trans Am. He watches Jim get out of his car and answer his phone. Jim starts walking. He bangs on the trunk of the Monte Carlo, waves and gets into the Cadillac.

"Fuck," says Leo.

"What's wrong?" says Brutus.

Jim comments on the Cadillac, tells Frank he's an idiot for driving a Cadillac into a parking lot to meet the rest of the boys. It's conspicuous, he tells him. He says he doesn't ride his Harley for that very reason. Imagine a Harley pulling into a parking lot to meet a shiny black Cadillac with smoked glass windows, he says. Next thing you know the SWAT team's pulling in too. Take it back, Frank, he says, take it back.

Jim gets out of the car. Leo and Brutus watch him as he walks past the Monte Carlo, gets into his Trans Am and drives away. Leo looks at his phone, looks at the Cadillac.

He gets out of the Monte Carlo, knocks on the window of the Cadillac, opens the door and gets in. Frank's slumped down in his seat listening to the radio.

"Sinatra?" says Leo.

"I think it's Perry Como."

"Oh."

Leo looks around. "It's comfortable, Frank."

"Yeah? I don't think it's as comfortable as the Carlo though, you know, Leo. I don't know, it's tough to say."

"Hmm," says Leo.

There's a knock on the window. Brutus gets in.

Frank turns around in his seat. "You want to go for a drive?" he says. "You want to feel how it drives."

"Yeah, yeah, sure," says Brutus.

"Uh, yeah, sure, Frank," says Leo. "That'd be great."

Frank starts the car. He pulls out of the parking lot and heads out of town. Brutus natters on about the smoothness of the ride. Leo watches the road.

The Day of the Locust

by NATHANAEL WEST

from New Directions

Miss Lonelyhearts

The Day of the Locust

The Day of the Locust

NATHANAEL WEST

A NEW DIRECTIONS PAPERBOOK

First published clothbound by New Directions in 1950.
Published with *Miss Lonelyhearts* as a New Directions Paperbook (NDP125) in 1962,
and reissued as a New Directions Paperbook (NDP1259) in 2013.
Manufactured in the United States of America
New Directions Books are printed on acid-free paper

Library of Congress Cataloging-in-Publication Data
West, Nathanael, 1903–1940.
The day of the locust / Nathanael West. — Paperback edition.
pages ; cm
ISBN 978-0-8112-2461-1 (softcover : acid-free paper)
1. Motion picture industry—Fiction. 2. Hollywood (Los Angeles, Calif.)—Fiction. I. Title.
PS3545.E8334D39 2015
813'.54—dc23   2015006842

10 9 8 7 6 5 4 3 2 1

New Directions Books are published for James Laughlin
by New Directions Publishing Corporation
80 Eighth Ave, New York 10011

The Day of the Locust

Around quitting time, Tod Hackett heard a great din on the road outside his office. The groan of leather mingled with the jangle of iron and over all beat the tattoo of a thousand hooves. He hurried to the window.

An army of cavalry and foot was passing. It moved like a mob; its lines broken, as though fleeing from some terrible defeat. The dolmans of the hussars, the heavy shakos of the guards, Hanoverian light horse, with their flat leather caps and flowing red plumes, were all jumbled together in bobbing disorder. Behind the cavalry came the infantry, a wild sea of waving sabretaches, sloped muskets, crossed shoulder belts and swinging cartridge boxes. Tod recognized the scarlet infantry of England with their white shoulder pads, the black infantry of the Duke of Brunswick, the French grenadiers with their enormous white gaiters, the Scotch with bare knees under plaid skirts.

While he watched, a little fat man, wearing a cork sun-helmet, polo shirt and knickers, darted around the corner of the building in pursuit of the army.

"Stage Nine—you bastards—Stage Nine!" he screamed through a small megaphone.

The cavalry put spur to their horses and the infantry broke into a dogtrot. The little man in the cork hat ran after them, shaking his fist and cursing.

Tod watched until they had disappeared, behind half a Mississippi steamboat, then put away his pencils and drawing board, and left the office. On the sidewalk outside the studio he stood for a moment trying to decide whether to walk home or take a streetcar. He had been in Hollywood less than three months and still found it a very exciting place, but he was lazy and didn't like to walk. He decided to take the streetcar as far as Vine Street and walk the rest of the way.

A talent scout for National Films had brought Tod to the Coast after seeing some of his drawings in an exhibit of undergraduate work at the Yale School of Fine Arts. He had been hired by telegram. If the scout had met Tod, he probably wouldn't have sent him to Hollywood to learn set and costume designing. His large sprawling body, his slow blue eyes and sloppy grin made him seem completely without talent, almost doltish in fact.

Yes, despite his appearance, he was really a very complicated young man with a whole set of personalities, one

4

inside the other like a nest of Chinese boxes. And "The Burning of Los Angeles," a picture he was soon to paint, definitely proved he had talent.

He left the car at Vine Street. As he walked along, he examined the evening crowd. A great many of the people wore sports clothes which were not really sports clothes. Their sweaters, knickers, slacks, blue flannel jackets with brass buttons were fancy dress. The fat lady in the yachting cap was going shopping, not boating; the man in the Norfolk jacket and Tyrolean hat was returning, not from a mountain, but an insurance office; and the girl in slacks and sneaks with a bandanna around her head had just left a switchboard, not a tennis court.

Scattered among these masquerades were people of a different type. Their clothing was somber and badly cut, brought from mail-order houses. While the others moved rapidly, darting into stores and cocktail bars, they loitered on the corners or stood with their backs to the shop windows and stared at everyone who passed. When their stare was returned, their eyes filled with hatred. At this time Tod knew very little about them except that they had come to California to die.

He was determined to learn much more. They were the people he felt he must paint. He would never again do a fat red barn, old stone wall or sturdy Nantucket fisherman. From the moment he had seen them, he had known that, despite his race, training and heritage, neither Winslow Homer nor Thomas Ryder could be his masters and he turned to Goya and Daumier.

He had learned this just in time. During his last year in art school, he had begun to think that he might give up painting completely. The pleasures he received from the problems of composition and color had decreased as his facility had increased and he had realized that he was going the way of all his classmates, toward illustration or mere handsomeness. When the Hollywood job had come along, he had grabbed it despite the arguments of his friends who were certain that he was selling out and would never paint again.

He reached the end of Vine Street and began the climb into Pinyon Canyon. Night had started to fall.

The edges of the trees burned with a pale violet light and their centers gradually turned from deep purple to black. The same violet piping, like a Neon tube, outlined the tops of the ugly, hump-backed hills and they were almost beautiful.

But not even the soft wash of dusk could help the houses. Only dynamite would be of any use against the Mexican ranch houses, Samoan huts, Mediterranean villas, Egyptian and Japanese temples, Swiss chalets, Tudor cottages, and every possible combination of these styles that lined the slopes of the canyon.

When he noticed that they were all of plaster, lath and paper, he was charitable and blamed their shape on the materials used. Steel, stone and brick curb a builder's fancy a little, forcing him to distribute his stresses and weights and to keep his corners plumb, but plaster and paper know no law, not even that of gravity.

On the corner of La Huerta Road was a miniature Rhine castle with tarpaper turrets pierced for archers. Next to it was a highly colored shack with domes and minarets out of the *Arabian Nights*. Again he was charitable. Both houses were comic, but he didn't laugh. Their desire to startle was so eager and guileless.

It is hard to laugh at the need for beauty and romance, no matter how tasteless, even horrible, the results of that are. But it is easy to sigh. Few things are sadder than the truly monstrous.

2

The house he lived in was a nondescript affair called the San Bernardino Arms. It was an oblong three stories high, the back and sides of which were of plain, unpainted stucco, broken by even rows of unadorned windows. The façade was the color of diluted mustard and its windows, all double, were framed by pink Moorish columns which supported turnip-shaped lintels.

His room was on the third floor, but he paused for a moment on the landing of the second. It was on that floor that Faye Greener lived, in 208. When someone laughed in one of the apartments he started guiltily and continued upstairs.

As he opened his door a card fluttered to the floor. "Honest Abe Kusich," it said in large type, then underneath in smaller italics were several endorsements, printed to look like press notices.

'. . . the Lloyds of Hollywood'—Stanley Rose.

'Abe's word is better than Morgan's bonds'—Gail Brenshaw.

On the other side was a penciled message:

"Kingpin fourth, Solitair sixth. You can make some real dough on those nags."

After opening the window, he took off his jacket and lay down on the bed. Through the window he could see a square of enameled sky and a spray of eucalyptus. A light breeze stirred its long, narrow leaves, making them show first their green side, then their silver one.

He began to think of "Honest Abe Kusich" in order not to think of Faye Greener. He felt comfortable and wanted to remain that way.

Abe was an important figure in a set of lithographs called "The Dancers" on which Tod was working. He was one of the dancers. Faye Greener was another and her father, Harry, still another. They changed with each plate, but the group of uneasy people who formed their audience remained the same. They stood staring at the performers in just the way that they stared at the masqueraders on Vine Street. It was their stare that drove Abe and the others to spin crazily and leap into the air with twisted backs like hooked trout.

Despite the sincere indignation that Abe's grotesque depravity aroused in him, he welcomed his company. The little man excited him and in that way made him feel certain of his need to paint.

He had first met Abe when he was living on Ivar Street, in a hotel called the Chateau Mirabella. Another name for Ivar Street was "Lysol Alley," and the Chateau was mainly inhabited by hustlers, their managers, trainers and advance agents.

In the morning its halls reeked of antiseptic. Tod didn't like this odor. Moreover, the rent was high because it included police protection, a service for which he had no need. He wanted to move, but inertia and the fact that he didn't know where to go kept him in the Chateau until he met Abe. The meeting was accidental.

He was on the way to his room late one night when he saw what he supposed was a pile of soiled laundry lying in front of the door across the hall from his own. Just as he was passing it, the bundle moved and made a peculiar noise. He struck a match, thinking it might be a dog wrapped in a blanket. When the light flared up, he saw it was a tiny man.

The match went out and he hastily lit another. It was a male dwarf rolled up in a woman's flannel bathrobe. The round thing at the end was his slightly hydrocephalic head. A slow, choked snore bubbled from it.

The hall was cold and draughty. Tod decided to wake the man and stirred him with his toe. He groaned and opened his eyes.

"You oughtn't to sleep there."

"The hell you say," said the dwarf, closing his eyes again.

"You'll catch cold."

This friendly observation angered the little man still more.

"I want my clothes!" he bellowed.

The bottom of the door next to which he was lying filled with light. Tod decided to take a chance and knock. A few seconds later a woman opened it part way.

"What the hell do you want?" she demanded.

"There's a friend of yours out here who ..."

Neither of them let him finish.

"So what!" she barked, slamming the door.

"Give me my clothes, you bitch!' roared the dwarf.

She opened the door again and began to hurl things into the hall. A jacket and trousers, a shirt, socks, shoes and underwear, a tie and hat followed each other through the air in rapid succession. With each article went a special curse.

Tod whistled with amazement.

"Some gal!"

"You bet," said the dwarf. "A lollapalooza—all slut and a yard wide."

He laughed at his own joke, using a high-pitched cackle more dwarflike than anything that had come from him so far, then struggled to his feet and arranged the voluminous robe so that he could walk without tripping. Tod helped him gather his scattered clothing.

"Say, mister," he asked, "could I dress in your place?"

Tod let him into his bathroom. While waiting for him to reappear, he couldn't help imagining what had happened in the woman's apartment. He began to feel sorry for having interfered. But when the dwarf came out wearing his hat, Tod felt better.

The little man's hat fixed almost everything. That year Tyrolean hats were being worn a great deal along Hollywood Boulevard and the dwarf's was a fine specimen. It was the proper magic green color and had a high, conical crown. There should have been a brass buckle on the front, but otherwise it was quite perfect.

The rest of his outfit didn't go well with the hat. Instead of shoes with long points and a leather apron, he wore a blue, double-breasted suit and a black shirt with a yellow tie. Instead of a crooked thorn stick, he carried a rolled copy of the *Daily Running Horse*.

"That's what I get for fooling with four-bit broads," he said by way of greeting.

Tod nodded and tried to concentrate on the green hat. His ready acquiescence seemed to irritate the little man.

"No quiff can give Abe Kusich the fingeroo and get away with it," he said bitterly. "Not when I can get her leg broke for twenty bucks and I got twenty."

He took out a thick billfold and shook it at Tod.

"So she thinks she can give me the fingeroo, hah? Well, let me tell ..."

Tod broke in hastily.

"You're right, Mr. Kusich."

The dwarf came over to where Tod was sitting and for a moment Tod thought he was going to climb into his lap, but he only asked his name and shook hands. The little man had a powerful grip.

"Let me tell you something, Hackett, if you hadn't come along, I'da broke in the door. That dame thinks she can give me the fingeroo, but she's got another thinkola coming. But thanks anyway."

"Forget it."

"I don't forget nothing. I remember. I remember those who do me dirt and those who do me favors."

He wrinkled his brow and was silent for a moment.

"Listen," he finally said, "seeing as you helped me, I got to return it. I don't want anybody going around saying Abe Kusich owes him anything. So I'll tell you what. I'll give you a good one for the fifth at Caliente. You put a fiver on its nose and it'll get you twenty smackeroos. What I'm telling you is strictly correct."

Tod didn't know how to answer and his hesitation offended the little man.

"Would I give you a bum steer?" he demanded, scowling. "Would I?"

Tod walked toward the door to get rid of him.

"No," he said.

"Then why won't you bet, hah?"

"What's the name of the horse?" Tod asked, hoping to calm him.

The dwarf had followed him to the door, pulling the bathrobe after him by one sleeve. Hat and all, he came to a foot below Tod's belt.

"Tragopan. He's a certain, sure winner. I know the guy who owns him and he gave me the office."

"Is he a Greek?" Tod asked.

He was being pleasant in order to hide the attempt he was making to maneuver the dwarf through the door.

"Yeh, he's a Greek. Do you know him?"

"No."

"No?"

"No," said Tod with finality.

"Keep your drawers on," ordered the dwarf, "all I want

to know is how you know he's a Greek if you don't know him?"

His eyes narrowed with suspicion and he clenched his fists.

Tod smiled to placate him.

"I just guessed it."

"You did?"

The dwarf hunched his shoulders as though he were going to pull a gun or throw a punch. Tod backed off and tried to explain.

"I guessed he was a Greek because Tragopan is a Greek word that means pheasant."

The dwarf was far from satisfied.

"How do you know what it means? You ain't a Greek?"

"No, but I know a few Greek words."

"So you're a wise guy, hah, a know-it-all."

He took a short step forward, moving on his toes, and Tod got set to block a punch.

"A college man, hah? Well, let me tell ..."

His foot caught in the wrapper and he fell forward on his hands. He forgot Tod and cursed the bathrobe, then got started on the woman again.

"So she thinks she can give me the fingeroo."

He kept poking himself in the chest with his thumbs.

"Who gave her forty bucks for an abortion? Who? And another ten to go to the country for a rest that time. To a ranch I sent her. And who got her fiddle out of hock that time in Santa Monica? Who?"

"That's right," Tod said, getting ready to give him a quick shove through the door.

But he didn't have to shove him. The little man suddenly darted out of the room and ran down the hall, dragging the bathrobe after him.

A few days later, Tod went into a stationery store on Vine Street to buy a magazine. While he was looking through the rack, he felt a tug at the bottom of his jacket. It was Abe Kusich, the dwarf, again.

"How's things?" he demanded.

Tod was surprised to find that he was just as truculent as he had been the other night. Later, when he got to know him better, he discovered that Abe's pugnacity was often a joke. When he used it on his friends, they played with him like one does with a growling puppy, staving off his mad rushes and then baiting him to rush again.

"Fair enough," Tod said, "but I think I'll move."

He had spent most of Sunday looking for a place to live and was full of the subject. The moment he mentioned it, however, he knew that he had made a mistake. He tried to end the matter by turning away, but the little man blocked him. He evidently considered himself an expert on the housing situation. After naming and discarding a dozen possibilities without a word from Tod, he finally hit on the San Bernardino Arms.

"That's the place for you, the San Berdoo. I live there, so I ought to know. The owner's strictly from hunger. Come on, I'll get you fixed up swell."

"I don't know, I ..." Tod began.

The dwarf bridled instantly, and appeared to be mortally offended.

"I suppose it ain't good enough for you. Well, let me tell you something, you ..."

Tod allowed himself to be bullied and went with the dwarf to Pinyon Canyon. The rooms in the San Berdoo were small and not very clean. He rented one without hesitation, however, when he saw Faye Greener in the hall.

3

Tod had fallen asleep. When he woke again, it was after eight o'clock. He took a bath and shaved, then dressed in front of the bureau mirror. He tried to watch his fingers as he fixed his collar and tie, but his eyes kept straying to the photograph that was pushed into the upper corner of the frame.

It was a picture of Faye Greener, a still from a two-reel farce in which she had worked as an extra. She had given him the photograph willingly enough, had even autographed it in a large, wild hand, "Affectionately yours, Faye Greener," but she refused his friendship, or, rather, insisted on keeping it impersonal. She had told him why. He had nothing to offer her, neither money nor looks, and she could only love a handsome man and would only let a wealthy man love her. Tod was a "good-hearted man," and she liked "good-hearted men," but only as friends. She wasn't hard-boiled. It was just that she put love on a special plane, where a man without money or looks couldn't move.

Tod grunted with annoyance as he turned to the photograph. In it she was wearing a harem costume, full Turkish trousers, breastplates and a monkey jacket, and lay stretched out on a silken divan. One hand held a beer bottle and the other a pewter stein.

He had gone all the way to Glendale to see her in that movie. It was about an American drummer who gets lost in the seraglio of a Damascus merchant and has a lot of fun with the female inmates. Faye played one of the dancing girls. She had only one line to speak, "Oh, Mr. Smith!" and spoke it badly.

She was a tall girl with wide, straight shoulders and long, swordlike legs. Her neck was long, too, and columnar. Her face was much fuller than the rest of her body would lead you to expect and much larger. It was a moon face, wide at the cheek bones and narrow at chin and brow. She wore her "platinum" hair long, letting it fall almost to her shoulders in back, but kept it away from her face and ears with a narrow blue ribbon that went under it and was tied on top of her head with a little bow.

She was supposed to look drunk and she did, but not with alcohol. She lay stretched out on the divan with her arms and legs spread, as though welcoming a lover, and her lips were parted in a heavy, sullen smile. She was supposed to look inviting, but the invitation wasn't to pleasure.

Tod lit a cigarette and inhaled with a nervous gasp. He

started to fool with his tie again, but had to go back to the photograph.

Her invitation wasn't to pleasure, but to struggle, hard and sharp, closer to murder than to love. If you threw yourself on her, it would be like throwing yourself from the parapet of a skyscraper. You would do it with a scream. You couldn't expect to rise again. Your teeth would be driven into your skull like nails into a pine board and your back would be broken. You wouldn't even have time to sweat or close your eyes.

He managed to laugh at his language, but it wasn't a real laugh and nothing was destroyed by it.

If she would only let him, he would be glad to throw himself, no matter what the cost. But she wouldn't have him. She didn't love him and he couldn't further her career. She wasn't sentimental and she had no need for tenderness, even if he were capable of it.

When he had finished dressing, he hurried out of the room. He had promised to go to a party at Claude Estee's.

4

Claude was a successful screen writer who lived in a big house that was an exact reproduction of the old Dupuy mansion near Biloxi, Mississippi. When Tod came up the walk between the boxwood hedges, he greeted him from the enormous, two-story porch by doing the impersonation that went with the Southern colonial architecture. He teetered back and forth on his heels like a Civil War colonel and made believe he had a large belly.

He had no belly at all. He was a dried-up little man with the rubbed features and stooped shoulders of a postal clerk. The shiny mohair coat and nondescript trousers of that official would have become him, but he was dressed, as always, elaborately. In the buttonhole of his brown jacket was a lemon flower. His trousers were of reddish Harris tweed with a hound tooth check and on his feet were a pair of magnificent, rust-colored blüchers. His shirt was ivory flannel and his knitted tie a red that was almost black.

While Tod mounted the steps to reach his outstretched hand, he shouted to the butler.

"Here, you black rascal! A mint julep."

A Chinese servant came running with a Scotch and soda.

After talking to Tod for a moment, Claude started him in the direction of Alice, his wife, who was at the other end of the porch.

"Don't run off," he whispered. "We're going to a sporting house."

Alice was sitting in a wicker swing with a woman named Mrs. Joan Schwartzen. When she asked him if he was playing any tennis, Mrs. Schwartzen interrupted her.

"How silly, batting an inoffensive ball across something that ought to be used to catch fish on account of millions are starving for a bite of herring."

"Joan's a female tennis champ," Alice explained.

Mrs. Schwartzen was a big girl with large hands and feet and square, bony shoulders. She had a pretty, eighteen-year-old face and a thirty-five-year-old neck that was veined and sinewy. Her deep sunburn, ruby colored with a slight blue tint, kept the contrast between her face and neck from being too startling.

"Well, I wish we were going to a brothel this minute," she said. "I adore them."

She turned to Tod and fluttered her eyelids.

"Don't you, Mr. Hackett?"

"That's right, Joan darling," Alice answered for him.

"Nothing like a bagnio to set a fellow up. Hair of the dog that bit you."

"How dare you insult me!"

She stood up and took Tod's arm.

"Convoy me over there."

She pointed to the group of men with whom Claude was standing.

"For God's sake, convoy her," Alice said. "She thinks they're telling dirty stories."

Mrs. Schwartzen pushed right among them, dragging Tod after her.

"Are you talking smut?" she asked. "I adore smut."

They all laughed politely.

"No, shop," said someone.

"I don't believe it. I can tell from the beast in your voices. Go ahead, do say something obscene."

This time no one laughed.

Tod tried to disengage her arm, but she kept a firm grip on it. There was a moment of awkward silence, then the man she had interrupted tried to make a fresh start.

"The picture business is too humble," he said. "We ought to resent people like Coombes."

"That's right," said another man. "Guys like that come out here, make a lot of money, grouse all the time about the place, flop on their assignments, then go back East and tell dialect stories about producers they've never met."

"My God," Mrs. Schwartzen said to Tod in a loud, stagey whisper, "they *are* talking shop."

"Let's look for the man with the drinks," Tod said.

"No. Take me into the garden. Have you seen what's in the swimming pool?"

She pulled him along.

The air of the garden was heavy with the odor of mimosa and honeysuckle. Through a slit in the blue serge sky poked a grained moon that looked like an enormous bone button. A little flagstone path, made narrow by its border of oleander, led to the edge of the sunken pool. On the bottom, near the deep end, he could see a heavy, black mass of some kind.

"What is it?" he asked.

She kicked a switch that was hidden at the base of a shrub and a row of submerged floodlights illuminated the green water. The thing was a dead horse, or, rather, a life-size, realistic reproduction of one. Its legs stuck up stiff and straight and it had an enormous, distended belly. Its hammerhead lay twisted to one side and from its mouth, which was set in an agonized grin, hung a heavy, black tongue.

"Isn't it marvelous!" exclaimed Mrs. Schwartzen, clapping her hands and jumping up and down excitedly like a little girl.

"What's it made of?"

"Then you weren't fooled? How impolite! It's rubber, of course. It cost lots of money."

"But why?"

"To amuse. We were looking at the pool one day and somebody, Jerry Appis, I think, said that it needed a dead horse on the bottom, so Alice got one. Don't you think it looks cute?"

"Very."

"You're just an old meanie. Think how happy the Estees must feel, showing it to people and listening to their merriment and their oh's and ah's of unconfined delight."

She stood on the edge of the pool and "ohed and ahed" rapidly several times in succession.

"Is it still there?" someone called.

Tod turned and saw two women and a man coming down the path.

"I think its belly's going to burst," Mrs. Schwartzen shouted to them gleefully.

"Goody," said the man, hurrying to look.

"But it's only full of air," said one of the women.

Mrs. Schwartzen made believe she was going to cry.

"You're just like that mean Mr. Hackett. You just won't let me cherish my illusions."

Tod was half way to the house when she called after him. He waved but kept going.

The men with Claude were still talking shop.

"But how are you going to get rid of the illiterate mockies that run it? They've got a strangle hold on the industry. Maybe they're intellectual stumblebums, but they're damn good business men. Or at least they know how to go into receivership and come up with a gold watch in their teeth."

"They ought to put some of the millions they make back into the business again. Like Rockefeller does with his Foundation. People used to hate the Rockefellers, but now instead of hollering about their ill-gotten oil dough, everybody praises them for what the Foundation does. It's a swell stunt and pictures could do the same thing. Have a Cinema Foundation and make contributions to Science and Art. You know, give the racket a front."

Tod took Claude to one side to say good night, but he wouldn't let him go. He led him into the library and mixed two double Scotches. They sat down on the couch facing the fireplace.

"You haven't been to Audrey Jenning's place?" Claude asked.

"No, but I've heard tell of it."

"Then you've got to come along."

"I don't like pro-sport."

"We won't indulge in any. We're just going to see a movie."

"I get depressed."

"Not at Jenning's you won't. She makes a vice attractive by skillful packaging. Her dive's a triumph of industrial design."

Tod liked to hear him talk. He was master of an involved comic rhetoric that permitted him to express his moral indignation and still keep his reputation for worldliness and wit.

Tod fed him another lead. "I don't care how much cellophane she wraps it in," he said—"nautch joints are depressing, like all places for deposit, banks, mail boxes, tombs, vending machines."

"Love is like a vending machine, eh? Not bad. You insert a coin and press home the lever. There's some mechanical activity inside the bowels of the device. You receive a small sweet, frown at yourself in the dirty mirror, adjust your hat, take a firm grip on your umbrella and walk away, trying to look as though nothing had happened. It's good, but it's not for pictures."

Tod played straight again.

"That's not it. I've been chasing a girl and it's like carrying something a little too large to conceal in your pocket, like a briefcase or a small valise. It's uncomfortable."

"I know, I know. It's always uncomfortable. First your right hand gets tired, then your left. You put the valise down and sit on it, but people are surprised and stop to stare at you, so you move on. You hide it behind a tree and hurry away, but someone finds it and runs after you to return it. It's a small valise when you leave home in the morning, cheap and with a bad handle, but by evening it's a trunk with brass corners and many foreign labels. I know. It's good, but it won't film. You've got to remember your audience. What about the barber in Purdue? He's been cutting hair all day and he's tired. He doesn't want to see some dope carrying a valise or fooling with a nickel machine. What the barber wants is amour and glamor."

The last part was for himself and he sighed heavily. He was about to begin again when the Chinese servant came in and said that the others were ready to leave for Mrs. Jenning's.

5

They started out in several cars. Tod rode in the front of the one Claude drove and as they went down Sunset Boulevard he described Mrs. Jenning for him. She had been a fairly prominent actress in the days of silent films, but sound made it impossible for her to get work. Instead of becoming an extra or a bit player like many other old stars, she had shown excellent business sense and had opened a callhouse. She wasn't vicious. Far from it. She ran her business just as other women run lending libraries, shrewdly and with taste.

None of the girls lived on the premises. You telephoned and she sent a girl over. The charge was thirty dollars for a single night of sport and Mrs. Jenning kept fifteen of it. Some people might think that fifty per cent is a high brokerage fee, but she really earned every cent of it. There was a big overhead. She maintained a beautiful house for the girls to wait in and a car and a chauffeur to deliver them to the clients.

Then, too, she had to move in the kind of society where she could make the right contacts. After all, not every man can afford thirty dollars. She permitted her girls to service only men of wealth and position, not to say taste and discretion. She was so particular that she insisted on meeting the prospective sportsman before servicing him. She had often said, and truthfully, that she would not let a girl of hers go to a man with whom she herself would not be willing to sleep.

And she was really cultured. All the most distinguished visitors considered it quite a lark to meet her. They were disappointed, however, when they discovered how refined she was. They wanted to talk about certain lively matters of universal interest, but she insisted on discussing Gertrude Stein and Juan Gris. No matter how hard the distinguished visitor tried, and some had been known to go to really great lengths, he could never find a flaw in her refinement or make a breach in her culture.

Claude was still using his peculiar rhetoric on Mrs. Jenning when she came to the door of her house to greet them.

"It's so nice to see you again," she said. "I was telling Mrs. Prince at tea only yesterday—the Estees are my favorite couple."

She was a handsome woman, smooth and buttery, with fair hair and a red complexion.

She led them into a small drawing room whose color

scheme was violet, gray and rose. The Venetian blinds were rose, as was the ceiling, and the walls were covered with a pale gray paper that had a tiny, widely spaced flower design in violet. On one wall hung a silver screen, the kind that rolls up, and against the opposite wall, on each side of a cherrywood table, was a row of chairs covered with rose and gray, glazed chintz bound in violet piping. There was a small projection machine on the table and a young man in evening dress was fumbling with it.

She waved them to their seats. A waiter then came in and asked what they wanted to drink. When their orders had been taken and filled, she flipped the light switch and the young man started his machine. It whirred merrily, but he had trouble in getting it focused.

"What are we going to see first?" Mrs. Schwartzen asked.

"*Le Predicament de Marie.*"

"That sounds ducky."

"It's charming, utterly charming," said Mrs. Jenning.

"Yes," said the cameraman, who was still having trouble. "I love *Le Predicament de Marie*. It has a marvelous quality that is too exciting."

There was a long delay, during which he fussed desperately with his machine. Mrs. Schwartzen started to whistle

and stamp her feet and the others joined in. They imitated
a rowdy audience in the days of the nickelodeon.

"Get a move on, slow poke."

"What's your hurry? Here's your hat."

"Get a horse!"

"Get out and get under!"

The young man finally found the screen with his light
beam and the film began.

LE PREDICAMENT DE MARIE
ou
LA BONNE DISTRAITE

Marie, the "bonne," was a buxom young girl in a
tight-fitting black silk uniform with very short skirts. On her
head was a tiny lace cap. In the first scene, she was shown
serving dinner to a middle-class family in an oak-paneled
dining room full of heavy, carved furniture. The family was
very respectable and consisted of a bearded, frock-coated
father, a mother with a whalebone collar and a cameo
brooch, a tall, thin son with a long mustache and almost
no chin and a little girl wearing a large bow in her hair and
a crucifix on a gold chain around her neck.

After some low comedy with father's beard and the

soup, the actors settled down seriously to their theme. It was evident that while the whole family desired Marie, she only desired the young girl. Using his napkin to hide his activities, the old man pinched Marie, the son tried to look down the neck of her dress and the mother patted her knee. Marie, for her part, surreptitiously fondled the child.

The scene changed to Marie's room. She undressed and got into a chiffon negligee, leaving on only her black silk stockings and high-heeled shoes. She was making an elaborate night toilet when the child entered. Marie took her on her lap and started to kiss her. There was a knock on the door. Consternation. She hid the child in the closet and let in the bearded father. He was suspicious and she had to accept his advances. He was embracing her when there was another knock. Again consternation and tableau. This time it was the mustachioed son. Marie hid the father under the bed. No sooner had the son begun to grow warm than there was another knock. Marie made him climb into a large blanket chest. The new caller was the lady of the house. She, too, was just settling down to work when there was another knock.

Who could it be? A telegram? A policeman? Frantically Marie counted the different hiding places. The whole family was present. She tiptoed to the door and listened.

"Who can it be that wishes to enter now?" read the title card.

And there the machine stuck. The young man in evening dress became as frantic as Marie. When he got it running again, there was a flash of light and the film whizzed through the apparatus until it had all run out.

"I'm sorry, extremely," he said. "I'll have to rewind."

"It's a frameup," someone yelled.

"Fake!"

"Cheat!"

"The old teaser routine!"

They stamped their feet and whistled.

Under cover of the mock riot, Tod sneaked out. He want to get some fresh air. The waiter, whom he found loitering in the hall, showed him to the patio in back of the house.

On his return, he peeked into the different rooms. In one of them he found a large number of miniature dogs in a curio cabinet. There were glass pointers, silver beagles, porcelain schnauzers, stone dachshunds, aluminum bulldogs, onyx whippets, china bassets, wooden spaniels. Every recognized breed was represented and almost every material that could be sculptured, cast or carved.

While he was admiring the little figures, he heard a girl singing. He thought he recognized her voice and peeked into the hall. It was Mary Dove, one of Faye Greener's best friends.

Perhaps Faye also worked for Mrs. Jenning. If so, for thirty dollars ...

He went back to see the rest of the film.

6

Tod's hope that he could end his trouble by paying a small fee didn't last long. When he got Claude to ask Mrs. Jenning about Faye, that lady said she had never heard of the girl. Claude then asked her to inquire through Mary Dove. A few days later she phoned him to say there was nothing doing. The girl wasn't available.

Tod wasn't really disappointed. He didn't want Faye that way, not at least while he still had a chance some other way. Lately, he had begun to think he had a good one. Harry, her father, was sick and that gave him an excuse for hanging around their apartment. He ran errands and kept the old man company. To repay his kindness, she permitted him the intimacies of a family friend. He hoped to deepen her gratitude and make it serious.

Apart from this purpose, he was interested in Harry and enjoyed visiting him. The old man was a clown and Tod had all the painter's usual love of clowns. But what was more important, he felt that his clownship was a clue to the people who stared (a painter's clue, that is—a clue in the form of a symbol), just as Faye's dreams were another.

He sat near Harry's bed and listened to his stories by the hour. Forty years in vaudeville and burlesque had provided him with an infinite number of them. As he put it, his life had consisted of a lightning series of "nip-ups," "high-gruesomes," "flying-W's" and "hundred-and-eights" done to escape a barrage of "exploding stoves." An "exploding stove" was any catastrophe, natural or human, from a flood in Medicine Hat, Wyoming, to an angry policeman in Moose Factory, Ontario.

When Harry had first begun his stage career, he had probably restricted his clowning to the boards, but now he clowned continuously. It was his sole method of defense. Most people, he had discovered, won't go out of their way to punish a clown.

He used a set of elegant gestures to accent the comedy of his bent, hopeless figure and wore a special costume, dressing like a banker, a cheap, unconvincing, imitation banker. The costume consisted of a greasy derby with an unusually high crown, a wing collar and polka dot four-in-hand, a shiny double-breasted jacket and gray-striped trousers. His outfit fooled no one, but then he didn't intend it to fool anyone. His slyness was of a different sort.

On the stage he was a complete failure and knew it. Yet he claimed to have once come very close to success. To prove how close, he made Tod read an old clipping from the theatrical section of the Sunday *Times*.

"BEDRAGGLED HARLEQUIN," it was headed.

"The commedia dell'arte is not dead, but lives on in Brooklyn, or was living there last week on the stage of the Oglethorpe Theatre in the person of one Harry Greener. Mr. Greener is of a troupe called 'The Flying Lings,' who, by the time this reaches you, have probably moved on to Mystic, Connecticut, or some other place more fitting than the borough of large families. If you have the time and really love the theatre, by all means seek out the Lings wherever they may be.

"Mr. Greener, the bedraggled Harlequin of our caption, is not bedraggled but clean, neat and sweet when he first comes on. By the time the Lings, four muscular Orientals, finish with him, however, he is plenty bedraggled. He is tattered and bloody, but still sweet.

"When Mr. Greener enters, the trumpets are properly silent. Mama Ling is spinning a plate on the end of a stick held in her mouth, Papa Ling is doing cartwheels, Sister Ling is juggling fans and Sonny Ling is hanging from the proscenium arch by his pigtail. As he inspects his strenuous colleagues, Mr. Greener tries to hide his confusion under some much too obvious worldliness. He ventures to tickle Sister and receives a powerful kick in the belly in return for this innocent attention. Having been kicked, he is on familiar ground and begins to tell a dull joke. Father Ling sneaks up behind him and tosses him to Brother, who looks the other way. Mr. Greener lands on the back of his neck. He shows his mettle by finishing his dull story from a recumbent position. When he stands up, the audience, which failed to laugh at his joke, laughs at his limp, so he continues lame for the rest of the act.

"Mr. Greener begins another story, even longer and duller than his first. Just before he arrives at the gag line, the orchestra blares loudly and drowns him out. He is very patient and very brave. He begins again, but the orchestra will not let him finish. The pain that almost, not quite, thank God, crumples his stiff little figure would be unbearable if it were not obviously make-believe. It is gloriously funny.

"The finale is superb. While the Ling Family flies through the air, Mr. Greener, held to the ground by his sense of reality and his knowledge of gravitation, tries hard to make the audience think that he is neither surprised nor worried by the rocketing Orientals. It's familiar stuff, his hands signal, but his face denies this. As time goes on and no one is hurt, he regains his assurance. The acrobats ignore him, so he ignores the acrobats. His is the final victory; the applause is for him.

"My first thought was that some producer should put Mr. Greener into a big revue against a background of beautiful girls and glittering curtains. But my second was that this would be a mistake. I am afraid that Mr. Greener, like certain humble field plants which die when transferred to richer soil, had better be left to bloom in vaudeville against a background of ventriloquists and lady bicycle riders."

Harry had more than a dozen copies of this article, several on rag paper. After trying to get a job by inserting a small advertisement in *Variety* ("... 'some producer should put Mr. Greener into a big revue ...' The *Times*"), he had come to Hollywood, thinking to earn a living playing comedy bits in films. There proved to be little demand for his talents, however. As he himself put it, he "stank from hunger." To supplement his meager income from the studios, he peddled silver polish which he made in the bathroom of the apartment out of chalk, soap and yellow axle grease. When Faye wasn't at Central Casting, she took him around on his peddling trips in her Model T Ford. It was on their last expedition together that he had fallen sick.

It was on this trip that Faye acquired a new suitor by

the name of Homer Simpson. About a week after Harry had taken to his bed, Tod met Homer for the first time. He was keeping the old man company when their conversation was interrupted by a light knock on the apartment door. Tod answered it and found a man standing in the hall with flowers for Faye and a bottle of port wine for her father.

Tod examined him eagerly. He didn't mean to be rude but at first glance this man seemed an exact model for the kind of person who comes to California to die, perfect in every detail down to fever eyes and unruly hands.

"My name is Homer Simpson," the man gasped, then shifted uneasily and patted his perfectly dry forehead with a folded handkerchief.

"Won't you come in?" Tod asked.

He shook his head heavily and thrust the wine and flowers at Tod. Before Tod could say anything, he had lumbered off.

Tod saw that he was mistaken. Homer Simpson was only physically the type. The men he meant were not shy.

He took the gifts in to Harry, who didn't seem at all surprised. He said Homer was one of his grateful customers.

"That Miracle Polish of mine sure does fetch 'em."

Later, when Faye came home and heard the story, she was very much amused. They both told Tod how they had happened to meet Homer, interrupting themselves and each other every few seconds to laugh.

The next thing Tod saw Homer staring at the apartment house from the shadow of a date palm on the opposite side of the street. He watched him for a few minutes, then called out a friendly greeting. Without replying, Homer ran away. On the next day and the one after, Tod again saw him lurking near the palm tree. He finally caught him by approaching the tree silently from the rear.

"Hello, Mr. Simpson," Tod said softly. "The Greeners were very grateful for your gift."

This time Simpson didn't move, perhaps because Tod had him backed against the tree.

"That's fine," he blurted out. "I was passing ... I live up the street."

Tod managed to keep their conversation going for several minutes before he escaped again.

The next time Tod was able to approach him without the stalk. From then on, he responded very quickly to his advances. Sympathy, even of the most obvious sort, made him articulate, almost garrulous.

7

Tod was right about one thing at least. Like most of the people he was interested in, Homer was a Middle-Westerner. He came from a little town near Des Moines, Iowa, called Wayneville, where he had worked for twenty years in a hotel.

One day, while sitting in the park in the rain, he had caught cold and his cold developed into pneumonia. When he came out of the hospital, he found that the hotel had hired a new bookkeeper. They offered to take him on again, but his doctor advised him to go to California for a rest. The doctor had an authoritative manner, so Homer left Wayneville for the Coast.

After living for a week in a railroad hotel in Los Angeles, he rented a cottage in Pinyon Canyon. It was only the second house the real estate agent showed him, but he took it because he was tired and because the agent was a bully.

He rather liked the way the cottage was located. It was the last house in the canyon and the hills rose directly behind the garage. They were covered with lupines, Canterbury bells, poppies, and several varieties of large yellow daisy. There were also some scrub pines, Joshua and eu-calyptus trees. The agent told him that he would see doves and plumed quail, but during all the time he lived there, he saw only a few large, black velvet spiders and a lizard. He grew very fond of the lizard.

The house was cheap because it was hard to rent. Most of the people who took cottages in the neighborhood wanted them to be "Spanish" and this one, so the agent claimed, was "Irish." Homer thought that the place looked kind of queer, but the agent insisted that it was cute.

The house was queer. It had an enormous and very crooked stone chimney, little dormer windows with big hoods and a thatched roof that came down very low on both sides of the front door. This door was of gumwood painted like fumed oak and it hung on enormous hinges. Although made by machine, the hinges had been carefully stamped to appear hand-forged. The same kind of care and skill had been used to make the roof thatching, which was not really straw but heavy fireproof paper colored and ribbed to look like straw.

The prevailing taste had been followed in the living room. It was "Spanish." The walls were pale orange flecked with pink and on them hung several silk armorial banners in red and gold. A big galleon stood on the mantelpiece. Its hull was plaster, its sails paper and its rigging wire. In the fireplace was a variety of cactus in gaily colored Mexican pots. Some of the plants were made of rubber and cork; others were real.

The room was lit by wall fixtures in the shape of galleons with pointed amber bulbs projecting from their decks. The table held a lamp with a paper shade, oiled to look like parchment, that had several more galleons painted on it. On each side of the windows red velvet draperies hung from black, double-headed spears.

The furniture consisted of a heavy couch that had fat monks for legs and was covered with faded red damask, and three swollen armchairs, also red. In the center of the room was a very long mahogany table. It was of the trestle type and studded with large-headed bronze nails. Beside each of the chairs was a small end table, the same color and design as the big one, but with a colored tile let into the top.

In the two small bedrooms still another style had been used. This the agent had called "New England." There was a spool bed made of iron grained like wood, a Windsor chair of the kind frequently seen in tea shops, and a Governor Winthrop dresser painted to look like unpainted pine. On the floor was a small hooked rug. On the wall facing the dresser was a colored etching of a snowbound

Connecticut farmhouse, complete with wolf. Both of these rooms were exactly alike in every detail. Even the pictures were duplicates.

There was also a bathroom and a kitchen.

8

It took Homer only a few minutes to get settled in his new home. He unpacked his trunk, hung his two suits, both dark gray, in the closet of one of his bedrooms and put his shirts and underclothes into the dresser drawers. He made no attempt to rearrange the furniture.

After an aimless tour of the house and the yard, he sat down on the couch in the living room. He sat as though waiting for someone in the lobby of a hotel. He remained that way for almost half an hour without moving anything but his hands, then got up and went into the bedroom and sat down on the edge of the bed.

Although it was still early in the afternoon, he felt very sleepy. He was afraid to stretch out and go to sleep. Not because he had bad dreams, but because it was so hard for him to wake again. When he fell asleep, he was always afraid that he would never get up.

But his fear wasn't as strong as his need. He got his alarm clock and set it for seven o'clock, then lay down with it next to his ear. Two hours later, it seemed like seconds to him, the alarm went off. The bell rang for a full minute before he began to work laboriously toward consciousness. The struggle was a hard one. He groaned. His head trembled and his feet shot out. Finally his eyes opened, then widened. Once more the victory was his.

He lay stretched out on the bed, collecting his senses and testing the different parts of his body. Every part was awake but his hands. They still slept. He was not surprised. They demanded special attention, had always demanded it. When he had been a child, he used to stick pins into them and once had even thrust them into a fire. Now he used only cold water.

He got out of bed in sections, like a poorly made automaton, and carried his hands into the bathroom. He turned on the cold water. When the basin was full, he plunged his hands in up to the wrists. They lay quietly on the bottom like a pair of strange aquatic animals. When they were thoroughly chilled and began to crawl about, he lifted them out and hid them in a towel.

He was cold. He ran hot water into the tub and began to undress, fumbling with the buttons of his clothing as though he were undressing a stranger. He was naked before the tub was full enough to get in and he sat down on a stool to wait. He kept his enormous hands folded quietly on his belly. Although absolutely still, they seemed curbed rather than resting.

Except for his hands, which belonged on a piece of monumental sculpture, and his small head, he was well proportioned. His muscles were large and round and he had a full, heavy chest. Yet there was something wrong. For all his size and shape, he looked neither strong nor fertile. He was like one of Picasso's great sterile athletes, who brood hopelessly on pink sand, staring at veined marble waves.

When the tub was full, he got in and sank down in the hot water. He grunted his comfort. But in another moment he would begin to remember, in just another moment. He tried to fool his memory by overwhelming it with tears and brought up the sobs that were always lurking uneasily in his chest. He cried softly at first, then harder. The sound he made was like that of a dog lapping gruel. He concentrated on how miserable and lonely he was, but it didn't work. The thing he was trying so desperately to avoid kept crowding into his mind.

One day when he was working in the hotel, a guest called Romola Martin had spoken to him in the elevator.

"Mr. Simpson, you're Mr. Simpson, the bookkeeper?"

"Yes."

"I'm in six-eleven."

She was small and childlike, with a quick, nervous manner. In her arms she coddled a package which obviously contained a square gin bottle.

"Yes," said Homer again, working against his natural instinct to be friendly. He knew that Miss Martin owed several weeks' rent and had heard the room clerk say she was a drunkard.

"Oh! . . ." the girl went on coquettishly, making obvious their difference in size, "I'm sorry you're worried about your bill, I . . ."

The intimacy of her tone embarrassed Homer.

"You'll have to speak to the manager," he rapped out, turning away.

He was trembling when he reached his office.

How bold the creature was! She was drunk, of course, but not so drunk that she didn't know what she was doing. He hurriedly labeled his excitement disgust.

Soon afterwards the manager called and asked him to bring in Miss Martin's credit card. When he went into the manager's office, he found Miss Carlisle, the room clerk, there. Homer listened to what the manager was saying to her.

"You roomed six-eleven?"

"I did, yes sir."

"Why? She's obvious enough, isn't she?"

"Not when she's sober."

"Never mind that. We don't want her kind in this hotel."

"I'm sorry."

The manager turned to Homer and took the credit card he was holding.

"She owes thirty-one dollars," Homer said.

"She'll have to pay up and get out. I don't want her kind around here." He smiled. "Especially when they run up bills. Get her on the phone for me."

Homer asked the telephone operator for six-eleven and after a short time was told that the room didn't answer.

"She's in the house," he said. "I saw her in the elevator."

"I'll have the housekeeper look."

Homer was working on his books some minutes later when his phone rang. It was the manager again. He said that six-eleven had been reported in by the housekeeper and asked Homer to take her a bill.

"Tell her to pay up or get out," he said.

His first thought was to ask that Miss Carlisle be sent because he was busy, but he didn't dare to suggest it. While making out the bill, he began to realize how excited he was. It was terrifying. Little waves of sensation moved along his nerves and the base of his tongue tingled.

When he got off at the sixth floor, he felt almost gay. His step was buoyant and he had completely forgotten his troublesome hands. He stopped at six-eleven and made as though to knock, then suddenly took fright and lowered his fist without touching the door.

He couldn't go through with it. They would have to send Miss Carlisle.

The housekeeper, who had been watching from the end of the hall, came up before he could escape.

"She doesn't answer," Homer said hurriedly.

"Did you knock hard enough? That slut is in there."

Before Homer could reply, she pounded on the door.

"Open up!" she shouted.

Homer heard someone move inside, then the door opened a few inches.

"Who is it, please?" a light voice asked.

"Mr. Simpson, the bookkeeper," he gasped.

"Come in, please."

The door opened a little wider and Homer went in without daring to look around at the housekeeper. He stumbled to the center of the room and stopped. At first he was conscious only of the heavy odor of alcohol and stale tobacco, but then underneath he smelled a metallic perfume. His eyes moved in a slow circle. On the floor was a litter of clothing, newspapers, magazines and bottles. Miss Martin was huddled up on a corner of the bed. She was wearing a man's black silk dressing gown with light-blue cuffs and lapel facings. Her close-cropped hair was the color and texture of straw and she looked like a little boy. Her youthfulness was heightened by her blue button eyes, pink button nose and red button mouth.

Homer was too busy with his growing excitement to speak or even think. He closed his eyes to tend it better, nursing carefully what he felt. He had to be careful, for if he went too fast, it might wither and then he would be cold again. It continued to grow.

"Go away, please, I'm drunk," Miss Martin said.

Homer neither moved nor spoke.

She suddenly began to sob. The coarse, broken sounds she made seemed to come from her stomach. She buried her face in her hands and pounded the floor with her feet.

Homer's feelings were so intense that his head bobbed stiffly on his neck like that of a toy Chinese dragon.

"I'm broke. I haven't any money. I haven't a dime. I'm broke, I tell you."

Homer pulled out his wallet and moved on the girl as though to strike her with it.

She cowered away from him and her sobs grew stronger.

He dropped the wallet in her lap and stood over her, not knowing what else to do. When she saw the wallet, she smiled, but continued sobbing.

"Sit down," she said.

He sat down on the bed beside her.

"You strange man," she said coyly. "I could kiss you for being so nice."

He caught her in his arms and hugged her. His suddenness frightened her and she tried to pull away, but he held on and began awkwardly to caress her. He was completely unconscious of what he was doing. He knew only that what he felt was marvelously sweet and that he had to make the sweetness carry through to the poor, sobbing woman.

Miss Martin's sobs grew less and soon stopped altogether. He could feel her fidget and gather strength.

The telephone rang.

"Don't answer it," she said, beginning to sob once more.

He pushed her away gently and stumbled to the telephone. It was Miss Carlisle.

"Are you all right?" she asked, "or shall we send for the cops?"

"All right," he said, hanging up.

It was all over. He couldn't go back to the bed.

Miss Martin laughed at his look of acute distress.

"Bring the gin, you enormous cow," she shouted gaily. "It's under the table."

He saw her stretch herself out in a way that couldn't be mistaken. He ran out of the room.

Now in California, he was crying because he had never seen Miss Martin again. The next day the manager had told him that he had done a good job and that she had paid up and checked out.

Homer tried to find her. There were two other hotels in Wayneville, small run-down houses, and he inquired at both of them. He also asked in the few rooming places, but with no success. She had left town.

He settled back into his regular routine, working ten hours, eating two, sleeping the rest. Then he caught cold and had been advised to come to California. He could easily afford not to work for a while. His father had left him about six thousand dollars and during the twenty years he had kept books in the hotel, he had saved at least ten more.

9

He got out of the tub, dried himself hurriedly with a rough towel, then went into the bedroom to dress. He felt even more stupid and washed out than usual. It was always like that. His emotions surged up in an enormous wave, curving and rearing, higher and higher, until it seemed as though the wave must carry everything before it. But the crash never came. Something always happened at the very top of the crest and the wave collapsed to run back like water down a drain, leaving, at the most, only the refuse of feeling.

It took him a long time to get all his clothing on. He stopped to rest after each garment with a desperation far out of proportion to the effort involved.

There was nothing to eat in the house and he had to go down to Hollywood Boulevard for food. He thought of waiting until morning, but then, although he was not hungry, decided against waiting. It was only eight o'clock and the trip would kill some time. If he just sat around, the temptation to go to sleep again would become irresistible.

The night was warm and very still. He started down

hill, walking on the outer edge of the pavement. He hurried between lamp-posts, where the shadows were heaviest, and came to a full stop for a moment at every circle of light. By the time he reached the boulevard, he was fighting the desire to run. He stopped for several minutes on the corner to get his bearings. As he stood there, poised for flight, his fear made him seem almost graceful.

When several other people passed without paying any attention to him, he quieted down. He adjusted the collar of his coat and prepared to cross the street. Before he could take two steps someone called to him.

"Hey, you, mister."

It was a beggar who had spotted him from the shadow of a doorway. With the infallible instinct of his kind, he knew that Homer would be easy.

"Can you spare a nickel?"

"No," Homer said without conviction.

The beggar laughed and repeated his question, threateningly.

"A nickel, mister!"

He poked his hand into Homer's face.

Homer fumbled in his change pocket and dropped several coins on the sidewalk. While the man scrambled for them, he made his escape across the street.

The SunGold Market into which he turned was a large, brilliantly lit place. All the fixtures were chromium and the floors and walls were lined with white tile. Colored spotlights played on the showcases and counters, heightening the natural hues of the different foods. The oranges were bathed in red, the lemons in yellow, the fish in pale green, the steaks in rose and the eggs in ivory.

Homer went directly to the canned goods department and bought a can of mushroom soup and another of sardines. These and a half a pound of soda crackers would be enough for his supper.

Out on the street again with his parcel, he started to walk home. When he reached the corner that led to Pinyon Canyon and saw how steep and black the hill looked, he turned back along the lighted boulevard. He thought of waiting until someone else started up the hill, but finally took a taxicab.

10

Although Homer had nothing to do but prepare his scanty meals, he was not bored. Except for the Romola Martin incident and perhaps one or two other widely spaced events, the forty years of his life had been entirely without variety or excitement. As a bookkeeper, he had worked mechanically, totaling figures and making entries with the same impersonal detachment that he now opened cans of soup and made his bed.

Someone watching him go about his little cottage might have thought him sleep-walking or partially blind. His hands seemed to have a life and a will of their own. It was they who pulled the sheets tight and shaped the pillows.

One day, while opening a can of salmon for lunch, his thumb received a nasty cut. Although the wound must have hurt, the calm, slightly querulous expression he usually wore did not change. The wounded hand writhed about on the kitchen table until it was carried to the sink by its mate and bathed tenderly in hot water.

When not keeping house, he sat in the back yard, called the patio by the real estate agent, in an old broken deck chair. He went out to it immediately after breakfast to bake himself in the sun. In one of the closets he had found a tattered book and he held it in his lap without looking at it.

There was a much better view to be had in any direction other than the one he faced. By moving his chair in a quarter circle he could have seen a large part of the canyon twisting down to the city below. He never thought of making this shift. From where he sat, he saw the closed door of the garage and a patch of its shabby, tarpaper roof. In the foreground was a sooty, brick incinerator and a pile of rusty cans. A little to the right of them were the remains of a cactus garden in which a few ragged, tortured plants still survived.

One of these, a clump of thick, paddlelike blades, covered with ugly needles, was in bloom. From the tip of several of its topmost blades protruded a bright yellow flower, somewhat like a thistle blossom but coarser. No matter how hard the wind blew, its petals never trembled.

A lizard lived in a hole near the base of this plant. It was about five inches long and had a wedge-shaped head from which darted a fine, forked tongue. It earned a hard living catching the flies that strayed over to the cactus from the pile of cans.

The lizard was self-conscious and irritable, and Homer

found it very amusing to watch. Whenever one of its elaborate stalks was foiled, it would shift about uneasily on its short legs and puff out its throat. Its coloring matched the cactus perfectly, but when it moved over to the cans where the flies were thick, it stood out very plainly. It would sit on the cactus by the hour without moving, then become impatient and start for the cans. The flies would spot it immediately and after several misses, it would sneak back sheepishly to its original post.

Homer was on the side of the flies. Whenever one of them, swinging too widely, would pass the cactus, he prayed silently for it to keep on going or turn back. If it lighted, he watched the lizard begin its stalk and held his breath until it had killed, hoping all the while that something would warn the fly. But no matter how much he wanted the fly to escape, he never thought of interfering, and was careful not to budge or make the slightest noise. Occasionally the lizard would miscalculate. When that happened Homer would laugh happily.

Between the sun, the lizard and the house, he was fairly well occupied. But whether he was happy or not it is hard to say. Probably he was neither, just as a plant is neither. He had memories to disturb him and a plant hasn't, but after the first bad night his memories were quiet.

11

He had been living this way for almost a month, when, one day, just as he was about to prepare his lunch, the door bell rang. He opened it and found a man standing on the step with a sample case in one hand and a derby hat in the other. Homer hurriedly shut the door again.

The bell continued to ring. He put his head out of the window nearest the door to order the fellow away, but the man bowed very politely and begged for a drink of water. Homer saw that he was old and tired and thought that he looked harmless. He got a bottle of water from the icebox, then opened the door and asked him in.

"The name, sir, is Harry Greener," the man announced in sing-song, stressing every other syllable.

Homer handed him a glass of water. He swallowed it quickly, then poured himself another.

"Much obliged," he said with an elaborate bow. "That was indeed refreshing."

Homer was astonished when he bowed again, did several quick jig steps, then let his derby hat roll down his arm. It fell to the floor. He stooped to retrieve it, straightening up with a jerk as though he had been kicked, then rubbed the seat of his trousers ruefully.

Homer understood that this was to amuse, so he laughed.

Harry thanked him by bowing again, but something went wrong. The exertion had been too much for him. His face blanched and he fumbled with his collar.

"A momentary indisposition," he murmured, wondering himself whether he was acting or sick.

"Sit down," Homer said.

But Harry wasn't through with his performance. He assumed a gallant smile and took a few unsteady steps toward the couch, then tripped himself. He examined the carpet indignantly, made believe he had found the object that had tripped him and kicked it away. He then limped to the couch and sat down with a whistling sigh like air escaping from a toy balloon.

Homer poured more water. Harry tried to stand up, but Homer pressed him back and made him drink sitting. He drank this glass as he had the other two, in quick gulps, then wiped his mouth with his handkerchief, imitating a man with a big mustache who had just drunk a glass of foamy beer.

"You are indeed kind, sir," he said. "Never fear, some day I'll repay you a thousandfold."

Homer clucked.

From his pocket Harry brought out a small can and held it out for him to take.

"Compliments of the house," he announced. "'Tis a box of Miracle Solvent, the modern polish par excellence, the polish without peer or parallel, used by all the movie stars . . ."

He broke off his spiel with a trilling laugh.

Homer took the can.

"Thank you," he said, trying to appear grateful. "How much is it?"

"The ordinary price, the retail price, is fifty cents, but you can have it for the extraordinary price of a quarter, the wholesale price, the price I pay at the factory."

"A quarter?" asked Homer, habit for the moment having got the better of his timidity. "I can buy one twice that size for a quarter in the store."

Harry knew his man.

"Take it, take it for nothing," he said contemptuously.

Homer was tricked into protesting.

"I guess maybe this is a much better polish."

"No," said Harry, as though he were spurning a bribe. "Keep your money. I don't want it."

He laughed, this time bitterly.

Homer pulled out some change and offered it.

"Take it, please. You need it, I'm sure. I'll have two cans."

Harry had his man where he wanted him. He began to practice a variety of laughs, all of them theatrical, like a musician tuning up before a concert. He finally found the right one and let himself go. It was a victim's laugh.

"Please stop," Homer said.

But Harry couldn't stop. He was really sick. The last block that held him poised over the runway of self-pity had been knocked away and he was sliding down the chute, gaining momentum all the time. He jumped to his feet and began doing Harry Greener, poor Harry, honest Harry, well-meaning, humble, deserving, a good husband, a model father, a faithful Christian, a loyal friend.

Homer didn't appreciate the performance in the least. He was terrified and wondered whether to phone the police. But he did nothing. He just held up his hand for Harry to stop.

At the end of his pantomime, Harry stood with his head thrown back, clutching his throat, as though waiting for the curtain to fall. Homer poured him still another glass of water. But Harry wasn't finished. He bowed, sweeping his hat to his heart, then began again. He didn't get very far this time and had to gasp painfully for breath. Suddenly, like a mechanical toy that had been overwound, something snapped inside of him and he began to spin through his entire repertoire. The effort was purely muscular, like the dance of a paralytic. He jigged, juggled his hat, made believe he had been kicked, tripped, and shook hands with himself. He went through it all in one dizzy spasm, then reeled to the couch and collapsed.

He lay on the couch with his eyes closed and his chest heaving. He was even more surprised than Homer. He had put on his performance four or five times already that day and nothing like this had happened. He was really sick.

"You've had a fit," Homer said when Harry opened his eyes.

As the minutes passed, Harry began to feel better and his confidence returned. He pushed all thought of sickness out of his mind and even went so far as to congratulate himself on having given the finest performance of his career. He should be able to get five dollars out of the big dope who was leaning over him.

"Have you any spirits in the house?" he asked weakly.

The grocer had sent Homer a bottle of port wine on approval and he went to get it. He filled a tumbler half full and handed it to Harry, who drank it in small sips, making the faces that usually go with medicine.

Speaking slowly, as though in great pain, he then asked Homer to bring in his sample case.

66

"It's on the doorstep. Somebody might steal it. The greater part of my small capital in invested in those cans of polish."

When Homer stepped outside to obey, he saw a girl near the curb. It was Faye Greener. She was looking at the house.

"Is my father in there?" she called out.

"Mr. Greener?"

She stamped her foot.

"Tell him to get a move on, damn it. I don't want to stay here all day."

"He's sick."

The girl turned away without giving any sign that she either heard or cared.

Homer took the sample case back into the house with him. He found Harry pouring himself another drink.

"Pretty fair stuff," he said, smacking his lips over it. "Pretty fair, all right, all right. Might I be so bold as to ask what you pay for a ..."

Homer cut him short. He didn't approve of people who drank and wanted to get rid of him.

"Your daughter's outside," he said with as much firmness as he could muster. "She wants you."

Harry collapsed on the couch and began to breathe heavily. He was acting again.

"Don't tell her," he gasped. "Don't tell her how sick her old daddy is. She must never know."

Homer was shocked by his hypocrisy.

"You're better," he said as coldly as he could. "Why don't you go home?"

Harry smiled to show how offended and hurt he was by the heartless attitude of his host. When Homer said nothing, his smile became one expressing boundless courage. He got carefully to his feet, stood erect for a minute, then began to sway weakly and tumbled back on the couch.

"I'm faint," he groaned.

Once again he was surprised and frightened. He was faint.

"Get my daughter," he gasped.

Homer found her standing at the curb with her back to the house. When he called her, she whirled and came running toward him. He watched her for a second, then went in, leaving the door unlatched.

Faye burst into the room. She ignored Homer and went straight to the couch.

"Now what in hell's the matter?" she exploded.

"Darling daughter," he said. "I have been badly taken, and this gentleman has been kind enough to let me rest for a moment."

"He had a fit or something," Homer said.

She whirled around on him so suddenly that he was startled.

"How do you do?" she said, holding her hand forward and high up.

He shook it gingerly.

"Charmed," she said, when he mumbled something.

She spun around once more.

"It's my heart," Harry said. "I can't stand up."

The little performance he put on to sell polish was familiar to her and she knew that this wasn't part of it. When she turned to face Homer again, she looked quite tragic. Her head, instead of being held far back, now drooped forward.

"Please let him rest there," she said.

"Yes, of course."

Homer motioned her toward a chair, then got her a match for her cigarette. He tried not to stare at her, but his good manners were wasted. Faye enjoyed being stared at.

He thought her extremely beautiful, but what affected him still more was her vitality. She was taut and vibrant. She was as shiny as a new spoon.

Although she was seventeen, she was dressed like a child of twelve in a white cotton dress with a blue sailor collar. Her long legs were bare and she had blue sandals on her feet.

"I'm so sorry," she said when Homer looked at her father again.

He made a motion with his hand to show that it was nothing.

"He has a vile heart, poor dear," she went on. "I've begged and begged him to go to a specialist, but you men are all alike."

"Yes, he ought to go to a doctor," Homer said.

Her odd mannerisms and artificial voice puzzled him.

"What time is it?" she asked.

"About one o'clock."

She stood up suddenly and buried both her hands in her hair at the sides of her head, making it bunch at the top in a shiny ball.

"Oh," she gasped prettily, "and I had a luncheon date."

Still holding her hair, so that her snug dress twisted even tighter and Homer could see her dainty, arched ribs and little, dimpled belly. This elaborate gesture, like all her others, was so completely meaningless, almost formal, that she seemed a dancer rather than an affected actress.

"Do you like salmon salad?" Homer ventured to ask.

"Salmon sal-ahde?"

She seemed to be repeating the question to her stomach. The answer was yes.

"With plenty of mayonnaise, huh? I adore it."

"I was going to have some for lunch. I'll finish making it."

"Let me help."

They looked at Harry, who appeared to be asleep, then went into the kitchen. While he opened a can of salmon, she climbed on a chair and straddled it with her arms folded across the top of its back and rested her chin on her arms. Whenever he looked at her, she smiled intimately and tossed her pale, glittering hair first forward, then back.

Homer was excited and his hands worked quickly. He soon had a large bowl of salad ready. He set the table with his best cloth and his best silver and china.

"It makes me hungry just to look," she said.

The way she said this seemed to mean that it was Homer who made her hungry and he beamed at her. But before he had a chance to sit down, she was already eating. She buttered a slice of bread, covered the butter with sugar and took a big bite. Then she quickly smeared a gob of mayonnaise on the salmon and went to work. Just as he was about to sit down, she asked for something to drink. He poured her a glass of milk and stood watching her like a waiter. He was unaware of her rudeness.

As soon as she had gobbled up her salad, he brought her a large red apple. She ate the fruit more slowly, nibbling daintily, her smallest finger curled away from the rest of her hand. When she had finished it, she went back to the living room and Homer followed her.

Harry still lay as they had left him, stretched out on the sofa. The heavy noon-day sun hit directly on his face, beating down on him like a club. He hardly felt its blows, however. He was busy with the stabbing pain in his chest. He was so busy with himself that he had even stopped trying to plan how to get money out of the big dope.

Homer drew the window curtain to shade his face. Harry didn't even notice. He was thinking about death. Faye bent over him. He saw, from under his partially closed eyelids, that she expected him to make a reassuring gesture. He refused. He examined the tragic expression that she had assumed and didn't like it. In a serious moment like this, her ham sorrow was insulting.

"Speak to me, Daddy," she begged.

She was baiting him without being aware of it.

"What the hell is this," he snarled, "a Tom show?"

His sudden fury scared her and she straightened up with a jerk. He didn't want to laugh, but a short bark escaped before he could stop it. He waited anxiously to see what would happen. When it didn't hurt he laughed again. He kept on, timidly at first, then with growing assurance. He laughed with his eyes closed and the sweat pouring down his brow. Faye knew only one way to stop him and that was to do something he hated as much as she hated his laughter. She began to sing.

> *"Jeepers Creepers!*
> *Where'd ya get those peepers? . . ."*

She trucked, jerking her buttocks and shaking her head from side to side.

Homer was amazed. He felt that the scene he was witnessing had been rehearsed. He was right. Their bitterest quarrels often took this form; he laughing, she singing.

> *"Jeepers Creepers!*
> *Where'd ya get those eyes?*
> *Gosh, all git up!*
> *How'd they get so lit up?*
> *Gosh all git . . ."*

When Harry stopped, she stopped and flung herself into a chair. But Harry was only gathering strength for a final effort. He began again. This new laugh was not critical; it was horrible. When she was a child, he used to punish her with it. It was his masterpiece. There was a director who always called on him to give it when he was shooting a scene in an insane asylum or a haunted castle.

It began with a sharp, metallic crackle, like burning sticks, then gradually increased in volume until it became a rapid bark, then fell away again to an obscene chuckle. After a slight pause, it climbed until it was the nicker of a horse, then still higher to become a machinelike screech.

Faye listened helplessly with her head cocked on one side. Suddenly, she too laughed, not willingly, but fighting the sound.

"You bastard!" she yelled.

She leaped to the couch, grabbed him by the shoulders and tried to shake him quiet.

He kept laughing.

Homer moved as though he meant to pull her away, but he lost courage and was afraid to touch her. She was so naked under her skimpy dress.

"Miss Greener," he pleaded, making his big hands dance at the end of his arms. "Please, please ..."

Harry couldn't stop laughing now. He pressed his belly with his hands, but the noise poured out of him. It had begun to hurt again.

Swinging her hand as though it held a hammer, she

brought her fist down hard on his mouth. She hit him only once. He relaxed and was quiet.

"I had to do it," she said to Homer when he took her arm and led her away.

He guided her to a chair in the kitchen and shut the door. She continued to sob for a long time. He stood behind her chair, helplessly, watching the rhythmical heave of her shoulders. Several times his hands moved forward to comfort her, but he succeeded in curbing them.

When she was through crying, he handed her a napkin and she dried her face. The cloth was badly stained by her rouge and mascara.

"I've spoilt it," she said, keeping her face averted. "I'm very sorry."

"It was dirty," Homer said.

She took a compact from her pocket and looked at herself in its tiny mirror.

"I'm a fright."

She asked if she could use the bathroom and he showed her where it was. He then tiptoed into the living room to see Harry. The old man's breathing was noisy but regular and he seemed to be sleeping quietly. Homer put a cushion under his head without disturbing him and went back into the kitchen. He lit the stove and put the coffeepot on the flame, then sat down to wait for the girl to return. He heard her go into the living room. A few seconds later she came into the kitchen.

She hesitated apologetically in the doorway.

"Won't you have some coffee?"

Without waiting for her to reply, he poured a cup and moved the sugar and cream so that she could reach them.

"I had to do it," she said. "I just had to."

"That's all right."

To show her that it wasn't necessary to apologize, he busied himself at the sink.

"No, I had to," she insisted. "He laughs that way just to drive me wild. I can't stand it. I simply can't."

"Yes."

"He's crazy. We Greeners are all crazy."

She made this last statement as though there were merit in being crazy.

"He's pretty sick," Homer said, apologizing for her. "Maybe he had a sunstroke."

"No, he's crazy."

He put a plate of gingersnaps on the table and she ate them with her second cup of coffee. The dainty crunching sound she made chewing fascinated him.

When she remained quiet for several minutes, he turned

from the sink to see if anything was wrong. She was smoking a cigarette and seemed lost in thought.

He tried to be gay.

"What are you thinking?" he said awkwardly, then felt foolish.

She sighed to show how dark and foreboding her thoughts were, but didn't reply.

"I'll bet you would like some candy," Homer said. "There isn't any in the house, but I could call the drugstore and they'd send it right over. Or some ice cream?"

"No, thanks, please."

"It's no trouble."

"My father isn't really a peddler," she said, abruptly. "He's an actor. I'm an actress. My mother was also an actress, a dancer. The theatre is in our blood."

"I haven't seen many shows. I ..."

He broke off because he saw that she wasn't interested.

"I'm going to be a star some day," she announced as though daring him to contradict her.

"I'm sure you ..."

"It's my life. It's the only thing in the whole world that I want."

"It's good to know what you want. I used to be a bookkeeper in a hotel, but ..."

"If I'm not, I'll commit suicide."

She stood up and put her hands to her hair, opened her eyes wide and frowned.

"I don't go to shows very often," he apologized, pushing the gingersnaps toward her. "The lights hurt my eyes."

She laughed and took a cracker.

"I'll get fat."

"Oh, no."

"They say fat women are going to be popular next year. Do you think so? I don't. It's just publicity for Mae West."

He agreed with her.

She talked on and on, endlessly, about herself and about the picture business. He watched her, but didn't listen, and whenever she repeated a question in order to get a reply, he nodded his head without saying anything.

His hands began to bother him. He rubbed them against the edge of the table to relieve their itch, but it only stimulated them. When he clasped them behind his back, the strain became intolerable. They were hot and swollen. Using the dishes as an excuse, he held them under the cold water tap of the sink.

Faye was still talking when Harry appeared in the doorway. He leaned weakly against the door jamb. His nose was very red, but the rest of his face was drained white and he seemed to have grown too small for his clothing. He was smiling, however.

To Homer's amazement, they greeted each other as though nothing had happened.

"You okay now, Pop?"

"Fine and dandy, baby. Right as rain, fit as a fiddle and lively as a flea, as the feller says."

The nasal twang he used in imitation of a country yokel made Homer smile.

"Do you want something to eat?" he asked. "A glass of milk, maybe?"

"I could do with a snack."

Faye helped him over to the table. He tried to disguise how weak he was by doing an exaggerated Negro shuffle.

Homer opened a can of sardines and sliced some bread. Harry smacked his lips over the food, but ate slowly and with an effort.

"That hit the spot, all righty right," he said when he had finished.

He leaned back and fished a crumpled cigar butt out of his vest pocket. Faye lit it for him and he playfully blew a puff of smoke in her face.

"We'd better go, Daddy," she said.

"In a jiffy, child."

He turned to Homer.

"Nice place you've got here. Married?"

Faye tried to interfere.

"Dad!"

He ignored her.

"Bachelor, eh?"

"Yes."

"Well, well, a young fellow like you."

"I'm here for my health," Homer found it necessary to say.

"Don't answer his questions," Faye broke in.

"Now, now, daughter, I'm just being friendly like. I don't mean no harm."

He was still using an exaggerated backwoods accent. He spat dry into an imaginary spittoon and made believe he was shifting a cud of tobacco from cheek to cheek.

Homer thought his mimicry funny.

"I'd be lonesome and scared living alone in a big house like this," Harry went on. "Don't you ever get lonesome?"

Homer looked at Faye for his answer. She was frowning with annoyance.

"No," he said, to prevent Harry from repeating the uncomfortable question.

"No? Well, that's fine."

He blew several smoke rings at the ceiling and watched their behavior judiciously.

"Did you ever think of taking boarders?" he asked. "Some nice, sociable folks, I mean. It'll bring in a little extra money and make things more homey."

Homer was indignant, but underneath his indignation lurked another idea, a very exciting one. He didn't know what to say.

Faye misunderstood his agitation.

"Cut it out, Dad," she exclaimed before Homer could reply. "You've been a big enough nuisance already."

"Just chinning," he protested innocently. "Just chewing the fat."

"Well, then, let's get going," she snapped.

"There's plenty of time," Homer said.

He wanted to add something stronger, but didn't have the courage. His hands were braver. When Faye shook good-by, they clutched and refused to let go.

Faye laughed at their warm insistence.

"Thanks a million, Mr. Simpson," she said. "You've been very kind. Thanks for the lunch and for helping Daddy."

"We're very grateful," Harry chimed in. "You've done a Christian deed this day. God will reward you."

He had suddenly become very pious.

"Please look us up," Faye said. "We live close-by in the San Berdoo Apartments, about five blocks down the canyon. It's the big yellow house."

When Harry stood, he had to lean against the table for support. Faye and Homer each took him by the arm and helped him into the street. Homer held him erect, while Faye went to get their Ford which was parked across the street.

"We're forgetting your order of Miracle Salve," Harry said, "the polish without peer or parallel."

Homer found a dollar and slipped it into his hand. He hid the money quickly and tried to become businesslike.

"I'll leave the goods tomorrow."

"Yes, that'll be fine," Homer said. "I really need some silver polish."

Harry was angry because it hurt him to be patronized by a sucker. He made an attempt to re-establish what he considered to be their proper relationship by bowing ironically, but didn't get very far with the gesture and began to fumble with his Adam's apple. Homer helped him into the car and he slumped down in the seat beside Faye.

They drove off. She turned to wave, but Harry didn't even look back.

12

Homer spent the rest of the afternoon in the broken deck chair. The lizard was on the cactus, but he took little interest in its hunting. His hands kept his thoughts busy. They trembled and jerked, as though troubled by dreams. To hold them still, he clasped them together. Their fingers twined like a tangle of thighs in miniature. He snatched them apart and sat on them.

When the days passed and he couldn't forget Faye, he began to grow frightened. He somehow knew that his only defense was chastity, that it served him, like the shell of a tortoise, as both spine and armor. He couldn't shed it even in thought. If he did, he would be destroyed.

He was right. There are men who can lust with parts of themselves. Only their brain or their hearts burn and then not completely. There are others, still more fortunate, who are like the filaments of an incandescent lamp. They burn fiercely, yet nothing is destroyed. But in Homer's case it would be like dropping a spark into a barn full of hay. He had escaped in the Romola Martin incident, but he wouldn't escape again. Then, for one thing, he had had his job in the hotel, a daily all-day task that protected him by tiring him, but now he had nothing.

His thoughts frightened him and he bolted into the house, hoping to leave them behind like a hat. He ran into his bedroom and threw himself down on the bed. He was simple enough to believe that people don't think while asleep.

In his troubled state, even this delusion was denied him and he was unable to fall asleep. He closed his eyes and tried to make himself drowsy. The approach to sleep which had once been automatic had somehow become a long, shining tunnel. Sleep was at the far end of it, a soft bit of shadow in the hard glare. He couldn't run, only crawl toward the black patch. Just as he was about to give up, habit came to his rescue. It collapsed the shining tunnel and hurled him into the shadow.

When he awoke it was without a struggle. He tried to fall asleep once more, but this time couldn't even find the tunnel. He was throughly awake. He tried to think of how very tired he was, but he wasn't tired. He felt more alive than he had at any time since Romola Martin.

Outside a few birds still sang intermittently, starting and breaking off, as though sorry to acknowledge the end of another day. He thought that he heard the lisp of silk against silk, but it was only the wind playing in the trees. How empty the house was! He tried to fill it by singing.

> *"Oh, say can you see,*
> *By the dawn's early light ..."*

It was the only song he knew. He thought of buying a victrola or a radio. He knew, however, that he would buy neither. This fact made him very sad. It was a pleasant sadness, very sweet and calm.

But he couldn't let well enough alone. He was impatient and began to prod at his sadness, hoping to make it acute and so still more pleasant. He had been getting pamphlets in the mail from a travel bureau and he thought of the trips he would never take. Mexico was only a few hundred miles away. Boats left daily for Hawaii.

His sadness turned to anguish before he knew it and became sour. He was miserable again. He began to cry.

Only those who still have hope can benefit from tears. When they finish, they feel better. But to those without hope, like Homer, whose anguish is basic and permanent, no good comes from crying. Nothing changes for them. They usually know this, but still can't help crying.

Homer was lucky. He cried himself to sleep.

But he awoke again in the morning with Faye uppermost in his mind. He bathed, ate breakfast and sat in his deck chair. In the afternoon, he decided to go for a walk. There was only one way for him to go and that led past the San Bernardino Apartments.

Some time during his long sleep, he had given up the battle. When he came to the apartment house, he peered into the amber-lit hallway and read the Greener card on the letter box, then turned and went home. On the next night, he repeated the trip, carrying a gift of flowers and wine.

13

Harry Greener's condition didn't improve. He remained in bed, staring at the ceiling with his hands folded on his chest.

Tod went to see him almost every night. There were usually other guests. Sometimes Abe Kusich, sometimes Anna and Annabelle Lee, a sister act of the nineteen-tens, more often the four Gingos, a family of performing Eskimos from Point Barrow, Alaska.

If Harry were asleep or there were visitors, Faye usually invited Tod into her room for a talk. His interest in her grew despite the things she said and he continued to find her very exciting. Had any other girl been so affected, he would have thought her intolerable. Faye's affectations, however, were so completely artificial that he found them charming.

Being with her was like being backstage during an amateurish, ridiculous play. From in front, the stupid lines and grotesque situations would have made him squirm with annoyance, but because he saw the perspiring stagehands and the wires that held up the tawdry summerhouse with its tangle of paper flowers, he accepted everything and was anxious for it to succeed.

He found still another way to excuse her. He believed that while she often recognized the falseness of an attitude, she persisted in it because she didn't know how to be simpler or more honest. She was an actress who had learned from bad models in a bad school.

Yet Faye did have some critical ability, almost enough to recognize the ridiculous. He had often seen her laugh at herself. What was more, he had even seen her laugh at her dreams.

One evening they talked about what she did with herself when she wasn't working as an extra. She told him that she often spent the whole day making up stories. She laughed as she said it. When he questioned her, she described her method quite willingly.

She would get some music on the radio, then lie down on her bed and shut her eyes. She had a large assortment of stories to choose from. After getting herself in the right mood, she would go over them in her mind, as though they were a pack of cards, discarding one after another until she found the one that suited. On some days, she would run through the whole pack without making a choice. When that happened, she would either go to Vine Street for an ice cream soda or, if she was broke, thumb over the pack again and force herself to choose.

While she admitted that her method was too mechanical for the best results and that it was better to slip into a dream naturally, she said that any dream was better than no dream and beggars couldn't be choosers. She hadn't exactly said this, but he was able to understand it from what she did say. He thought it important that she smiled while telling him, not with embarrassment, but critically. However, her critical powers ended there. She only smiled at the mechanics.

The first time he had ever heard one of her dreams was late at night in her bedroom. About half an hour earlier, she had knocked on his door and had asked him to come and help her with Harry because she thought he was dying. His noisy breathing, which she had taken for the death rattle, had awakened her and she was badly frightened. Tod put on his bathrobe and followed her downstairs. When he got to the apartment, Harry had managed to clear his throat and his breathing had become quiet again.

She invited him into her room for a smoke. She sat on the bed and he sat beside her. She was wearing an old beach robe of white toweling over her pajamas and it was very becoming.

He wanted to beg her for a kiss but was afraid, not because she would refuse, but because she would insist on making it meaningless. To flatter her, he commented on her appearance. He did a bad job of it. He was incapable of direct flattery and got bogged down in a much too roundabout observation. She didn't listen and he broke off feeling like an idiot.

"I've got a swell idea," she said suddenly. "An idea how we can make some real money."

He made another attempt to flatter her. This time by assuming an attitude of serious interest.

"You're educated," she said. "Well, I've got some swell ideas for pictures. All you got to do is write them up and then we'll sell them to the studios."

He agreed and she described her plan. It was very vague until she came to what she considered would be its results, then she went into concrete details. As soon as they had sold one story, she would give him another. They would make loads and loads of money. Of course she wouldn't give up acting, even if she was a big success as a writer, because acting was her life.

He realized as she went on that she was manufacturing another dream to add to her already very thick pack. When she finally got through spending the money, he asked her to tell him the idea he was to "write up," keeping all trace of irony out of his voice.

On the wall of the room beyond the foot of her bed was a large photograph that must have once been used in the lobby of a theatre to advertise a Tarzan picture. It showed a beautiful young man with magnificent muscles, wearing only a narrow loin cloth, who was ardently squeezing a slim girl in a torn riding habit. They stood in a jungle clearing and all around the pair writhed great vines loaded with fat orchids. When she told her story, he knew that this photograph had a lot to do with inspiring it.

A young girl is cruising on her father's yacht in the South Seas. She is engaged to marry a Russian count, who is tall, thin and old, but with beautiful manners. He is on the yacht, too, and keeps begging her to name the day. But she is spoiled and won't do it. Maybe she became engaged to him in order to spite another man. She becomes interested in a young sailor who is far below her in station, but very handsome. She flirts with him because she is bored. The sailor refuses to be toyed with no matter how much money she's got and tells her that he only takes orders from the captain and to go back to her foreigner. She gets sore as hell and threatens to have him fired, but he only laughs at her. How can he be fired in the middle of the ocean? She falls in love with him, although maybe she doesn't realize it herself, because he is the first man who has ever said no to one of her whims and because he is so handsome. Then there is a big storm and the yacht is wrecked near an island. Everybody is drowned, but she manages to swim to shore. She makes herself a hut of boughs and lives on fish and fruit. It's the tropics. One morning, while she is bathing naked in a brook, a big snake grabs her. She struggles but the snake is too strong for her and it looks like curtains. But the sailor, who has been watching her from behind some bushes, leaps to her rescue. He fights the snake for her and wins.

Tod was to go on from there. He asked her how she thought the picture should end, but she seemed to have lost interest. He insisted on hearing, however.

"Well, he marries her, of course, and they're rescued. First they're rescued and then they're married, I mean. Maybe he turns out to be a rich boy who is being a sailor just for the adventure of it, or something like that. You can work it out easy enough."

"It's sure-fire," Tod said earnestly, staring at her wet lips and the tiny point of her tongue which she kept moving between them.

'I've got just hundreds and hundreds more."

He didn't say anything and her manner changed. While telling the story, she had been full of surface animation and her hands and face were alive with little illustrative grimaces and gestures. But now her excitement narrowed and became deeper and its play internal. He guessed that she must be thumbing over her pack and that she would soon select another card to show him.

He had often seen her like this, but had never before understood it. All these little stories, these little daydreams of hers, were what gave such extraordinary color and mystery to her movements. She seemed always to be struggling in their soft grasp as though she were trying to run in a swamp. As he watched her, he felt sure that her lips must taste of blood and salt and that there must be a delicious weakness in her legs. His impulse wasn't to aid her to get free, but to throw her down in the soft, warm mud and to keep her there.

He expressed some of his desire by a grunt. If he only had the courage to throw himself on her. Nothing less violent than rape would do. The sensation he felt was like that he got when holding an egg in his hand. Not that she was fragile or even seemed fragile. It wasn't that. It was her completeness, her egglike self-sufficiency, that made him want to crush her.

But he did nothing and she began to talk again.

"I've got another swell idea that I want to tell you.

Maybe you had better write this one up first. It's a backstage story and they're making a lot of them this year."

She told him about a young chorus girl who gets her big chance when the star of the show falls sick. It was a familiar version of the Cinderella theme, but her technique was much different from the one she had used for the South Sea tale. Although the events she described were miraculous, her description of them was realistic. The effect was similar to that obtained by the artists of the Middle Ages, who, when doing a subject like the raising of Lazarus from the dead or Christ walking on water, were careful to keep all the details intensely realistic. She, like them, seemed to think that fantasy could be made plausible by a humdrum technique.

"I like that one, too," he said when she had finished.

"Think them over and do the one that has the best chance."

She was dismissing him and if he didn't act at once the opportunity would be gone. He started to lean toward her, but she caught his meaning and stood up. She took his arm with affectionate brusqueness—they were now business partners—and guided him to the door.

In the hall, when she thanked him for coming down and apologized for having disturbed him, he tried again.

She seemed to melt a little and he reached for her. She kissed him willingly enough, but when he tried to extend the caress, she tore free.

"Whoa there, palsy-walsy," she laughed. "Mama spank."

He started for the stairs.

"Good-by now," she called after him, then laughed again.

He barely heard her. He was thinking of the drawings he had made of her and of the new one he would do as soon as he got to his room.

In "The Burning of Los Angeles" Faye is the naked girl in the left foreground being chased by the group of men and women who have separated from the main body of the mob. One of the women is about to hurl a rock at her to bring her down. She is running with her eyes closed and a strange half-smile on her lips. Despite the dreamy repose of her face, her body is straining to hurl her along at top speed. The only explanation for this contrast is that she is enjoying the release that wild flight gives in much the same way that a game bird must when, after hiding for several tense minutes, it bursts from cover in complete, unthinking panic.

14

Tod had other and more successful rivals than Homer Simpson. One of the most important was a young man called Earle Shoop.

Earle was a cowboy from a small town in Arizona. He worked occasionally in horse-operas and spent the rest of his time in front of a saddlery store on Sunset Boulevard. In the window of this store was an enormous Mexican saddle covered with carved silver, and around it was arranged a large collection of torture instruments. Among other things there were fancy, braided quirts, spurs with great spiked wheels, and double bits that looked as though they could break a horse's jaw without trouble. Across the back of the window ran a low shelf on which was a row of boots, some black, some red and some a pale yellow. All of the boots had scalloped tops and very high heels.

Earle always stood with his back to the window, his eyes fixed on a sign on the roof of a one-story building across the street that read: "Malted Milks Too Thick For a Straw." Regularly, twice every hour, he pulled a sack of tobacco and a sheaf of papers from his shirt pocket and rolled a cigarette.

Then he tightened the cloth of his trousers by lifting his knee and struck a match along the underside of his thigh.

He was over six feet tall. The big Stetson hat he wore added five inches more to his height and the heels of his boots still another three. His polelike appearance was further exaggerated by the narrowness of his shoulders and by his lack of either hips or buttocks. The years he had spent in the saddle had not made him bowlegged. In fact, his legs were so straight that his dungarees, bleached a very light blue by the sun and much washing, hung down without a wrinkle, as though they were empty.

Tod could see why Faye thought him handsome. He had a two-dimensional face that a talented child might have drawn with a ruler and a compass. His chin was perfectly round and his eyes, which were wide apart, were also round. His thin mouth ran at right angles to his straight, perpendicular nose. His reddish tan complexion was the same color from hairline to throat, as though washed in by an expert, and it completed his resemblance to a mechanical drawing.

Tod had told Faye that Earle was a dull fool. She agreed laughing, but then said that he was "criminally handsome," an expression she had picked up in the chatter column of a trade paper.

Meeting her on the stairs one night, Tod asked if she would go to dinner with him.

"I can't. I've got a date. But you can come along."

"With Earle?"

"Yes, with Earle," she repeated, mimicking his annoyance.

"No, thanks."

She misunderstood, perhaps on purpose, and said, "He'll treat this time."

Earle was always broke and whenever Tod went with them he was the one who paid.

"That isn't it, and you damn well know it."

"Oh, isn't it?" she asked archly, then, absolutely sure of herself, added, "Meet us at Hodge's around five."

Hodge's was the saddlery store. When Tod got there, he found Earle Shoop at his usual post, just standing and just looking at the sign across the street. He had on his ten-gallon hat and his high-heeled boots. Neatly folded over his left arm was a dark gray jacket. His shirt was navy-blue cotton with large polka dots, each the size of a dime. The sleeves of his shirt were not rolled, but pulled to the middle of his forearm and held there by a pair of fancy, rose armbands. His hands were the same clean reddish tan as his face.

"Lo, thar," was the way he returned Tod's salute.

Tod found his Western accent amusing. The first time he had heard it, he had replied, "Lo, thar, stranger," and had been surprised to discover that Earle didn't know he was being kidded. Even when Tod talked about "cayuses," "mean hombres" and "rustlers," Earle took him seriously.

"Howdy, partner," Tod said.

Next to Earle was another Westerner in a big hat and boots, sitting on his heels and chewing vigorously on a little twig. Close behind him was a battered paper valise held together by heavy rope tied with professional-looking knots.

Soon after Tod arrived a third man came along. He made a thorough examination of the merchandise in the window, then turned and began to stare across the street like the other two.

He was middle-aged and looked like an exercise boy from a racing stable. His face was completely covered with a fine mesh of wrinkles, as though he had been sleeping with it pressed against a roll of rabbit wire. He was very shabby and had probably sold his big hat, but he still had his boots.

"Lo, boys," he said.

"Lo, Hink," said the man with the paper valise.

Tod didn't know whether he was included in the greeting, but took a chance and replied.

"Howdy."

Hink prodded the valise with his toe.

"Goin' some place, Calvin?" he asked.

"Azusa, there's a rodeo."

"Who's running it?"

"A fellow calls himself 'Badlands Jack.'"

"That grifter! . . . You goin', Earle?"

"Nope."

"I gotta eat," said Calvin.

Hink carefully considered all the information he had received before speaking again.

"Mono's makin' a new Buck Stevens," he said. "Will Ferris told me they'd use more than forty riders."

Calvin turned and looked up at Earle.

"Still got the piebald vest?" he asked slyly.

"Why?"

"It'll cinch you a job as a road agent."

Tod understood that this was a joke of some sort because Calvin and Hink chuckled and slapped their thighs loudly while Earle frowned.

There was another long silence, then Calvin spoke again.

"Ain't your old man still got some cows?" he asked Earle.

But Earle was wary this time and refused to answer.

Calvin winked at Tod, slowly and elaborately, contorting one whole side of his face.

"That's right, Earle," Hink said. "Your old man's still got some stock. Why don't you go home?"

They couldn't get a rise out of Earle, so Calvin answered the question.

"He dassint. He got caught in a sheep car with a pair of rubber boots on."

It was another joke. Calvin and Hink slapped their thighs and laughed, but Tod could see that they were waiting for something else. Earle, suddenly, without even shifting his weight, shot his foot out and kicked Calvin solidly in the rump. This was the real point of the joke. They were delighted by Earle's fury. Tod also laughed. The way Earle had gone from apathy to action without the usual transition was funny. The seriousness of his violence was even funnier.

A little while later, Faye drove by in her battered Ford touring car and pulled into the curb some twenty feet away. Calvin and Hink waved, but Earle didn't budge. He took his time, as befitted his dignity. Not until she tooted her horn did he move. Tod followed a short distance behind him.

"Hi, cowboy," said Faye gaily.

"Lo, honey," he drawled, removing his hat carefully and replacing it with even greater care.

Faye smiled at Tod and motioned for them both to climb in. Tod got in the back. Earle unfolded the jacket he was carrying, slapped it a few times to remove the wrinkles, then put it on and adjusted its collar and shaped the roll of its lapels. He then climbed in beside Faye.

She started the car with a jerk. When she reached LaBrea, she turned right to Hollywood Boulevard and then left along it. Tod could see that she was watching Earle out of the corner of her eye and that he was preparing to speak.

"Get going," she said, trying to hurry him. "What is it?"

"Looka here, honey, I ain't got any dough for supper."

She was very much put out.

"But I told Tod we'd treat him. He's treated us enough times."

"That's all right," Tod interposed. "Next time'll do. I've got plenty of money."

"No, damn it," she said without looking around. "I'm sick of it."

She pulled into the curb and slammed on the brakes.

"It's always the same story," she said to Earle.

He adjusted his hat, his collar and his sleeves, then spoke.

"We've got some grub at camp."

"Beans, I suppose."

"Nope."

She prodded him.

"Well, what've you got?"

"Mig and me's set some traps."

Faye laughed.

"Rat traps, eh? We're going to eat rats."

Earle didn't say anything.

"Listen, you big, strong, silent dope," she said, "either make sense, or God damn it, get out of this car."

"They're quail traps," he said without the slightest change in his wooden, formal manner.

She ignored his explanation.

"Talking to you is like pulling teeth. You wear me out."

Tod knew that there was no hope for him in this quarrel. He had heard it all before.

"I didn't mean nothing," Earle said. "I was only funning. I wouldn't feed you rats."

She slammed off the emergency brake and started the car again. At Zacarias Street, she turned into the hills. After climbing steadily for a quarter of a mile, she reached a dirt road and followed it to its end. They all climbed out, Earle helping Faye.

"Give me a kiss," she said, smiling her forgiveness.

He took his hat off ceremoniously and placed it on the hood the car, then wrapped his long arms around her. They paid no attention to Tod, who was standing off to one side watching them. He saw Earle close his eyes and pucker up his lips like a little boy. But there was nothing boyish about what he did to her. When she had had as much as she wanted, she pushed him away.

"You, too?" she called gaily to Tod, who had turned his back.

"Oh, some other time," he replied, imitating her casualness.

She laughed, then took out a compact and began to fix her mouth. When she was ready, they started along a little path that was a continuation of the dirt road. Earle led, Faye came next and Tod brought up the rear.

It was full spring. The path ran along the bottom of a narrow canyon and wherever weeds could get a purchase in its steep banks they flowered in purple, blue and yellow. Orange poppies bordered the path. Their petals were wrinkled like crepe and their leaves were heavy with talcumlike dust.

They climbed until they reached another canyon. This one was sterile, but its bare ground and jagged rocks were even more brilliantly colored than the flowers of the first.

The path was silver, grained with streaks of rose-gray, and the walls of the canyon were turquoise, mauve, chocolate and lavender. The air itself was vibrant pink.

They stopped to watch a hummingbird chase a bluejay. The jay flashed by squawking with its tiny enemy on its tail like a ruby bullet. The gaudy birds burst the colored air into a thousand glittering particles like metal confetti.

When they came out of this canyon, they saw below them a little green valley thick with trees, mostly eucalyptus, with here and there a poplar and one enormous black live-oak. Sliding and stumbling down a dry wash, they made for the valley.

Tod saw a man watching their approach from the edge of the wood. Faye also saw him and waved.

"Hi, Mig!" she shouted.

"Chinita!" he called back.

She ran the last ten yards of the slope and the man caught her in his arms.

He was toffee-colored with large Armenian eyes and pouting black lips. His head was a mass of tight, ordered curls. He wore a long-haired sweater, called a "gorilla" in and around Los Angeles, with nothing under it. His soiled duck trousers were held up by a red bandanna handkerchief. On his feet were a pair of tattered tennis sneakers.

They moved on to the camp which was located in a clearing in the center of the wood. It consisted of little more than a ramshackle hut patched with tin signs that had been stolen from the highway and a stove without legs or bottom set on some rocks. Near the hut was a row of chicken coops.

Earle started a fire under the stove while Faye sat down on a box and watched him. Tod went over to look at the chickens. There was one old hen and a half a dozen game cocks. A great deal of pains had been taken in making the coops, which were of grooved boards, carefully matched and joined. Their floors were freshly spread with peat moss.

The Mexican came over and began to talk about the cocks. He was very proud of them.

"That's Hermano, five times winner. He's one of Street's Butcher Boys. Pepe and El Negro are still stags. I fight them next week in San Pedro. That's Villa, he's a blinker, but still good. And that one's Zapata, twice winner, a Tassel Dom he is. And that's Jujutla. My champ."

He opened the coop and lifted the bird out for Tod.

"A murderer is what the guy is. Speedy and how!"

The cock's plummage was green, bronze and copper. Its beak was lemon and its legs orange.

"He's beautiful," Tod said.

"I'll say."

Mig tossed the bird back into the coop and they went back to join the others at the fire.

"When do we eat?" Faye asked.

Miguel tested the stove by spitting on it. He next found a large iron skillet and began to scour it with sand. Earle gave Faye a knife and some potatoes to peel, then picked up a burlap sack.

"I'll get the birds," he said.

Tod went along with him. They followed a narrow path that looked as though it had been used by sheep until they came to a tiny field covered with high, tufted grass. Earle stopped behind a gum bush and held up his hand to warn Tod.

A mocking bird was singing near by. Its song was like pebbles being dropped one by one from a height into a pool of water. Then a quail began to call, using two soft guttural notes. Another quail answered and the birds talked back and forth. Their call was not like the cheerful whistle of the Eastern bobwhite. It was full of melancholy and weariness, yet marvelously sweet. Still another quail joined the duet. This one called from near the center of the field. It was a trapped bird, but the sound it made had no anxiety in it, only sadness, impersonal and without hope.

When Earle was satisfied that no one was there to spy

on his poaching, he went to the trap. It was a wire basket about the size of a washtub with a small door in the top. He stooped over and began to fumble with the door. Five birds ran wildly along the inner edge and threw themselves at the wire. One of them, a cock, had a dainty plume on his head that curled forward almost to his beak.

Earle caught the birds one at a time and pulled their heads off before dropping them into his sacks. Then he started back. As he walked along, he held the sack under his left arm. He lifted the birds out with his right hand and plucked them one at a time. Their feathers fell to the ground, point first, weighed down by the tiny drop of blood that trembled on the tips of their quills.

The sun went down before they reached the camp again. It grew chilly and Tod was glad of the fire. Faye shared her seat on the box with him and they both leaned forward into the heat.

Mig brought a jug of tequila from the hut. He filled a peanut butter jar for Faye and passed the jug to Tod. The liquor smelled like rotten fruit, but he liked the taste. When he had had enough, Earle took it and then Miguel. They continued to pass it from hand to hand.

Earle tried to show Faye how plump the game was, but

she wouldn't look. He gutted the birds, then began cutting them into quarters with a pair of heavy tin shears. Faye held her hands over her ears in order not to hear the soft click made by the blades as they cut through flesh and bone. Earle wiped the pieces with a rag and dropped them into the skillet where a large piece of lard was already sputtering.

For all her squeamishness, Faye ate as heartily as the men did. There was no coffee and they finished with tequila. They smoked and kept the jug moving. Faye tossed away the peanut butter jar and drank like the others, throwing her head back and tilting the jug.

Tod could sense her growing excitement. The box on which they were sitting was so small that their backs touched and he could feel how hot she was and how restless. Her neck and face had turned from ivory to rose. She kept reaching for his cigarettes.

Earle's features were hidden in the shadow of his big hat, but the Mexican sat full in the light of the fire. His skin glowed and the oil in his black curls sparkled. He kept smiling at Faye in a manner that Tod didn't like. The more he drank, the less he liked it.

Faye kept crowding Tod, so he left the box to sit on the ground where he could watch her better. She was smiling back at the Mexican. She seemed to know what he was thinking and to be thinking the same thing. Earle, too, became aware of what was passing between them. Tod heard him curse softly and saw him lean forward into the light and pick up a thick piece of firewood.

Mig laughed guiltily and began to sing.

> *"Las palmeras lloran por tu ausencia,*
> *Las laguna se seco—ay!*
> *La cerca de alambre que estaba en*
> *El patio tambien se cayo!"*

His voice was a plaintive tenor and it turned the revolutionary song into a sentimental lament, sweet and cloying. Faye joined in when he began another stanza. She didn't know the words, but she was able to carry the melody and to harmonize.

> *"Pues mi madre las cuidaba, ay!*
> *Toditito se acabo—ay!"*

Their voices touched in the thin, still air to form a minor chord and it was as though their bodies had touched. The song was transformed again. The melody remained the same, but the rhythm broke and its beat became ragged. It was a rumba now.

Earle shifted uneasily and played with his stick. Tod saw her look at him and saw that she was afraid, but instead of becoming wary, she grew still more reckless. She took a long pull at the jug and stood up. She put one hand on each of her buttocks and began to dance.

Mig seemed to have completely forgotten Earle. He clapped his hands, cupping them to make a hollow, drumlike sound, and put all he felt into his voice. He had changed to a more fitting song.

> "Tony's wife,
> The boys in Havana love Tony's wife ..."

Faye had her hands clasped behind her head now and she rolled her hips to the broken beat. She was doing the "bump."

> "Tony's wife,
> They're fightin' their duels about Tony's wife ..."

Perhaps Tod had been mistaken about Earle. He was using his club on the back of the skillet, using it to bang out the rhythm.

The Mexican stood up, still singing, and joined her in the dance. They approached each other with short mincing steps. She held her skirt up and out with her thumbs and forefingers and he did the same with his trousers. They met head on, blue-black against pale-gold, and used their heads to pivot, then danced back to back with their buttocks touching, their knees bent and wide apart. While Faye shook her breasts and her head, holding the rest of her body rigid, he struck the soft ground heavily with his feet and circled her. They faced each other again and made believe they were cradling their behinds in a shawl.

Earle pounded the skillet harder and harder until it rang like an anvil. Suddenly he, too, jumped up and began to dance. He did a crude hoe-down. He leaped into the air and knocked his heels together. He whooped. But he couldn't become part of their dance. Its rhythm was like a smooth glass wall between him and the dancers. No matter how loudly he whooped or threw himself around, he was unable to disturb the precision with which they retreated and advanced, separated and came together again.

Tod saw the blow before it fell. He saw Earle raise his stick and bring it down on the Mexican's head. He heard the crack and saw the Mexican go to his knees still dancing, his body unwilling or unable to acknowledge the interruption.

Faye had her back to Mig when he fell, but she didn't turn to look. She ran. She flashed by Tod. He reached for her ankle to pull her down, but missed. He scrambled to his feet and ran after her.

If he caught her now, she wouldn't escape. He could hear her on the hill a little way ahead of him. He shouted to her, a deep, agonized bellow, like that a hound makes when it strike a fresh line after hours of cold trailing. Already he could feel how it would be when he pulled her to the ground.

But the going was heavy and the stones and sand moved under his feet. He fell prone with his face in a clump of wild mustard that smelled of the rain and sun, clean, fresh and sharp. He rolled over on his back and stared up at the sky. The violent exercise had driven most of the heat out of his blood, but enough remained to make him tingle pleasantly. He felt comfortably relaxed, even happy.

Somewhere farther up the hill a bird began to sing. He listened. At first the low, rich music sounded like water dripping on something hollow, the bottom of a silver pot perhaps, then like a stick dragged slowly over the string of a harp. He lay quietly, listening.

When the bird grew silent, he made a effort to put Faye out of his mind and began to think about the series of cartoons he was making for his canvas of Los Angeles on fire. He was going to show the city burning at high noon, so that the flames would have to compete with the desert sun and thereby appear less fearful, more like bright flags flying from roofs and windows than a terrible holocaust. He wanted the city to have quite a gala air as it burned, to appear almost gay. And the people who set it on fire would be a holiday crowd.

The bird began to sing again. When it stopped, Faye was forgotten and he only wondered if he weren't exaggerating the importance of the people who come to California to die. Maybe they weren't really desperate enough to set a single city on fire, let alone the whole country. Maybe they were only the pick of America's madmen and not at all typical of the rest of the land.

He told himself that it didn't make any difference because he was an artist, not a prophet. His work would not be judged by the accuracy with which it foretold a future event but by its merit as painting. Nevertheless, he refused to give up the role of Jeremiah. He changed "pick of America's madmen" to "cream" and felt almost certain that the milk from which it had been skimmed was just as rich in violence. The Angelenos would be first, but their comrades all over the country would follow. There would be civil war.

He was amused by the strong feeling of satisfaction this dire conclusion gave him. Were all prophets of doom and destruction such happy men?

He stood up without trying to answer. When he reached the dirt road at the top of the canyon, Faye and the car were gone.

15

"She went to the pictures with that Simpson guy," Harry told him when he called to see her the next night.

He sat down to wait for her. The old man was very ill and lay on the bed with extreme care as though it were a narrow shelf from which he might fall if he moved.

"What are they making on your lot?" he asked slowly, rolling his eyes toward Tod without budging his head.

"'Manifest Destiny,' 'Sweet and Low Down,' 'Waterloo,' 'The Great Divide,' 'Begging Your . . .'"

"'The Great Divide'—" Harry said, interrupting eagerly. "I remember that vehicle."

Tod realized he shouldn't have got him started, but there was nothing he could do about it now. He had to let him run down like a clock.

"When it opened I was playing the Irving in a little number called 'Enter Two Gents,' a trifle, but entertainment, real entertainment. I played a Jew comic, a Ben Welch effect, derby and big pants—'Pat, dey hoffered me a chob in de Heagle Laundreh' . . . 'Faith now, Ikey, and did you take it?' . . . 'No, who vants to vash heagles?' Joe Parvos played straight for me in a cop's suit. Well, the night 'The Great Divide' opened, Joe was laying up with a whisker in the old Fifth Avenue when the stove exploded. It was the broad's husband who blew the whistle. He was ..."

He hadn't run down. He had stopped and was squeezing his left side with both hands.

Tod leaned over anxiously.

"Some water?"

Harry framed the word "no" with his lips, then groaned skillfully. It was a second-act curtain groan, so phony that Tod had to hide a smile. And yet, the old man's pallor hadn't come from a box.

Harry groaned again, modulating from pain to exhaustion, then closed his eyes. Tod saw how skillfully he got the maximum effect out of his agonized profile by using the pillow to set it off. He also noticed that Harry, like many actors, had very little back or top to his head. It was almost all face, like a mask, with deep furrows between the eyes, across the forehead and on either side of the nose and mouth, plowed there by years of broad grinning and heavy frowning. Because of them, he could never express anything either subtly or exactly. They wouldn't permit degrees of feeling, only the furthest degree.

Tod began to wonder if it might not be true that actors

117

suffer less than other people. He thought about this for a while, then decided that he was wrong. Feeling is of the heart and nerves and the crudeness of its expression has nothing to do with its intensity. Harry suffered as keenly as anyone, despite the theatricality of his groans and grimaces.

He seemed to enjoy suffering. But not all kinds, certainly not sickness. Like many people, he only enjoyed the sort that was self-inflicted. His favorite method was to bare his soul to strangers in barrooms. He would make believe he was drunk, and stumble over to where some strangers were sitting. He usually began by reciting a poem.

> *"Let me sit down for a moment,*
> *I have a stone in my shoe.*
> *I was once blithe and happy,*
> *I was once young like you."*

If his audience shouted, "scram, bum!" he only smiled humbly and went on with his act.

> *"Have pity, folks, on my gray hair ..."*

The bartender or someone else had to stop him by force, otherwise he would go on no matter what was said to him. Once he got started everyone in the bar usually listened, for he gave a great performance. He roared and whispered, commanded and cajoled. He imitated the whimper of a little girl crying for her vanished mother, as well as the different dialects of the many cruel managers he had known. He even did the off-stage noises, twittering like birds to herald the dawn of Love and yelping like a pack of bloodhounds when describing how an Evil Fate ever pursued him.

He made his audience see him start out in his youth to play Shakespeare in the auditorium of the Cambridge Latin School, full of glorious dreams, burning with ambition. Follow him, as still a mere stripling, he starved in a Broadway rooming house, an idealist who desired only to share his art with the world. Stand with him, as, in the prime of manhood, he married a beautiful dancer, a headliner on the Gus Sun time. Be close behind him as, one night, he returned home unexpectedly to find her in the arms of a head usher. Forgive, as he forgave, out of the goodness of his heart and the greatness of his love. Then laugh, tasting the bitter gall, when the very next night he found her in the arms of a booking agent. Again he forgave her and again she sinned. Even then he didn't cast her out, no, though she jeered, mocked and even struck him repeatedly with an umbrella. But she ran off with a foreigner, a swarthy magician fellow. Behind she left memories and their baby daughter. He made his audience shadow him still as misfortune followed misfortune and, a middle-aged man, he haunted the booking offices, only a ghost of his former self. He who had hoped to play Hamlet, Lear, Othello, must needs become the Co. in an act called Nat Plumstone & Co., light quips and breezy patter. He made them dog his dragging feet as, an aged and trembling old man, he ...

Faye came in quietly. Tod started to greet her, but she put her finger to her lips for him to be silent and motioned toward the bed.

The old man was asleep. Tod thought his worn, dry skin looked like eroded ground. The few beads of sweat that glistened on his forehead and temples carried no promise of relief. It might rot, like rain that comes too late to a field, but could never refresh.

They both tiptoed out of the room.

In the hall he asked if she had had a good time with Homer.

"That dope!" she exclaimed, making a wry face. "He's strictly home-cooking."

Tod started to ask some more questions, but she dismissed him with a curt, "I'm tired, honey."

16

The next afternoon, Tod was on his way upstairs when he saw a crowd in front of the door of the Greeners' apartment. They were excited and talked in whispers.

"What's happened?" he asked.

"Harry's dead."

He tried the door of the apartment. It wasn't locked, so he went in. The corpse lay stretched out on the bed, completely covered with a blanket. From Faye's room came the sound of crying. He knocked softly on her door. She opened it for him, then turned without saying a word, and stumbled to her bed. She was sobbing into a face towel.

He stood in the doorway, without knowing what to do or say. Finally, he went over to the bed and tried to comfort her. He patted her shoulder.

"You poor kid."

She was wearing a tattered, black lace negligee that had large rents in it. When he leaned over her, he noticed that her skin gave off a warm, sweet odor, like that of buckwheat in flower.

He turned away and lit a cigarette. There was a knock

on the door. When he opened it, Mary Dove rushed past him to take Faye in her arms.

Mary also told Faye to be brave. She phrased it differently than he had done, however, and made it sound a lot more convincing.

"Show some guts, kid. Come on now, show some guts."

Faye shoved her away and stood up. She took a few wild steps, then sat down on the bed again.

"I killed him," she groaned.

Mary and he both denied this emphatically.

"I killed him, I tell you! I did! I did!"

She began to call herself names. Mary wanted to stop her, but Tod told her not to. Faye had begun to act and he felt that if they didn't interfere she would manage an escape for herself.

"She'll talk herself quiet," he said.

In a voice heavy with self-accusation, she began to tell what had happened. She had come home from the studio and found Harry in bed. She asked him how he was, but didn't wait for an answer. Instead, she turned her back on him to examine herself in the wall mirror. While fixing her face, she told him that she had seen Ben Murphy and that Ben had said that if Harry were feeling better he might be able to use him in a Bowery sequence. She had been surprised when he didn't shout as he always did when Ben's name was mentioned. He was jealous of Ben and always shouted, "To hell with that bastard; I knew him when he cleaned spittoons in a nigger barroom."

She realized that he must be pretty sick. She didn't turn around because she noticed what looked like the beginning of a pimple. It was only a speck of dirt and she wiped it off, but then she had to do her face all over again. While she was working at it, she told him that she could get a job as a dress extra if she had a new evening gown. Just to kid him, she looked tough and said, "If you can't buy me an evening gown, I'll find someone who can."

When he didn't say anything, she got sore and began to sing, "Jeepers Creepers." He didn't tell her to shut up, so she knew something must be wrong. She ran over to the couch. He was dead.

As soon as she had finished telling all this, she began to sob in a lower key, almost a coo, and rocked herself back and forth.

'Poor papa ... Poor darling ..."

The fun they used to have together when she was little. No matter how hard up he was, he always brought her dolls and candy, and no matter how tired, he always played with her. She used to ride piggy-back and they would roll on the floor and laugh and laugh.

Mary's sobs made Faye speed up her own and they both began to get out of hand.

There was a knock on the door. Tod answered it and found Mrs. Johnson, the janitress. Faye shook her head for him not to let her in.

"Come back later," Tod said.

He shut the door in her face. A minute later it opened again and Mrs. Johnson entered boldly. She had used a pass-key.

"Get out," he said.

She tried to push past him, but he held her until Faye told him to let her go.

He disliked Mrs. Johnson intensely. She was an officious, bustling woman with a face like a baked apple, soft and blotched. Later he found out that her hobby was funerals. Her preoccupation with them wasn't morbid; it was formal. She was interested in the arrangement of the flowers, the order of the procession, the clothing and deportment of the mourners.

She went straight to Faye and stopped her sobs with a firm, "Now, Miss Greener."

124

There was so much authority in her voice and manner that she succeeded where Mary and Tod had failed.

Faye looked up at her respectfully.

"First, my dear," Mrs. Johnson said, counting one with the thumb of her right hand on the index finger of her left, "first, I want you to understand that my sole desire in this matter is to help you."

She looked hard at Mary, then at Tod.

"I don't get anything out of it, and it's just a lot of trouble."

"Yes," Faye said.

"All right. There are several things I have to know, if I'm to help you. Did the deceased leave any money or insurance?"

"No."

"Have you any money?"

"No."

"Can you borrow any?"

"I don't think so."

Mrs. Johnson sighed.

"Then the city will have to bury him."

Faye didn't comment.

"Don't you understand, child, the city will have to bury him in a pauper's grave?"

She put so much contempt into "city" and horror into "pauper" that Faye flushed and began to sob again.

Mrs. Johnson made as though to walk out, even took several steps in the direction of the door, then changed her mind and came back.

"How much does a funeral cost?" Faye asked.

"Two hundred dollars. But you can pay on the installment plan—fifty dollars down and twenty-five a month."

Mary and Tod both spoke together.

"I'll get the money."

"I've got some."

"That's fine," Mrs. Johnson said. "You'll need at least fifty more for incidental expenses. I'll go ahead and take care of everything. Mr. Holsepp will bury your father. He'll do it right."

She shook hands with Faye, as though she were congratulating her, and hurried out of the room.

Mrs. Johnson's little business talk had apparently done Faye some good. Her lips were set and her eyes dry.

"Don't worry," Tod said. "I can raise the money."

"No, thanks," she said.

Mary opened her purse and took out a roll of bills.

"Here's some."

"No," she said, pushing it away.

She sat thinking for a while, then went to the dressing table and began to fix her tear-stained face. She wore a hard smile as she worked. Suddenly she turned, lipstick in air, and spoke to Mary.

"Can you get me into Mrs. Jenning's?"

"What for?" Tod demanded. "I'll get the money."

Both girls ignored him.

"Sure," said Mary, "you ought to done that long ago. It's a soft touch."

Faye laughed.

"I was saving it."

The change that had come over both of them startled Tod. They had suddenly become very tough.

"For a punkola like that Earle. Get smart, girlie, and lay off the cheapies. Let him ride a horse, he's a cowboy, ain't he?"

They laughed shrilly and went into the bathroom with their arms around each other.

Tod thought he understood their sudden change to slang. It made them feel worldly and realistic, and so more able to cope with serious things.

He knocked on the bathroom door.

"What do you want?" Faye called out.

"Listen, kid," he said, trying to imitate them. "Why go on the turf? I can get the dough."

"Oh, yeah! No thanks," Faye said.

"But listen ..." he began again.

"Go peddle your tripe!" Mary shouted.

17

On the day of Harry's funeral Tod was drunk. He hadn't seen Faye since she went off with Mary Dove, but he knew that he was certain to find her at the undertaking parlor and he wanted to have the courage to quarrel with her. He started drinking at lunch. When he got to Holsepp's in the late afternoon, he had passed the brave state and was well into the ugly one.

He found Harry in his box, waiting to be wheeled out for exhibition in the adjoining chapel. The casket was open and the old man looked quite snug. Drawn up to a little below his shoulders and folded back to show its fancy lining was an ivory satin coverlet. Under his head was a tiny lace cushion. He was wearing a Tuxedo, or at least had on a black bow tie with his stiff shirt and wing collar. His face had been newly shaved, his eyebrows shaped and plucked and his lips and cheeks rouged. He looked like the interlocutor in a minstrel show.

Tod bowed his head as though in silent prayer when he heard someone come in. He recognized Mrs. Johnson's voice and turned carefully to face her. He caught her eye and nodded, but she ignored him. She was busy with a man in a badly fitting frock coat.

"It's the principle of the thing," she scolded. "Your estimate said bronze. Those handles ain't bronze and you know it."

"But I asked Miss Greener," whined the man. "She okayed them."

"I don't care. I'm surprised at you, trying to save a few dollars by fobbing off a set of cheap gun-metal handles on the poor child."

Tod didn't wait for the undertaker to answer. He had seen Faye pass the door on the arm of one of the Lee sisters. When he caught up with her, he didn't know what to say. She misunderstood his agitation and was touched. She sobbed a little for him.

She had never looked more beautiful. She was wearing a new, very tight black dress and her platinum hair was tucked up in a shining bun under a black straw sailor. Ever so often, she carried a tiny lace handkerchief to her eyes and made it flutter there for a moment. But all he could think of was that she had earned the money for her outfit on her back.

She grew uneasy under his stare and started to edge away. He caught her arm.

"May I speak with you for a minute, alone?"

Miss Lee took the hint and left.

"What is it?" Faye asked.

"Not here," he whispered, making mystery out of his uncertainty.

He led her along the hall until he found an empty showroom. On the walls were framed photographs of important funerals and on little stands and tables were samples of coffin materials and models of tombstones and mausoleums.

Not knowing what to say, he accented his awkwardness, playing the inoffensive fool.

She smiled and became almost friendly.

"Give out, you big dope."

"A kiss . . ."

"Sure, baby," she laughed, "only don't muss me." They pecked at each other.

She tried to get away, but he held her. She became annoyed and demanded an explanation. He searched his head for one. It wasn't his head he should have searched, however.

She was leaning toward him, drooping slightly, but not from fatigue. He had seen young birches droop like that at midday when they are over-heavy with sun.

"You're drunk," she said, pushing him away.

"Please," he begged.

"Le'go, you bastard."

Raging at him, she was still beautiful. That was because her beauty was structural like a tree's, not a quality of her mind or heart. Perhaps even whoring couldn't damage it for that reason, only age or accident or disease.

In a minute she would scream for help. He had to say something. She wouldn't understand the aesthetic argument and with what values could he back up the moral one? The economic didn't make sense either. Whoring certainly paid. Half of the customer's thirty dollars. Say ten men a week.

She kicked at his shins, but he held on to her. Suddenly he began to talk. He had found an argument. Disease would destroy her beauty. He shouted at her like a Y.M.C.A. lecturer on sex hygiene.

She stopped struggling and held her head down, sobbing fitfully. When he was through, he let go of her arms and she bolted from the room. He groped his way to a carved, marble coffin.

He was still sitting there when a young man in a black jacket and gray striped trousers came in.

"Are you here for the Greener funeral?"

Tod stood up and nodded vaguely.

"The services are beginning," the man said, then opened

132

a little casket covered with grosgrain satin and took out a dust cloth. Tod watched him go around the showroom wiping off the samples.

"Services have probably started," the man repeated with a wave at the door.

Tod understood this time and left. The only exit he could find led through the chapel. The moment he entered it, Mrs. Johnson caught him and directed him to a seat. He wanted badly to get away, but it was impossible to do so without making a scene.

Faye was sitting in the front row of benches, facing the pulpit. She had the Lee sisters on one side and Mary Dove and Abe Kusich on the other. Behind them sat the tenants of the San Berdoo, occupying about six rows. Tod was alone in the seventh. After him were several empty rows and then a scattering of men and women who looked very much out of place.

He turned in order not to see Faye's jerking shoulders and examined the people in the last rows. He knew their kind. While not torchbearers themselves, they would run behind the fire and do a great deal of the shouting. They had come to see Harry buried, hoping for a dramatic incident of some sort, hoping at least for one of the mourners to be led weeping hysterically from the chapel. It seemed to Tod that they stared back at him with an expression of vicious, acrid boredom that trembled on the edge of violence. When they began to mutter among themselves, he half turned and watched them out of the corner of his eyes.

An old woman with a face pulled out of shape by badly fitting store teeth came in and whispered to a man sucking on the handle of a home-made walking stick. He passed her message along and they all stood up and went out hurriedly. Tod guessed that some star had been seen going into a restaurant by one of their scouts. If so, they would wait outside the place for hours until the star came out again or the police drove them away.

The Gingo family arrived soon after they had left. The Gingos were Eskimos who had been brought to Hollywood to make retakes for a picture about polar exploration. Although it had been released long ago, they refused to return to Alaska. They liked Hollywood.

Harry had been a good friend of theirs and had eaten with them quite regularly, sharing the smoked salmon, white fish, marinated and maatjes herrings they bought at Jewish delicatessen stores. He also shared the great quantities of cheap brandy they mixed with hot water and salt butter and drank out of tin cups.

Mama and Papa Gingo, trailed by their son, moved

down the center aisle of the chapel, bowing and waving to everyone, until they reached the front row. Here they gathered around Faye and shook hands with her, each one in turn. Mrs. Johnson tried to make them go to one of the back rows, but they ignored her orders and sat down in front.

The overhead lights of the chapel were suddenly dimmed. Simultaneously other lights went on behind imitation stained-glass windows which hung on the fake oak-paneled walls. There was a moment of hushed silence, broken only by Faye's sobs, then an electric organ started to play a recording of one of Bach's chorales, "Come Redeemer, Our Saviour."

Tod recognized the music. His mother often played a piano adaptation of it on Sundays at home. It very politely asked Christ to come, in clear and honest tones with just the proper amount of supplication. The God it invited was not the King of Kings, but a shy and gentle Christ, a maiden surrounded by maidens, and the invitation was to a lawn fete, not to the home of some weary, suffering sinner. It didn't plead; it urged with infinite grace and delicacy, almost as though it were afraid of frightening the prospective guest.

So far as Tod could tell, no one was listening to the music. Faye was sobbing and the others seemed busy inside themselves. Bach politely serenading Christ was not for them.

The music would soon change its tone and grow exciting. He wondered if that would make any difference. Already the bass was beginning to throb. He noticed that it made the Eskimos uneasy. As the bass gained in power and began to dominate the treble, he heard Papa Gingo grunt with pleasure. Mama caught Mrs. Johnson eyeing him, and put her fat hand on the back of his head to keep him quiet.

"Now come, O our Saviour," the music begged. Gone was its diffidence and no longer was it polite. Its struggle with the bass had changed it. Even a hint of a threat crept in and a little impatience. Of doubt, however, he could not detect the slightest trace.

If there was a hint of a threat, he thought, just a hint, and a tiny bit of impatience, could Bach be blamed? After all, when he wrote this music, the world had already been waiting for its lover more than seventeen hundred years. But the music changed again and both threat and impatience disappeared. The treble soared free and triumphant and the bass no longer struggled to keep it down. It had become a rich accompaniment. "Come or don't come," the music seemed to say, "I love you and my love is enough." It was a simple statement of fact, neither cry nor serenade, made without arrogance or humility.

Perhaps Christ heard. If He did, He gave no signs. The

attendants heard, for it was their cue to trundle on Harry in his box. Mrs. Johnson followed close behind and saw to it that the casket was properly placed. She raised her hand and Bach was silenced in the middle of a phrase.

"Will those of you who wish to view the deceased before the sermon please step forward?" she called out.

Only the Gingos stood up immediately. They made for the coffin in a group. Mrs. Johnson held them back and motioned for Faye to look first. Supported by Mary Dove and the Lee girls, she took a quick peek, increased the tempo of her sobs for a moment, then hurried back to the bench.

The Gingos had their chance next. They leaned over the coffin and told each other something in a series of thick, explosive gutturals. When they tried to take another look, Mrs. Johnson herded them firmly to their seats.

The dwarf sidled up to the box, made a play with his handkerchief and retreated. When no one followed him, Mrs. Johnson lost patience, seeming to take what she understood as a lack of interest for a personal insult.

"Those who wish to view the remains of the late Mr. Greener must do so at once," she barked.

There was a little stir, but no one stood up.

"You, Mrs. Gail," she finally said, looking directly at the person named. "How about you? Don't you want a last look? Soon all that remains of your neighbor will be buried forever."

There was no getting out of it. Mrs. Gail moved down the aisle, trailed by several others.

Tod used them to cover his escape.

18

Faye moved out of the San Berdoo the day after the funeral. Tod didn't know where she had gone and was getting up the courage to call Mrs. Jenning when he saw her from the window of his office. She was dressed in the costume of a Napoleonic vivandière. By the time he got the window open, she had almost turned the corner of the building. He shouted for her to wait. She waved, but when he got downstairs she was gone.

From her dress, he was sure that she was working in the picture called "Waterloo." He asked a studio policeman where the company was shooting and was told on the back lot. He started toward it at once. A platoon of cuirassiers, big men mounted on gigantic horses, went by. He knew that they must be headed for the same set and followed them. They broke into a gallop and he was soon outdistanced.

The sun was very hot. His eyes and throat were choked with the dust thrown up by the horses' hooves and his head throbbed. The only bit of shade he could find was under an ocean liner made of painted canvas with real life boats hanging from its davits. He stood in its narrow shadow for a while, then went on toward a great forty-foot papier mâché sphinx that loomed up in the distance. He had to cross a desert to reach it, a desert that was continually being made larger by a fleet of trucks dumping white sand. He had gone only a few feet when a man with a megaphone ordered him off.

He skirted the desert, making a wide turn to the right, and came to a Western street with a plank sidewalk. On the porch of the "Last Chance Saloon" was a rocking chair. He sat down on it and lit a cigarette.

From there he could see a jungle compound with a water buffalo tethered to the side of a conical grass hut. Every few seconds the animal groaned musically. Suddenly an Arab charged by on a white stallion. He shouted at the man, but got no answer. A little while later he saw a truck with a load of snow and several malamute dogs. He shouted again. The driver shouted something back, but didn't stop.

Throwing away his cigarette, he went through the swinging doors of the saloon. There was no back to the building and he found himself in a Paris street. He followed it to its end, coming out in a Romanesque courtyard. He heard voices a short distance away and went toward them. On a lawn of fiber, a group of men and women in riding costume were picnicking. They were eating cardboard food in front of a cellophane waterfall. He started toward them to ask his way, but was stopped by a man who scowled and held up a sign—"Quiet, Please, We're Shooting." When Tod took another step forward, the man shook his fist threateningly.

Next he came to a small pond with large celluloid swans floating on it. Across one end was a bridge with a sign that read, "To Kamp Komfit." He crossed the bridge and followed a little path that ended at a Greek temple dedicated to Eros. The god himself lay face downward in a pile of old newspapers and bottles.

From the steps of the temple, he could see in the distance a road lined with Lombardy poplars. It was the one on which he had lost the cuirassiers. He pushed his way through a tangle of briars, old flats and iron junk, skirting the skeleton of a Zeppelin, a bamboo stockade, an adobe fort, the wooden horse of Troy, a flight of baroque palace stairs that started in a bed of weeds and ended against the branches of an oak, part of the Fourteenth Street elevated station, a Dutch windmill, the bones of a dinosaur, the upper half of the Merrimac, a corner of a Mayan temple, until he finally reached the road.

He was out of breath. He sat down under one of the poplars on a rock made of brown plaster and took off his jacket. There was a cool breeze blowing and he soon felt more comfortable.

He had lately begun to think not only of Goya and Daumier but also of certain Italian artists of the seventeenth and eighteenth centuries, of Salvator Rosa, Francesco Guardi and Monsu Desiderio, the painters of Decay and Mystery. Looking down hill now, he could see compositions that might have actually been arranged from the Calabrian work of Rosa. There were partially demolished buildings and broken monuments, half hidden by great, tortured trees, whose exposed roots writhed dramatically in the arid ground, and by shrubs that carried, not flowers or berries, but armories of spikes, hooks and swords.

For Guardi and Desiderio there were bridges which bridged nothing, sculpture in trees, palaces that seemed of marble until a whole stone portico began to flap in the light breeze. And there were figures as well. A hundred yards from where Tod was sitting a man in a derby hat leaned drowsily against the gilded poop of a Venetian barque and peeled an apple. Still farther on, a charwoman on a stepladder was scrubbing with soap and water the face of a Buddha thirty feet high.

He left the road and climbed across the spine of the hill to look down on the other side. From there he could see a ten-acre field of cockleburs spotted with clumps of sunflowers and wild gum. In the center of the field was a gigantic pile of sets, flats and props. While he watched, a ten-ton truck added another load to it. This was the final dumping ground. He thought of Janvier's "Sargasso Sea." Just as that imaginary body of water was a history of civilization in the form of a marine junkyard, the studio lot was one in the form of a dream dump. A Sargasso of the imagination! And the dump grew continually, for there wasn't a dream afloat somewhere which wouldn't sooner or later turn up on it, having first been made photographic by plaster, canvas, lath and paint. Many boats sink and never reach the Sargasso, but no dream ever entirely disappears. Somewhere it troubles some unfortunate person and some day, when that person has been sufficiently troubled, it will be reproduced on the lot.

When he saw a red glare in the sky and heard the rumble of cannon, he knew it must be Waterloo. From around a bend in the road trotted several cavalry regiments. They wore casques and chest armor of black cardboard and carried long horse pistols in their saddle holsters. They were Victor Hugo's soldiers. He had worked on some of the drawings for their uniforms himself, following carefully the descriptions in "Les Miserables."

He went in the direction they took. Before long he was passed by the men of Lefebvre-Desnouttes, followed by a regiment of gendarmes d'élite, several companies of chasseurs of the guard and a flying detachment of Rimbaud's lancers.

They must be moving up for the disastrous attack on La Haite Santée. He hadn't read the scenario and wondered if it had rained yesterday. Would Grouchy or Blucher arrive? Grotenstein, the producer, might have changed it.

The sound of cannon was becoming louder all the time and the red fan in the sky more intense. He could smell the sweet, pungent odor of blank powder. It might be over before he could get there. He started to run. When he topped a rise after a sharp bend in the road, he found a great plain below him covered with early nineteenth-century troops, wearing all the gay and elaborate uniforms that used to please him so much when he was a child and spent long hours looking at the soldiers in an old dictionary. At the far end of the field, he could see an enormous hump around which the English and their allies were gathered. It was Mont St. Jean and they were getting ready to defend it gallantly. It wasn't quite finished, however, and swarmed with grips, property men, set dressers, carpenters and painters.

Tod stood near a eucalyptus tree to watch, concealing himself behind a sign that read, " 'Waterloo'—A Charles H. Grotenstein Production." Nearby a youth in a carefully torn horse guard's uniform was being rehearsed in his lines by one of the assistant directors.

"Vive l'Empereur!" the young man shouted, then clutched his breast and fell forward dead. The assistant director was a hard man to please and made him do it over and over again.

In the center of the plain, the battle was going ahead briskly. Things looked tough for the British and their allies. The Prince of Orange commanding the center, Hill the right and Picton the left wing, were being pressed hard by the veteran French. The desperate and intrepid Prince was in an especially bad spot. Tod heard him cry hoarsely above the din of battle, shouting to the Hollande-Belgians, "Nassau! Brunswick! Never retreat!" Nevertheless, the retreat began. Hill, too, fell back. The French killed General Picton with a ball through the head and he returned to his dressing room. Alten was put to the sword and also retired. The colors of the Lunenberg battalion, borne by a prince of the family of Deux-Ponts, were captured by a famous child star in the uniform of a Parisian drummer boy. The Scotch Grays were destroyed and went to change into another uniform. Ponsonby's heavy dragoons were also cut to ribbons. Mr. Grotenstein would have a large bill to pay at the Western Costume Company.

Neither Napoleon nor Wellington was to be seen. In Wellington's absence, one of the assistant directors, a Mr. Crane, was in command of the allies. He reinforced his center with one of Chasse's brigades and one of Wincke's. He supported these with infantry from Brunswick, Welsh foot, Devon yeomanry and Hanoverian light horse with oblong leather caps and flowing plumes of horsehair.

For the French, a man in a checked cap ordered Milhaud's cuirassiers to carry Mont St. Jean. With their sabers in their teeth and their pistols in their hands, they charged. It was a fearful sight.

The man in the checked cap was making a fatal error. Mont St. Jean was unfinished. The paint was not yet dry and all the struts were not in place. Because of the thickness of the cannon smoke, he had failed to see that the hill was still being worked on by property men, grips and carpenters.

It was the classic mistake, Tod realized, the same one Napoleon had made. Then it had been wrong for a different reason. The Emperor had ordered the cuirassiers to charge Mont St. Jean not knowing that a deep ditch was hidden at its foot to trap his heavy cavalry. The result had been disaster for the French; the beginning of the end.

This time the same mistake had a different outcome. Waterloo, instead of being the end of the Grand Army, resulted in a draw. Neither side won, and it would have to be fought over again the next day. Big losses, however, were sustained by the insurance company in workmen's compensation. The man in the checked cap was sent to the dog house by Mr. Grotenstein just as Napoleon was sent to St. Helena.

When the front rank of Milhaud's heavy division started up the slope of Mont St. Jean, the hill collapsed. The noise was terrific. Nails screamed with agony as they pulled out of joists. The sound of ripping canvas was like that of little children whimpering. Lath and scantling snapped as though they were brittle bones. The whole hill folded like an enormous umbrella and covered Napoleon's army with painted cloth.

It turned into a rout. The victors of Bersina, Leipsic, Austerlitz, fled like schoolboys who had broken a pane of glass. "Sauve qui peut!" they cried, or, rather, "Scram!"

The armies of England and her allies were too deep in scenery to flee. They had to wait for the carpenters and ambulances to come up. The men of the gallant Seventy-Fifth Highlanders were lifted out of the wreck with block and tackle. They were carted off by the stretcher-bearers, still clinging bravely to their claymores.

19

Tod got a lift back to his office in a studio car. He had to ride on the running board because the seats were occupied by two Walloon grenadiers and four Swabian foot. One of the infantrymen had a broken leg, the other extras were only scratched and bruised. They were quite happy about their wounds. They were certain to receive several extra days' pay, and the man with the broken leg thought he might get as much as five hundred dollars.

When Tod arrived at his office, he found Faye waiting to see him. She hadn't been in the battle. At the last moment, the director had decided not to use any vivandières.

To his surprise, she greeted him with warm friendliness. Nevertheless, he tried to apologize for his behavior in the funeral parlor. He had hardly started before she interrupted him. She wasn't angry, but grateful for his lecture on venereal disease. It had brought her to her senses.

She had still another surprise for him. She was living in Homer Simpson's house. The arrangement was a business one. Homer had agreed to board and dress her until she became a star. They were keeping a record of every cent he spent and as soon as she clicked in pictures, she would pay him back with six per cent interest. To make it absolutely legal, they were going to have a lawyer draw up a contract.

She pressed Tod for an opinion and he said it was a splendid idea. She thanked him and invited him to dinner for the next night.

After she had gone, he wondered what living with her would do to Homer. He thought it might straighten him out. He fooled himself into believing this with an image, as though a man were a piece of iron to be heated and then straightened with hammer blows. He should have known better, for if anyone ever lacked malleability Homer did.

He continued to make this mistake when he had dinner with them. Faye seemed very happy, talking about charge accounts and stupid sales clerks. Homer had a flower in his buttonhole, wore carpet slippers and beamed at her continually.

After they had eaten, while Homer was in the kitchen washing dishes, Tod got her to tell him what they did with themselves all day. She said that they lived quietly and that she was glad because she was tired of excitement. All she wanted was a career. Homer did the housework and she was getting a real rest. Daddy's long sickness had tired her out completely. Homer liked to do housework and anyway he wouldn't let her go into the kitchen because of her hands.

"Protecting his investment," Tod said.

"Yes," she replied seriously, "they have to be beautiful."

They had breakfast around ten, she went on. Homer brought it to her in bed. He took a housekeeping magazine and fixed the tray like the pictures in it. While she bathed and dressed, he cleaned the house. Then they went downtown to the stores and she bought all sorts of things, mostly clothes. They didn't eat lunch on account of her figure, but usually had dinner out and went to the movies.

"Then, ice cream sodas," Homer finished for her, as he came out of the kitchen.

Faye laughed and excused herself. They were going to a picture and she wanted to change her dress. When she had left, Homer suggested that they get some air in the patio. He made Tod take the deck chair while he sat on an upturned orange crate.

If he had been careful and had acted decently, Tod couldn't help thinking, she might be living with him. He was at least better looking than Homer. But then there was her other prerequisite. Homer had an income and lived in a house, while he earned thirty dollars a week and lived in a furnished room.

The happy grin on Homer's face made him feel ashamed of himself. He was being unfair. Homer was a humble, grateful man who would never laugh at her, who was incapable of laughing at anything. Because of this great quality, she could live with him on what she considered a much higher plane.

"What's the matter?" Homer asked softly, laying one of his heavy hands on Tod's knee.

"Nothing. Why?"

Tod moved so that the hand slipped off.

"You were making faces."

"I was thinking of something."

"Oh," Homer said sympathetically.

Tod couldn't resist asking an ugly question.

"When are you two getting married?"

Homer looked hurt.

"Didn't Faye tell about us?"

"Yes, sort of."

"It's a business arrangement."

"Yes?"

To make Tod believe it, he poured out a long, disjointed argument, the one he must have used on himself. He even went further than the business part and claimed that they were doing it for poor Harry's sake. Faye had nothing left in the world except her career and she must succeed for her daddy's sake. The reason she wasn't a star was because she didn't have the right clothes. He had money and believed in her talent, so it was only natural for them to enter into a business arrangement. Did Tod know a good lawyer?

It was a rhetorical question, but would become a real one, painfully insistent, if Tod smiled. He frowned. That was wrong, too.

"We must see a lawyer this week and have papers drawn up."

His eagerness was pathetic. Tod wanted to help him, but didn't know what to say. He was still fumbling for an answer when they heard a woman shouting from the hill behind the garage.

"Adore! Adore!"

She had a high soprano voice, very clear and pure.

"What a funny name," Tod said, glad to change the subject.

"Maybe it's a foreigner," Homer said.

The woman came into the yard from around the corner of the garage. She was eager and plump and very American.

"Have you seen my little boy?" she asked, making a gesture of helplessness. "Adore's such a wanderer."

Homer surprised Tod by standing up and smiling at the woman. Faye had certainly helped his timidity.

"Is your son lost?" Homer said.

"Oh, no—just hiding to tease me."

She held out her hand.

"We're neighbors. I'm Maybelle Loomis."

"Glad to know you, ma'am. I'm Homer Simpson and this is Mr. Hackett."

Tod also shook hands with her.

"Have you been living here long?" she asked.

"No. I've just come from the East," Homer said.

"Oh, have you? I've been here ever since Mr. Loomis passed on six years ago. I'm an old settler."

"You like it then?" Tod asked.

"Like California?" she laughed at the idea that anyone might not like it. "Why, it's a paradise on earth!"

"Yes," Homer agreed gravely.

"And anyway," she went on, "I have to live here on account of Adore."

"Is he sick?"

"Oh, no. On account of his career. His agent calls him the biggest little attraction in Hollywood."

She spoke so vehemently that Homer flinched.

"He's in the movies?" Tod asked.

"I'll say," she snapped.

Homer tried to placate her.

"That's very nice."

"If it weren't for favoritism," she said bitterly, "he'd be a star. It ain't talent. It's pull. What's Shirley Temple got that he ain't got?"

"Why, I don't know," Homer mumbled.

She ignored this and let out a fearful bellow.

"Adore! Adore!"

Tod had seen her kind around the studio. She was one of that army of women who drag their children from casting office to casting office and sit for hours, weeks, months, waiting for a chance to show what Junior can do. Some of them are very poor, but no matter how poor, they always manage to scrape together enough money, often by making great sacrifices, to send their children to one of the innumerable talent schools.

"Adore!" she yelled once more, then laughed and became a friendly housewife again, a chubby little person with dimples in her fat cheeks and fat elbows.

"Have you any children, Mr. Simpson?" she asked.

"No," he replied, blushing.

"You're lucky—they're a nuisance."

154

She laughed to show that she didn't really mean it and called her child again.

"Adore . . . Oh, Adore . . ."

Her next question surprised them both.

"Who do you follow?"

"What?" said Tod.

"I mean—in the Search for Health, along the Road of Life?"

They both gaped at her.

"I'm a raw-foodist, myself," she said. "Dr. Pierce is our leader. You must have seen his ads—'Know-All Pierce-All.'"

"Oh, yes," Tod said, "you're vegetarians."

She laughed at his ignorance.

"Far from it. We're much stricter. Vegetarians eat cooked vegetables. We eat only raw ones. Death comes from eating dead things."

Neither Tod nor Homer found anything to say.

"Adore," she began again. "Adore . . ."

This time there was an answer from around the corner of the garage.

"Here I am, Mama."

A minute later, a little boy appeared dragging behind

him a small sailboat on wheels. He was about eight years old, with a pale, peaked face and a large, troubled forehead. He had great staring eyes. His eyebrows had been plucked and shaped carefully. Except for his Buster Brown collar, he was dressed like a man, in long trousers, vest and jacket.

He tried to kiss his mother, but she fended him off and pulled at his clothes, straightening and arranging them with savage little tugs.

"Adore," she said sternly, "I want you to meet Mr. Simpson, our neighbor."

Turning like a soldier at the command of a drill sergeant, he walked up to Homer and grasped his hand.

"A pleasure, sir," he said, bowing stiffly with his heels together.

"That's the way they do it in Europe," Mrs. Loomis beamed, "Isn't he cute?"

"What a pretty sailboat!" Homer said, trying to be friendly.

Both mother and son ignored his comment. She pointed to Tod, and the child repeated his bow and heel-click.

"Well, we've got to go," she said.

Tod watched the child, who was standing a little to one side of his mother and making faces at Homer. He rolled his eyes back in his head so that only the whites showed and twisted his lips in a snarl.

Mrs. Loomis noticed Tod's glance and turned sharply. When she saw what Adore was doing, she yanked him by the arm, jerking him clear off the ground.

"Adore!" she yelled.

To Tod she said apologetically, "He thinks he's the Frankenstein monster."

She picked the boy up, hugging and kissing him ardently. Then she set him down again and fixed his rumpled clothing.

"Won't Adore sing something for us?" Tod asked.

"No," the little boy said sharply.

"Adore," his mother scolded, "sing at once."

"That's all right, if he doesn't feel like it," Homer said.

But Mrs. Loomis was determined to have him sing. She could never permit him to refuse an audience.

"Sing, Adore," she repeated with quiet menace. "Sing 'Mama Doan Wan' No Peas.'"

His shoulders twitched as though they already felt the strap. He tilted his straw sailor over one eye, buttoned up his jacket and did a little strut, then began:

> *"Mama doan wan' no peas,*
> *An' rice, an' cocoanut oil,*

Just a bottle of brandy handy all the day.
Mama doan wan' no peas,
Mama doan wan' no cocoanut oil."

His singing voice was deep and rough and he used the broken groan of the blues singer quite expertly. He moved his body only a little, against rather than in time with the music. The gestures he made with his hands were extremely suggestive.

"Mama doan wan' no gin,
Because gin do make her sin,
Mama doan wan' no glass of gin,
Because it boun' to make her sin,
An' keep her hot and bothered all the day."

He seemed to know what the words meant, or at least his body and his voice seemed to know. When he came to the final chorus, his buttocks writhed and his voice carried a top-heavy load of sexual pain.

Tod and Homer applauded. Adore grabbed the string of his sailboat and circled the yard. He was imitating a tugboat. He tooted several times, then ran off.

"He's just a baby," Mrs. Loomis said proudly, "but he's got loads of talent."

Tod and Homer agreed.

She saw that he was gone again and left hurriedly. They could hear her calling in the brush back of the garage.

"Adore! Adore ..."

"That's a funny woman," Tod said.

Homer sighed.

"I guess it's hard to get a start in pictures. But Faye is awfully pretty."

Tod agreed. She appeared a moment later in a new flower print dress and picture hat and it was his turn to sigh. She was much more than pretty. She posed, quivering and balanced, on the doorstep and looked down at the two men in the patio. She was smiling, a subtle half-smile uncontaminated by thought. She looked just born, everything moist and fresh, volatile and perfumed. Tod suddenly became very conscious of his dull, insensitive feet bound in dead skin and of his hands, sticky and thick, holding a heavy, rough felt hat.

He tried to get out of going to the pictures with them, but couldn't. Sitting next to her in the dark proved the ordeal he expected it to be. Her self-sufficiency made him squirm and the desire to break its smooth surface with a blow, or at least a sudden gesture, became irresistible.

He began to wonder if he himself didn't suffer from

the ingrained, morbid apathy he liked to draw in others. Maybe he could only be galvanized into sensibility and that was why he was chasing Faye.

He left hurriedly, without saying good-by. He had decided to stop running after her. It was an easy decision to make, but a hard one to carry out. In order to manage it, he fell back on one of the oldest tricks in the very full bag of the intellectual. After all, he told himself, he had drawn her enough times. He shut the portfolio that held the drawings he had made of her, tied it with a string, and put it away in his trunk.

It was a childish trick, hardly worthy of a primitive witch doctor, yet it worked. He was able to avoid her for several months. During this time, he took his pad and pencils on a continuous hunt for other models. He spent his nights at the different Hollywood churches, drawing the worshipers. He visited the "Church of Christ, Physical" where holiness was attained through the constant use of chestweights and spring grips; the "Church Invisible" where fortunes were told and the dead made to find lost objects; the "Tabernacle of the Third Coming" where a woman in male clothing preached the "Crusade Against Salt" and the "Temple Moderne" under whose glass and chromium roof "Brain-Breathing, the Secret of the Aztecs" was taught.

As he watched these people writhe on the hard seats of their churches, he thought of how well Alessandro Magnasco would dramatize the contrast between their drained-out, feeble bodies and their wild, disordered minds. He would not satirize them as Hogarth or Daumier might, nor would he pity them. He would paint their fury with respect, appreciating its awful, anarchic power and aware that they had it in them to destroy civilization.

One Friday night in the "Tabernacle of the Third Coming," a man near Tod stood up to speak. Although his name most likely was Thompson or Johnson and his home town Sioux City, he had the same countersunk eyes, like the heads of burnished spikes, that a monk by Magnasco might have. He was probably just in from one of the colonies in the desert near Soboba Hot Springs where he had been conning over his soul on a diet of raw fruit and nuts. He was very angry. The message he had brought to the city was one that an illiterate anchorite might have given decadent Rome. It was a crazy jumble of dietary rules, economics and Biblical threats. He claimed to have seen the Tiger of Wrath stalking the walls of the citadel and the Jackal of Lust skulking in the shrubbery, and he connected these omens with "thirty dollars every Thursday" and meat eating.

Tod didn't laugh at the man's rhetoric. He knew it was

unimportant. What mattered were his messianic rage and the emotional response of his hearers. They sprang to their feet, shaking their fists and shouting. On the altar someone began to beat a bass drum and soon the entire congregation was singing "Onward Christian Soldiers."

20

As time went on, the relationship between Faye and Homer began to change. She became bored with the life they were leading together and as her boredom deepened, she began to persecute him. At first she did it unconsciously, later maliciously.

Homer realized that the end was in sight even before she did. All he could do to prevent its coming was to increase his servility and his generosity. He waited on her hand and foot. He bought her a coat of summer ermine and a light blue Buick runabout.

His servility was like that of a cringing, clumsy dog, who is always anticipating a blow, welcoming it even, and in a way that makes overwhelming the desire to strike him. His generosity was still more irritating. It was so helpless and unselfish that it made her feel mean and cruel, no matter how hard she tried to be kind. And it was so bulky that she was unable to ignore it. She had to resent it. He was destroying himself, and although he didn't mean it that way, forcing her to accept the blame.

They had almost reached a final crisis when Tod saw

them again. Late one night, just as he was preparing for bed, Homer knocked on his door and said that Faye was downstairs in the car and that they wanted him to go to a night club with them.

The outfit Homer wore was very funny. He had on loose blue linen slacks and a chocolate flannel jacket over a yellow polo shirt. Only a Negro could have worn it without looking ridiculous, and no one was ever less a Negro than Homer.

Tod drove with them to the "Cinderella Bar," a little stucco building in the shape of a lady's slipper, on Western Avenue. Its floor show consisted of female impersonators.

Faye was in a nasty mood. When the waiter took their order, she insisted on a champagne cocktail for Homer. He wanted coffee. The waiter brought both, but she made him take the coffee back.

Homer explained painstakingly, as he must have done many times, that he could not drink alcohol because it made him sick. Faye listened with mock patience. When he finished, she laughed and lifted the cocktail to his mouth.

"Drink it, damn you," she said.

She tilted the glass, but he didn't open his mouth and the liquor ran down his chin. He wiped himself, using the napkin without unfolding it.

Faye called the waiter again.

"He doesn't like champagne cocktails," she said. "Bring him brandy."

Homer shook his head.

"Please, Faye," he whimpered.

She held the brandy to his lips, moving the glass when he turned away.

"Come on, sport—bottoms up."

"Let him alone," Tod finally said.

She ignored him as though she hadn't even heard his protest. She was both furious and ashamed of herself. Her shame strengthened her fury and gave it a target.

"Come on, sport," she said savagely, "or Mama'll spank."

She turned to Tod.

"I don't like people who won't drink. It isn't sociable. They feel superior and I don't like people who feel superior."

"I don't feel superior," Homer said.

"Oh, yes, you do. I'm drunk and you're sober and so you feel superior. God-damned, stinking superior."

He opened his mouth to reply and she poured the brandy into it, then clapped her hand over his lips so that he couldn't spit it back. Some of it came out of his nose.

Still without unfolding the napkin, he wiped himself.

Faye ordered another brandy. When it came, she held it to his lips again, but this time he took it and drank it himself, fighting the stuff down.

"That's the boy," Faye laughed. "Well done, sloppy-boppy."

Tod asked her to dance in order to give Homer a moment alone. When they reached the floor, she made an attempt to defend herself.

"That guy's superiority is driving me crazy."

"He loves you," Tod said.

"Yeah, I know, but he's such a slob."

She started to cry on his shoulder and he held her very tight. He took a long chance.

"Sleep with me."

"No, baby," she said sympathetically.

"Please, please ... just once."

"I can't, honey. I don't love you."

"You worked for Mrs. Jenning. Make believe you're still working for her."

She didn't get angry.

"That was a mistake. And anyway, that was different. I only went on call enough times to pay for the funeral and besides those men were complete strangers. You know what I mean?"

"Yes. But please, darling. I'll never bother you again. I'll go East right after. Be kind."

"I can't."

"Why . . . ?"

"I just can't. I'm sorry, darling. I'm not a tease, but I can't like that."

"I love you."

"No, sweetheart, I can't."

They danced until the number finished without saying anything else. He was grateful to her for having behaved so well, for not having made him feel too ridiculous.

When they returned to the table, Homer was sitting exactly as they had left him. He held the folded napkin in one hand and the empty brandy glass in the other. His helplessness was extremely irritating.

"You're right about the brandy, Faye," Homer said. "It's swell! Whoopee!"

He made a little circular gesture with the hand that held the glass.

"I'd like a Scotch," Tod said.

"Me, too," Faye said.

Homer made another gallant attempt to get into the spirit of the evening.

"Garsoon," he called to the waiter, "more drinks."

He grinned at them anxiously. Faye burst out laughing and Homer did his best to laugh with her. When she stopped suddenly, he found himself laughing alone and turned his laugh into a cough, then hid the cough in his napkin.

She turned to Tod.

"What the devil can you do with a slob like that?"

The orchestra started and Tod was able to ignore her question. All three of them turned to watch a young man in a tight gown of red silk sing a lullaby.

> *"Little man, you're crying,*
> *I know why you're blue,*
> *Someone took your kiddycar away;*
> *Better go to sleep now,*
> *Little man, you've had a busy day ..."*

He had a soft, throbbing voice and his gestures were matronly, tender and aborted, a series of unconscious caresses. What he was doing was in no sense parody; it was too simple and too restrained. It wasn't even theatrical. This dark young man with his thin, hairless arms and soft, rounded shoulders, who rocked an imaginary cradle as he crooned, was really a woman.

When he had finished, there was a great deal of applause. The young man shook himself and became an actor again. He tripped on his train, as though he weren't used to it, lifted his skirts to show he was wearing Paris garters, then strode off swinging his shoulders. His imitation of a man was awkward and obscene.

Homer and Tod applauded him.

"I hate fairies," Faye said.

"All women do."

Tod meant it as a joke, but Faye was angry.

"They're dirty," she said.

He started to say something else, but Faye had turned to Homer again. She seemed unable to resist nagging him. This time she pinched his arm until he gave a little squeak.

"Do you know what a fairy is?" she demanded.

"Yes," he said hesitatingly.

"All right, then," she barked. "Give out! What's a fairy?"

Homer twisted uneasily, as though he already felt the ruler on his behind, and looked imploring at Tod, who tried to help him by forming the word "homo" with his lips.

"Momo," Homer said.

Faye burst out laughing. But his hurt look made it impossible not to relent, so she patted his shoulder.

"What a hick," she said.

169

He grinned gratefully and signaled the waiter to bring another round of drinks.

The orchestra began to play and a man came over to ask Faye to dance. Without saying a word to Homer, she followed him to the floor.

"Who's that?" Homer asked, chasing them with his eyes.

Tod made believe he knew and said that he had often seen him around the San Berdoo. His explanation satisfied Homer, but at the same time set him to thinking of something else. Tod could almost see him shaping a question in his head.

"Do you know Earle Shoop?" Homer finally asked.

"Yes."

Homer then poured out a long, confused story about a dirty black hen. He kept referring to the hen again and again, as though it were the one thing he couldn't stand about Earle and the Mexican. For a man who was incapable of hatred, he managed to draw a pretty horrible picture of the bird.

"You never saw such a disgusting thing, the way it squats and turns its head. The roosters have torn all the feathers off its neck and made its comb all bloody and it has scabby feet covered with warts and it cackles so nasty when they drop it into the pen."

"Who drops it into what pen?"

"The Mexican."

"Miguel?"

"Yes. He's almost as bad as his hen."

"You've been to their camp?"

"Camp?"

"In the mountains?"

"No. They're living in the garage. Faye asked me if I minded if a friend of hers lived in the garage for a while because he was broke. But I didn't know about the chickens or the Mexican ... Lots of people are out of work nowadays."

"Why don't you throw them out?"

"They're broke and they have no place to go. It isn't very comfortable living in a garage."

"But if they don't behave?"

"It's just that hen. I don't mind the roosters, they're pretty, but that dirty hen. She shakes her dirty feathers each time and clucks so nasty."

"You don't have to look at it."

"They do it every afternoon at the same time when I'm usually sitting in the chair in the sun after I get back from shopping with Faye and just before dinner. The Mexican knows I don't like to see it so he tries to make me look just

171

for spite. I go into the house, but he taps on the windows and calls me to come out and watch. I don't call that fun. Some people have funny ideas of what's fun."

"What's Faye say?"

"She doesn't mind the hen. She says it's only natural."

Then, in case Tod should mistake this for criticism, he told him what a fine, wholesome child she was. Tod agreed, but brought him back to the subject.

"If I were you," he said, "I'd report the chickens to the police. You have to have a permit to keep chickens in the city. I'd do something and damned quick."

Homer avoided a direct answer.

"I wouldn't touch that thing for all the money in the world. She's all over scabs and almost naked. She looks like a buzzard. She eats meat. I saw her one time eating some meat that the Mexican got out of the garbage can. He feeds the roosters grain but the hen eats garbage and he keeps her in a dirty box."

"If I were you, I'd throw those bastards out and their birds with them."

"No, they're nice enough young fellows, just down on their luck, like a lot of people these days, you know. It's just that hen ..."

172

He shook his head wearily, as though he could smell and taste her.

Faye was coming back. Homer saw that Tod was going to speak to her about Earle and the Mexican and signaled desperately for him not to do it. She, however, caught at it and was curious.

"What have you guys been chinning about?"

"You, darling," Tod said. "Homer has a t.l. for you."

"Tell me, Homer."

"No, first you tell me one."

"Well, the man I just danced with asked me if you were a movie big shot."

Tod saw that Homer was unable to think of a return compliment so he spoke for him.

"I said you were the most beautiful girl in the place."

"Yes," Homer agreed. "That's what Tod said."

"I don't believe it. Tod hates me. And anyway, I caught you telling him to keep quiet. You were shushing him."

She laughed.

"I bet I know what you were talking about." She mimicked Homer's excited disgust. "'That dirty black hen, she's all over scabs and almost naked.'"

Homer laughed apologetically, but Tod was angry.

"What's the idea of keeping those guys in the garage?" he demanded.

"What the hell is it your business?" she replied, but not with real anger. She was amused.

"Homer enjoys their company. Don't you, sloppy-boppy?"

"I told Tod they were nice fellows just down on their luck like a lot of people these days. There's an awful lot of unemployment going around."

"That's right," she said. "If they go, I go."

Tod had guessed as much. He realized there was no use in saying anything. Homer was again signaling for him to keep quiet.

For some reason or other, Faye suddenly became ashamed of herself. She apologized to Tod by offering to dance with him again, flirting as she suggested it. Tod refused.

She broke the silence that followed by a eulogy of Miguel's chickens, which was really meant to be an excuse for herself. She described what marvelous fighters the birds were, how much Miguel loved them and what good care he took of them.

Homer agreed enthusiastically. Tod remained silent. She asked him if he had ever seen a cock fight and invited him to the garage for the next night. A man from San

Diego was coming North with his birds to pit them against Miguel's.

When she turned to Homer again, he leaned away as though she were going to hit him. She flushed with shame at this and looked at Tod to see if he had noticed. The rest of the evening, she tried to be nice to Homer. She even touched him a little, straightening his collar and patting his hair smooth. He beamed happily.

21

When Tod told Claude Estee about the cock fight, he wanted to go with him. They drove to Homer's place together.

It was one of those blue and lavender nights when the luminous color seems to have been blown over the scene with an air brush. Even the darkest shadows held some purple.

A car stood in the driveway of the garage with its headlights on. They could see several men in the corner of the building and could hear their voices. Someone laughed, using only two notes, ha-ha and ha-ha, over and over again.

Tod stepped ahead to make himself known, in case they were taking precautions against the police. When he entered the light, Abe Kusich and Miguel greeted him, but Earle didn't.

"The fights are off," Abe said. "That stinkola from Diego didn't get here."

Claude came up and Tod introduced him to the three men. The dwarf was arrogant, Miguel gracious and Earle his usual wooden, surly self.

Most of the garage floor had been converted into a pit, an

oval space about nine feet long and seven or eight wide. It was floored with an old carpet and walled by a low, ragged fence made of odd pieces of lath and wire. Faye's coupe stood in the driveway, placed so that its headlights flooded the arena.

Claude and Tod followed Abe out of the glare and sat down with him on an old trunk in the back of the garage. Earle and Miguel came in and squatted on their heels facing them. They were both wearing blue denims, polka-dot shirts, big hats and high-heeled boots. They looked very handsome and picturesque.

They sat smoking silently, all of them calm except the dwarf, who was fidgety. Although he had plenty of room, he suddenly gave Tod a shove.

"Get over, lard-ass," he snarled.

Tod moved, crowded against Claude, without saying anything. Earle laughed at Tod rather than the dwarf, but the dwarf turned on him anyway.

"Why, you punkola! Who you laughing at?"

"You," Earle said.

"That so, hah? Well, listen to me, you pee-hole bandit, for two cents I'd knock you out of them prop boots."

Earle reached into his shirt pocket and threw a coin on the ground.

"There's a nickel," he said.

The dwarf started to get off the trunk, but Tod caught him by the collar. He didn't try to get loose, but leaned forward against his coat, like a terrier in a harness, and wagged his great head from side to side.

"Go on," he sputtered, "you fugitive from the Western Costume Company, you . . . you louse in a fright-wig, you."

Earle would have been much less angry if he could have thought of a snappy comeback. He mumbled something about a half-pint bastard, then spat. He hit the instep of the dwarf's shoe with a big gob of spittle.

"Nice shot," Miguel said.

This was apparently enough for Earle to consider himself the winner, for he smiled and became quiet. The dwarf slapped Tod's hand away from his collar with a curse and settled down on the trunk again.

"He ought to wear gaffs," Miguel said.

"I don't need them for a punk like that."

They all laughed and everything was fine again.

Abe leaned across Tod to speak to Claude.

"It would have been a swell main," he said. "There was more than a dozen guys here before you come and some of them with real dough. I was going to make book."

He took out his wallet and gave him one of his business cards.

"It was in the bag," Miguel said. "I got five birds that would of won easy and two sure losers. We would of made a killing."

"I've never seen a chicken fight," Claude said. "In fact, I've never even seen a game chicken."

Miguel offered to show him one of his birds and left to get it. Tod went down to the car for the bottle of whiskey they had left in a side pocket. When he got back, Miguel was holding Jujutla in the light. They all examined the bird.

Miguel held the cock firmly with both hands, somewhat in the manner that a basketball is held for an underhand toss. The bird had short, oval wings and a heart-shaped tail that stood at right angles to its body. It had a triangular head, like a snake's, terminating in a slightly curved beak, thick at the base and fine at the point. All its feathers were so tight and hard that they looked as though they had been varnished. They had been thinned out for fighting and the lines of its body, which was like a truncated wedge, stood out plainly. From between Miguel's fingers dangled its long, bright orange legs and its slightly darker feet with their horn nails.

"Juju was bred by John R. Bowes of Lindale, Texas,"
Miguel said proudly. "He's a six times winner. I give fifty
dollars and a shotgun for him."

"He's a nice bird," the dwarf said grudgingly, "but
looks ain't everything."

Claude took out his wallet.

"I'd like to see him fight," he said. "Suppose you sell me
one of your other birds and I put it against him."

Miguel thought a while and looked at Earle, who told
him to go ahead.

"I've got a bird I'll sell you for fifteen bucks," he said.

The dwarf interfered.

"Let me pick the bird."

"Oh, I don't care," Claude said, "I just want to see a
fight. Here's your fifteen."

Earle took the money and Miguel told him to get Hermano, the big red.

"That red'll go over eight pounds," he said, "while Juju
won't go more than six."

Earle came back carrying a large rooster that had a
silver shawl. He looked like an ordinary barnyard fowl.

When the dwarf saw him, he became indignant.

"What do you call that, a goose?"

"That's one of Street's Butcher Boys," Miguel said.

"I wouldn't bait a hook with him," the dwarf said.

"You don't have to bet," Earle mumbled.

The dwarf eyed the bird and the bird eyed him. He turned to Claude.

"Let me handle him for you, mister," he said.

Miguel spoke quickly.

"Earle'll do it. He knows the cock."

The dwarf exploded at this.

"It's a frame-up!" he yelled.

He tried to take the red, but Earle held the bird high in the air out of the little man's reach.

Miguel opened the trunk and took out a small wooden box, the kind chessmen are kept in. It was full of curved gaffs, small squares of chamois with holes in their centers and bits of waxed string like that used by a shoemaker.

They crowded around to watch him arm Juju. First he wiped the short stubs on the cock's legs to make sure they were clean and then placed a leather square over one of them so that the stub came through the hole. He then fitted a gaff over it and fastened it with a bit of the soft string, wrapping very carefully. He did the same to the other leg.

When he had finished, Earle started on the big red.

"That's a bird with lots of cojones," Miguel said. "He's won plenty fights. He don't look fast maybe, but he's fast all right and he packs an awful wallop."

"Strictly for the cook stove, if you ask me," the dwarf said.

Earle took out a pair of shears and started to lighten the red's plumage. The dwarf watched him cut away most of the bird's tail, but when he began to work on the breast, he caught his hand.

"Leave him be!" he barked. "You'll kill him fast that way. He needs that stuff for protection."

He turned to Claude again.

"Please, mister, let me handle him."

"Make him buy a share in the bird," Miguel said.

Claude laughed and motioned for Earle to give Abe the bird. Earle didn't want to and looked meaningly at Miguel.

The dwarf began to dance with rage.

"You're trying to cold-deck us!" he screamed.

"Aw, give it to him," Miguel said.

The little man tucked the bird under his left arm so that his hands were free and began to look over the gaffs in the box. They were all the same length, three inches, but some had more pronounced curves than the others. He selected a pair and explained his strategy to Claude.

"He's going to do most of his fighting on his back. This

pair'll hit right that way. If he could get over the other bird, I wouldn't use them."

He got down on his knees and honed the gaffs on the cement floor until they were like needles.

"Have we a chance?" Tod asked.

"You can't ever tell," he said, shaking his extra large head. "He feels almost like a dead bird."

After adjusting the gaffs with great care, he looked the bird over, stretching its wings and blowing its feathers in order to see its skin.

"The comb ain't bright enough for fighting condition," he said, pinching it, "but he looks strong. He may have been a good one once."

He held the bird in the light and looked at its head. When Miguel saw him examining its beak, he told him anxiously to quit stalling. But the dwarf paid no attention and went on muttering to himself. He motioned for Tod and Claude to look.

"What'd I tell you!" he said, puffing with indignation. "We've been cold-decked."

He pointed to a hair line running across the top of the bird's beak.

"That's not a crack," Miguel protested, "it's just a mark."

He reached for the bird as though to rub its beak and the bird pecked savagely at him. This pleased the dwarf.

"We'll fight," he said, "but we won't bet."

Earle was to referee. He took a piece of chalk and drew three lines in the center of the pit, a long one in the middle and two shorter ones parallel to it and about three feet away.

"Pit your cocks," he called.

"No, bill them first," the dwarf protested.

He and Miguel stood at arm's length and thrust their birds together to anger them. Juju caught the big red by the comb and held on viciously until Miguel jerked him away. The red, who had been rather apathetic, came to life and the dwarf had trouble holding him. The two men thrust their birds together again, and again Juju caught the red's comb. The big cock became frantic with rage and struggled to get at the smaller bird.

"We're ready," the dwarf said.

He and Miguel climbed into the pit and set their birds down on the short lines so that they faced each other. They held them by the tails and waited for Earle to give the signal to let go.

"Pit them," he ordered.

The dwarf had been watching Earle's lips and he had his bird off first, but Juju rose straight in the air and sank one spur in the red's breast. It went through the feathers into the flesh. The red turned with the gaff still stuck in him and pecked twice at his opponent's head.

They separated the birds and held them to the lines again.

"Pit 'em!" Earle shouted.

Again Juju got above the other bird, but this time he missed with his spurs. The red tried to get above him, but couldn't. He was too clumsy and heavy to fight in the air. Juju climbed again, cutting and hitting so rapidly that his legs were a golden blur. The red met him by going back on his tail and hooking upward like a cat. Juju landed again and again. He broke one of the red's wings, then practically severed a leg.

"Handle them," Earle called.

When the dwarf gathered the red up, its neck had begun to droop and it was a mass of blood and matted feathers. The little man moaned over the bird, then set to work. He spit into its gaping beak and took the comb between his lips and sucked the blood back into it. The red began to regain its fury, but not its strength. Its beak closed and its neck straightened. The dwarf smoothed and shaped its plumage. He could do nothing to help the broken wing or the dangling leg.

"Pit 'em," Earle said.

The dwarf insisted that the birds be put down beak to beak on the center line, so that the red would not have to move to get at his opponent. Miguel agreed.

The red was very gallant. When Abe let go of its tail, it made a great effort to get off the ground and meet Juju in the air, but it could only thrust with one leg and fell over on its side. Juju sailed above it, half turned and came down on its back, driving in both spurs. The red twisted free, throwing Juju, and made a terrific effort to hook with its good leg, but fell sideways again.

Before Juju could get into the air, the red managed to drive a hard blow with its beak to Juju's head. This slowed the smaller bird down and he fought on the ground. In the pecking match, the red's greater weight and strength evened up for his lack of a leg and a wing. He managed to give as good as he got. But suddenly his cracked beak broke off, leaving only the lower half. A large bubble of blood rose where the beak had been. The red didn't retreat an inch, but made a great effort to get into the air once more. Using its one leg skillfully, it managed to rise six or seven inches from the ground, not enough, however, to get its spurs into play. Juju went up with him and got well above, then drove both gaffs into the red's breast. Again one of the steel needles stuck.

"Handle them," Earle shouted.

Miguel freed his bird and gave the other back to the dwarf. Abe, moaning softly, smoothed its feathers and licked its eyes clean, then took its whole head in his mouth. The red was finished, however. It couldn't even hold its neck straight. The dwarf blew away the feathers from under its tail and pressed the lips of its vent together hard. When that didn't seem to help, he inserted his little finger and scratched the bird's testicles. It fluttered and made a gallant effort to straighten its neck.

"Pit birds."

Once more the red tried to rise with Juju, pushing hard with its remaining leg, but it only spun crazily. Juju rose, but missed. The red thrust weakly with its broken bill. Juju went into the air again and this time drove a gaff through one of the red's eyes into its brain. The red fell over stone dead.

The dwarf groaned with anguish, but no one else said anything. Juju pecked at the dead bird's remaining eye.

"Take off that stinking cannibal!" the dwarf screamed.

Miguel laughed, then caught Juju and removed its gaffs. Earle did the same for the red. He handled the dead cock gently and with respect.

Tod passed the whiskey.

22

They were well on their way to getting drunk when Homer came out to the garage. He gave a little start when he saw the dead chicken sprawled on the carpet. He shook hands with Claude after Tod introduced him, and with Abe Kusich, then made a little set speech about everybody coming in for a drink. They trooped after him.

Faye greeted them at the door. She was wearing a pair of green silk lounging pajamas and green mules with large pompons and very high heels. The top three buttons of her jacket were open and a good deal of her chest was exposed but nothing of her breasts; not because they were small, but because they were placed wide apart and their thrust was upward and outward.

She gave Tod her hand and patted the dwarf on the top of the head. They were old friends. In acknowledging Homer's awkward introduction of Claude, she was very much the lady. It was her favorite role and she assumed it whenever she met a new man, especially if he were someone whose affluence was obvious.

"Charmed to have you," she trilled.

The dwarf laughed at her.

In a voice stiff with hauteur, she then ordered Homer into the kitchen for soda, ice and glasses.

"A swell layout," announced the dwarf, putting on the hat he had taken off in the doorway.

He climbed into one of the big Spanish chairs, using his knees and hands to do it, and sat on the edge with his feet dangling. He looked like a ventriloquist's dummy.

Earle and Miguel had remained behind to wash up. When they came in, Faye welcomed them with stilted condescension.

"How do you do, boys? The refreshments will be along in a jiffy. But perhaps you prefer a liqueur, Miguel?"

"No, mum," he said, a little startled. "I'll have what the others have."

He followed Earle across the room to the couch. Both of them took long, wooden steps, as though they weren't used to being in a house. They sat down gingerly with their backs straight, their big hats on their knees and their hands under their hats. They had combed their hair before leaving the garage and their small round heads glistened prettily.

Homer took the drinks around on a small tray.

They all made a show of manners, all but the dwarf, that is, who remained as arrogant as ever. He even commented on the quality of the whiskey. As soon as everyone had been served, Homer sat down.

Faye alone remained standing. She was completely self-possessed despite their stares. She stood with one hip thrown out and her hand on it. From where Claude was sitting he could follow the charming line of her spine as it swooped into her buttocks, which were like a heart upside down.

He gave a low whistle of admiration and everyone agreed by moving uneasily or laughing.

"My dear," she said to Homer, "perhaps some of the men would like cigars?"

He was surprised and mumbled something about there being no cigars in the house but that he would go to the store for them if ... Having to say all this made him unhappy and he took the whiskey around again. He poured very generous shots.

"That's a becoming shade of green," Tod said.

Faye peacocked for them all.

"I thought maybe it was a little gaudy ... vulgar you know."

"No," Claude said enthusiastically, "it's stunning."

She repaid him for his compliment by smiling in a peculiar, secret way and running her tongue over her lips. It was one of her most characteristic gestures and very effective.

It seemed to promise all sorts of undefined intimacies, yet it was really as simple and automatic as the word thanks. She used it to reward anyone for anything, no matter how unimportant.

Claude made the same mistake Tod had often made and jumped to his feet.

"Won't you sit here?" he said, waving gallantly at his chair. She accepted by repeating the secret smile and the tongue caress. Claude bowed, but then, realized that everyone was watching him, added a little mock flourish to make himself less ridiculous. Tod joined them, then Earle and Miguel came over. Claude did the courting while the others stood by and stared at her.

"Do you work in pictures, Mr. Estee?" she asked.

"Yes. You're in pictures, of course?"

Everyone was aware of the begging note in his voice, but no one smiled. They didn't blame him. It was almost impossible to keep that note out when talking to her. Men used it just to say good morning.

"Not exactly, but I hope to be," she said. "I've worked as an extra, but I haven't had a real chance yet. I expect to get one soon. All I ask is a chance. Acting is in my blood. We Greeners, you know, were all theatre people from away back."

She didn't let Claude finish, but he didn't care.

"Not musicals, but real dramas. Of course, maybe light comedies at first. All I ask is a chance. I've been buying a lot of clothes lately to make myself one. I don't believe in luck. Luck is just hard work, they say, and I'm willing to work as hard as anybody."

"You have a delightful voice and you handle it well," he said.

He couldn't help it. Having once seen her secret smile and the things that accompanied it, he wanted to make her repeat it again and again.

"I'd like to do a show on Broadway," she continued. "That's the way to get a start nowadays. They won't talk to you unless you've had stage experience."

She went on and on, telling him how careers are made in the movies and how she intended to make hers. It was all nonsense. She mixed bits of badly understood advice from the trade papers with other bits out of the fan magazines and compared these with the legends that surrounded the activities of screen stars and executives. Without any noticeable transition, possibilities became probabilities and wound up as inevitabilities. At first she occasionally stopped and waited for Claude to chorus a hearty agreement, but when she had a good start, all her questions were rhetorical and the stream of words rippled on without a break.

None of them really heard her. They were all too busy watching her smile, laugh, shiver, whisper, grow indignant, cross and uncross her legs, stick out her tongue, widen and narrow her eyes, toss her head so that her platinum hair splashed against the red plush of the chair back. The strange thing about her gestures and expressions was that they didn't really illustrate what she was saying. They were almost pure. It was as though her body recognized how foolish her words were and tried to excite her hearers into being uncritical. It worked that night; no one even thought of laughing at her. The only move they made was to narrow their circle about her.

Tod stood on the outer edge, watching her through the opening between Earle and the Mexican. When he felt a light tap on his shoulder, he knew it was Homer, but didn't turn. When the tap was repeated, he shrugged the hand away. A few minutes later, he heard a shoe squeak behind him and turned to see Homer tiptoeing off. He reached a chair safely and sank into it with a sigh. He put his heavy hands on the knees, one on each, and stared for a while at their backs. He felt Tod's eyes on him and looked up and smiled.

His smile annoyed Tod. It was one of those irritating smiles that seem to say: "My friend, what can you know of suffering?" There was something very patronizing and superior about it, and intolerably snobbish.

He felt hot and a little sick. He turned his back on Homer and went out the front door. His indignant exit wasn't very successful. He wobbled quite badly and when he reached the sidewalk, he had to sit down on the curb with his back against a date palm.

From where he was sitting, he couldn't see the city in the valley below the canyon, but he could see the reflection of its lights, which hung in the sky above it like a batik parasol. The unlighted part of the sky at the edge of the parasol was a deep black with hardly a trace of blue.

Homer followed him out of the house and stood standing behind him, afraid to approach. He might have sneaked away without Tod's knowing it, if he had not suddenly looked down and seen his shadow.

"Hello," he said.

He motioned for Homer to join on the curb.

"You'll catch cold," Homer said.

Tod understood his protest. He made it because he wanted to be certain that his company was really welcome. Nevertheless, Tod refused to repeat the invitation. He didn't even turn to look at him again. He was sure he was wearing his long-suffering smile and didn't want to see it.

He wondered why all his sympathy had turned to malice. Because of Faye? It was impossible for him to admit it. Because he was unable to do anything to help him? This reason was a more comfortable one, but he dismissed it with even less consideration. He had never set himself up as a healer.

Homer was looking the other way, at the house, watching the parlor window. He cocked his head to one side when someone laughed. The four short sounds, ha-ha and again ha-ha, distinct musical notes, were made by the dwarf.

"You could learn from him," Tod said.

"What?" Homer asked, turning to look at him.

"Let it go."

His impatience both hurt and puzzled Homer. He saw that and motioned for him to sit down, this time emphatically.

Homer obeyed. He did a poor job of squatting and hurt himself. He sat nursing his knee.

"What is it?" Tod finally said, making an attempt to be kind.

"Nothing, Tod, nothing."

He was grateful and increased his smile. Tod couldn't help seeing all its annoying attributes, resignation, kindliness, and humility.

195

They sat quietly, Homer with his heavy shoulders hunched and the sweet grin on his face, Tod frowning, his back pressed hard against the palm tree. In the house the radio was playing and its blare filled the street.

They sat for a long time without speaking. Several times Homer started to tell Tod something but he didn't seem able to get the words out. Tod refused to help him with a question.

His big hands left his lap, where they had been playing "here's the church and here the steeple," and hid in his armpits. They remained there for a moment, then slid under his thighs. A moment later they were back in his lap. The right hand cracked the joints of the left, one by one, then the left did the same service for the right. They seemed easier for a moment, but not for long. They started "here's the church" again, going through the entire performance and ending with the joint manipulation as before. He started a third time, but catching Tod's eyes, he stopped and trapped his hands between his knees.

It was the most complicated tic Tod had ever seen. What made it particularly horrible was its precision. It wasn't pantomime, as he had first thought, but manual ballet.

When Tod saw the hands start to crawl out again, he exploded.

"For Christ's sake!"

The hands struggled to get free, but Homer clamped his knees shut and held them.

"I'm sorry," he said.

"Oh, all right."

"But I can't help it, Tod. I have to do it three times."

"Okay with me."

He turned his back on him.

Faye started to sing and her voice poured into the street.

> *"Dreamed about a reefer five feet long*
> *Not too mild and not too strong,*
> *You'll be high, but not for long,*
> *If you're a viper—a vi-paah."*

Instead of her usual swing delivery, she was using a lugubrious one, wailing the tune as though it were a dirge. At the end of every stanza, she shifted to an added minor.

> *"I'm the queen of everything,*
> *Gotta be high before I can swing,*
> *Light a tea and let it be,*
> *If you're a viper—a vi-paah."*

"She sings very pretty," Homer said.

"She's drunk."

"I don't know what to do, Tod," Homer complained. "She's drinking an awful lot lately. It's that Earle. We used to have a lot of fun before he came, but now we don't have any fun any more since he started to hang around."

"Why don't you get rid of him?"

"I was thinking about what you said about the license to keep chickens."

Tod understood what he wanted.

"I'll report them to the Board of Health tomorrow."

Homer thanked him, then insisted on explaining in detail why he couldn't do it himself.

"But that'll only get rid of the Mexican," Tod said. "You have to throw Earle out yourself."

"Maybe he'll go with his friend?"

Tod knew that Homer was begging him to agree so that he could go on hoping, but he refused.

"Not a chance. You'll have to throw him out."

Homer accepted this with his brave, sweet smile.

"Maybe . . ."

"Tell Faye to do it," Tod said.

"Oh, I can't."

"Why the hell not? It's your house."

"Don't be mad at me, Toddie."

"All right, Homie, I'm not mad at you."

Faye's voice came through the open window.

> *"And when our throat gets dry,*
> *You know you're high,*
> *If you're a viper."*

The others harmonized on the last word, repeating it.
"Vi-paah ..."

"Toddie," Homer began, "if ..."

"Stop calling me Toddie, for Christ's sake!"

Homer didn't understand. He took Tod's hand.

"I didn't mean nothing. Back home we call ..."

Tod couldn't stand his trembling signals of affection. He tore free with a jerk.

"Oh, but, Toddie, I ..."

"She's a whore!"

He heard Homer grunt, then heard his knees creak as he struggled to his feet.

Faye's voice came pouring through the window, a reedy wail that broke in the middle with a husky catch.

> *"High, high, high, high, when you're high,*
> *Everything is dandy,*
> *Truck on down to the candy store,*
> *Bust your conk on peppermint candy!*

199

Then you know your body's sent,
Don't care if you don't pay rent,
Sky is high and so am I,
If you're a viper—a vi-paah."

23

When Tod went back into the house, he found Earle, Abe Kusich and Claude standing together in a tight group, watching Faye dance with Miguel. She and the Mexican were doing a slow tango to music from the phonograph. He held her very tight, one of his legs thrust between hers, and they swayed together in long spirals that broke rhythmically at the top of each curve into a dip. All the buttons on her lounging pajamas were open and the arm he had around her waist was inside her clothes.

Tod stood watching the dancers from the doorway for a moment, then went to a little table on which the whiskey bottle was. He poured himself a quarter of a tumblerful, tossed it off, then poured another drink. Carrying the glass, he went over to Claude and the others. They paid no attention to him; their heads moved only to follow the dancers, like the gallery at a tennis match.

"Did you see Homer?" Tod asked, touching Claude's arm.

Claude didn't turn, but the dwarf did. He spoke as though hypnotized.

"What a quiff! What a quiff!"

Tod left them and went to look for Homer. He wasn't in the kitchen, so he tried the bedrooms. One of them was locked. He knocked lightly, waited, then repeated the knock. There was no answer, but he thought he heard someone move. He looked through the keyhole. The room was pitch dark.

"Homer," he called softly.

He heard the bed creak, then Homer replied.

"Who is it?"

"It's me—Toddie."

He used the dimunitive with perfect seriousness.

"Go away, please," Homer said.

"Let me in for a minute. I want to explain something."

"No," Homer said, "go away, please."

Tod went back to the living room. The phonograph record had been changed to a fox-trot and Earle was now dancing with Faye. He had both his arms around her in a bear hug and they were stumbling all over the room, bumping into the walls and furniture. Faye, her head thrown back, was laughing wildly. Earle had both eyes shut tight.

Miguel and Claude were also laughing, but not the dwarf. He stood with his fists clenched and his chin stuck out. When he couldn't stand any more of it, he ran after

202

the dancers to cut in. He caught Earle by the seat of his
trousers.

"Le'me dance," he barked.

Earle turned his head, looking down at the dwarf from
over his shoulder.

"Git! G'wan, git!"

Faye and Earle had come to a halt with their arms
around each other. When the dwarf lowered his head like
a goat and tried to push between them, she reached down
and tweaked his nose.

"Le'me dance," he bellowed.

They tried to start again, but Abe wouldn't let them.
He had his hands between them and was trying frantically
to pull them apart. When that wouldn't work, he kicked
Earle sharply in the shins. Earle kicked back and his boot
landed in the little man's stomach, knocking him flat on his
back. Everyone laughed.

The dwarf struggled to his feet and stood with his head
lowered like a tiny ram. Just as Faye and Earle started
to dance again, he charged between Earle's legs and dug
upward with both hands. Earle screamed with pain, and
tried to get at him. He screamed again, then groaned and
started to sink to the floor, tearing Faye's silk pajamas on
his way down.

Miguel grabbed Abe by the throat. The dwarf let go his hold and Earle sank to the floor. Lifting the little man free, Miguel shifted his grip to his ankles and dashed him against the wall, like a man killing a rabbit against a tree. He swung the dwarf back to slam him again, but Tod caught his arm. Then Claude grabbed the dwarf and together they pulled him away from the Mexican.

He was unconscious. They carried him into the kitchen and held him under the cold water. He came to quickly, and began to curse. When they saw he was all right, they went back to the living room.

Miguel was helping Earle over to the couch. All the tan had drained from his face and it was covered with sweat. Miguel loosened his trousers while Claude took off his necktie and opened his collar.

Faye and Tod watched from the side.

"Look," she said, "my new pajamas are ruined."

One of the sleeves had been pulled almost off and her shoulder stuck through it. The trousers were also torn. While he stared at her, she undid the top of the trousers and stepped out of them. She was wearing tight black lace drawers. Tod took a step toward her and hesitated. She threw the pajama bottoms over her arm, turned slowly and walked toward the door.

"Faye," Tod gasped.

She stopped and smiled at him.

"I'm going to bed," she said. "Get that little guy out of here."

Claude came over and took Tod by the arm.

"Let's blow," he said.

Tod nodded.

"We'd better take the homunculus with us or he's liable to murder the whole household."

Tod nodded again and followed him into the kitchen. They found the dwarf holding a big piece of ice to the side of his head.

"There's some lump where that greaser slammed me."

He made them finger and admire it.

"Let's go home," Claude said.

"No," said the dwarf, "let's go see some girls. I'm just getting started."

"To hell with that," snapped Tod. "Come on."

He pushed the dwarf toward the door.

"Take your hands off, punk!" roared the little man.

Claude stepped between them.

"Easy there, citizen," he said.

"All right, but no shoving."

He strutted out and they followed.

Earle still lay stretched on the couch. He had his eyes closed and was holding himself below the stomach with both hands. Miguel wasn't there.

Abe chuckled, wagging his big head gleefully.

"I fixed that buckeroo."

Out on the sidewalk he tried again to get them to go with him.

"Come on, you guys—we'll have some fun."

"I'm going home," Claude said.

They went with the dwarf to his car and watched him climb in behind the wheel. He had special extensions on the clutch and brake so that he could reach them with his tiny feet.

"Come to town?"

"No, thanks," Claude said politely.

"Then to hell with you!"

That was his farewell. He let out the brake and the car rolled away.

24

Tod woke up the next morning with a splitting headache. He called the studio to say he wouldn't be in and remained in bed until noon, then went downtown for breakfast. After several cups of hot tea, he felt a little better and decided to visit Homer. He still wanted to apologize.

Climbing the hill to Pinyon Canyon made his head throb and he was relieved when no one answered his repeated knocks. As he started away, he saw one of the curtains move and went back to knock once more. There was still no answer.

He went around to the garage. Faye's car was gone and so were the game chickens. He went to the back of the house and knocked on the kitchen door. Somehow the silence seemed too complete. He tried the handle and found that the door wasn't locked. He shouted hello a few times, as a warning, then went through the kitchen into the living room.

The red velvet curtains were all drawn tight, but he could see Homer sitting on the couch and staring at the backs of his hands which were cupped over his knees. He wore an old-fashioned cotton nightgown and his feet were bare.

"Just get up?"

Homer neither moved nor replied.

Tod tried again.

"Some party!"

He knew it was stupid to be hearty, but he didn't know what else to be.

"Boy, have I got a hang-over," he went on, even going so far as to attempt a chuckle.

Homer paid absolutely no attention to him.

The room was just as they had left it the night before. Tables and chairs were overturned and the smashed picture lay where it had fallen. To give himself a reason for staying, he began to tidy up. He righted the chairs, straightened the carpet and picked up the cigarette butts that littered the floor. He also threw aside the curtains and opened a window.

"There, that's better, isn't it?" he asked cheerfully.

Homer looked up for a second, then down at his hands again. Tod saw that he was coming out of his stupor.

"Want some coffee?" he asked.

He lifted his hands from his knees and hid them in his armpits, clamping them tight, but didn't answer.

"Some hot coffee—what do you say?"

He took his hands from under his arms and sat on them.

208

After waiting a little while he shook his head no, slowly, heavily, like a dog with a foxtail in its ear.

"I'll make some."

Tod went to the kitchen and put the pot on the stove. While it was boiling, he took a peek into Faye's room. It had been stripped. All the dresser drawers were pulled out and there were empty boxes all over the floor. A broken flask of perfume lay in the middle of the carpet and the place reeked of gardenia.

When the coffee was ready, he poured two cups and carried them into the living room on a tray. He found Homer just as he had left him, sitting on his hands. He moved a small table close to him and put the tray on it.

"I brought a cup for myself, too," he said. "Come on— drink it while it's hot."

Tod lifted a cup and held it out, but when he saw that he was going to speak, he put it down and waited.

"I'm going back to Wayneville," Homer said.

"A swell idea—great!"

He pushed the coffee at him again. Homer ignored it. He gulped several times, trying to swallow something that was struck in his throat, then began to sob. He cried without covering his face or bending his head. The sound was like an ax chopping pine, a heavy, hollow, chunking noise.

It was repeated rhythmically but without accent. There was no progress in it. Each chunk was exactly like the one that preceded. It would never reach a climax.

Tod realized that there was no use trying to stop him. Only a very stupid man would have the courage to try to do it. He went to the farthest corner of the room and waited.

Just as he was about to light a second cigarette, Homer called him.

"Tod!"

"I'm here, Homer."

He hurried over to the couch again.

Homer was still crying, but he suddenly stopped even more abruptly than he had started.

"Yes, Homer?" Tod asked encouragingly.

"She's left."

"Yes, I know. Drink some coffee."

"She's left."

Tod knew that he put a great deal of faith in sayings, so he tried one.

"Good riddance to bad rubbish."

"She left before I got up," he said.

"What the hell do you care? You're going back to Wayneville."

"You shouldn't curse," Homer said with the same lunatic calm.

"I'm sorry," Tod mumbled.

The word "sorry" was like dynamite set off under a dam. Language leaped out of Homer in a muddy, twisting torrent. At first, Tod thought it would do him a lot of good to pour out in this way. But he was wrong. The lake behind the dam replenished itself too fast. The more he talked the greater the pressure grew because the flood was circular and ran back behind the dam again.

After going on continuously for about twenty minutes, he stopped in the middle of a sentence. He leaned back, closed his eyes and seemed to fall asleep. Tod put a cushion under his head. After watching him for a while, he went back to the kitchen.

He sat down and tried to make sense out of what Homer had told him. A great deal of it was gibberish. Some of it, however, wasn't. He hit on a key that helped when he realized that a lot of it wasn't jumbled so much as timeless. The words went behind each other instead of after. What he had taken for long strings were really one thick word and not a sentence. In the same way several sentences were simultaneous and not a paragraph. Using this key, he was able to arrange a part of what he had heard so that it made the usual kind of sense.

After Tod had hurt him by saying that nasty thing about Faye, Homer ran around to the back of the house and let himself in through the kitchen, then went to peek into the parlor. He wasn't angry with Tod, just surprised and upset because Tod was a nice boy. From the hall that led into the parlor he could see everybody having a good time and he was glad because it was kind of dull for Faye living with an old man like him. It made her restless. No one noticed him peeking there and he was glad because he didn't feel much like joining the fun, although he liked to watch people enjoy themselves. Faye was dancing with Mr. Estee and they made a nice pair. She seemed happy. Her face shone like always when she was happy. Next she danced with Earle. He didn't like that because of the way he held her. He couldn't see what she saw in that fellow. He just wasn't nice, that's all. He had mean eyes. In the hotel business they used to watch out for fellows like that and never gave them credit because they would jump their bills. Maybe he couldn't get a job because nobody would trust him, although it was true as Faye said that a lot of people were out of work nowadays. Standing there peeking at the party, enjoying the laughing and singing, he saw Earle catch Faye and bend her back and kiss her and everybody laughed although you could see Faye didn't like it because she slapped his face. Earle didn't care, he just kissed her again, a long nasty one. She got away from him and ran toward the door where he was standing. He tried to hide, but she caught him. Although he didn't say anything, she said he was nasty spying on her and wouldn't listen when he tried to explain. She went into her room and he followed to tell about the peeking, but she carried on awful and cursed him some more as she put red on her lip. Then she knocked over the perfume. That made her twice as mad. He tried to explain but she wouldn't listen and just went on calling him all sorts of dirty things. So he went to his room and got undressed and tried to go to sleep. Then Tod woke him up and wanted to come in and talk. He wasn't angry, but didn't feel like talking just then, all he wanted to do was go to sleep. Tod went away and no sooner had he climbed back into bed when there was some awful screaming and banging. He was afraid to go out and see and he thought of calling the police, but he was scared to go in the hall where the phone was so he started to get dressed to climb out of the window and go for help because it sounded like murder but before he finished putting his shoes on, he heard Tod talking to Faye and he figured that it must be all right or she wouldn't be laughing so he got undressed and went back to bed again. He couldn't fall asleep wondering what had happened, so when the house was quiet, he took a chance and knocked on Faye's door to find out. Faye let him in. She was curled up in bed like a little girl. She called him Daddy and kissed him and said that she wasn't angry at him at all. She said there had been a fight but nobody got hurt much and for him to go back to bed and that they would talk more in the morning. He went back like she said and fell asleep, but he woke up again as it was just breaking daylight. At first he wondered why he was up because when he once fell asleep, usually he didn't get up before the alarm clock rang. He knew that something had happened, but he didn't know what until he heard a noise in Faye's room. It was a moan and he thought he was dreaming, but he heard it again. Sure enough, Faye was moaning all right. He thought she must be sick. She moaned again like in pain. He got out of bed and went to her door and knocked and asked if she was sick. She didn't answer and the moaning stopped so he went back to bed. A little later she moaned again so he got out of bed, thinking she might want the hot water bottle or some aspirin and a drink of water or something and knocked on her door again, only meaning to help her. She heard him and said something. He didn't understand what but he thought she meant for him to go in. Lots of times when she had a headache he brought her an aspirin and a glass of water in the middle of the night. The door wasn't locked. You'd have thought she would have locked the door because the Mexican was in bed with her, both of them naked and she had her arms around him. Faye saw him and pulled the sheets over her head without saying anything. He didn't know what to do, so he backed out of the room and closed the door. He was standing in the hall, trying to figure out what to do, feeling so ashamed, when Earle appeared with his boots in his hand. He must have been sleeping in the parlor. He wanted to know what the trouble was. "Faye's sick," he said, "and I'm getting her a glass of water." But then Faye moaned again and Earle heard it. He pushed open the door. Faye screamed. He could hear Earle and Miguel cursing each other and fighting. He was afraid to call the police on account of Faye and didn't know what to do. Faye kept on screaming. When he opened the door again, Miguel fell out with Earle on top of him and both of them tearing at each other. He ran inside the room and locked the door. She had the sheets over her head, screaming. He could hear Earle and Miguel fighting in the hall and then he couldn't hear them any more. She kept the sheets over her head. He tried to talk to her but she wouldn't answer. He sat down on a chair to guard her in case Earle and Miguel came back, but they didn't and after a while she pulled the sheets away from her face and told him to get out. She pulled the sheets over her face again when he answered, so then he waited a little longer and again she told him to get out without letting him see her face. He couldn't hear either Miguel or Earle. He opened the door and looked out. They were gone. He locked the doors and windows and went to his room and lay down on his bed. Before he knew it he fell asleep and when he woke up she was gone. All he could find was Earle's boots in the hall. He threw them out the back and this morning they were gone.

25

Tod went into the living room to see how Homer was getting on. He was still on the couch, but had changed his position. He had curled his big body into a ball. His knees were drawn up almost to his chin, his elbows were tucked in close and his hands were against his chest. But he wasn't relaxed. Some inner force of nerve and muscle was straining to make the ball tighter and still tighter. He was like a steel spring which has been freed of its function in a machine and allowed to use all its strength centripetally. While part of a machine the pull of the spring had been used against other and stronger forces, but now, free at last, it was striving to attain the shape of its original coil.

Original coil ... In a book of abnormal psychology borrowed from the college library, he had once seen a picture of a woman sleeping in a net hammock whose posture was much like Homer's. "Uterine Flight," or something like that, had been the caption under the photograph. The woman had been sleeping in the hammock without changing her position, that of the foetus in the womb, for a great many years. The doctors of the insane asylum had been able to awaken her for only short periods of time and those months apart.

He sat down to smoke a cigarette and wondered what he ought to do. Call a doctor? But after all Homer had been awake most of the night and was exhausted. The doctor would shake him a few times and he would yawn and ask what the matter was. He could try to wake him up himself. But hadn't he been enough of a pest already? He was so much better off asleep, even if it was a case of "Uterine Flight."

What a perfect escape the return of the womb was. Better by far than Religion or Art or the South Sea Islands. It was so snug and warm there, and the feeding was automatic. Everything perfect in that hotel. No wonder the memory of those accommodations lingered in the blood and nerves of everyone. It was dark, yes, but what a warm, rich darkness. The grave wasn't in it. No wonder one fought so desperately against being evicted when the nine months' lease was up.

Tod crushed his cigarette. He was hungry and wanted his dinner, also a double Scotch and soda. After he had eaten, he would come back and see how Homer was. If he was still asleep, he would try to wake him. If he couldn't, he might call a doctor.

He took another look at him, then tiptoed out of the cottage, shutting the door carefully.

26

Tod didn't go directly to dinner. He went first to Hodge's saddlery store thinking he might be able to find out something about Earle and through him about Faye. Calvin was standing there with a wrinkled Indian who had long hair held by a bead strap around his forehead. Hanging over the Indian's chest was a sandwich board that read—

TUTTLE'S TRADING POST
for
GENUINE RELICS OF THE OLD WEST
Beads, Silver, Jewelry, Moccasins,
Dolls, Toys, Rare Books, Postcards.
TAKE BACK A SOUVENIR
from
TUTTLE'S TRADING POST

Calvin was always friendly.

"Lo, thar," he called out, when Tod came up.

"Meet the chief," he added, grinning. "Chief Kiss-My-Towkus."

The Indian laughed heartily at the joke.

"You gotta live," he said.

"Earle been around today?" Tod asked.

"Yop. Went by an hour ago."

"We were at a party last night and I ..."

Calvin broke in by hitting his thigh a wallop with the flat of his palm.

"That must've been some shindig to hear Earle tell it. Eh, Skookum?"

"Vas you dere, Sharley?" the Indian agreed, showing the black inside of his mouth, purple tongue and broken orange teeth.

"I heard there was a fight after I left."

Calvin smacked his thigh again.

"Sure musta been. Earle got himself two black eyes, lulus."

"That's what comes of palling up with a dirty greaser," said the Indian excitedly.

He and Calvin got into a long argument about Mexicans. The Indian said that they were all bad. Calvin claimed he had known quite a few good ones in his time. When the Indian cited the case of the Hermanos brothers who had killed a lonely prospector for half a dollar, Calvin countered with a long tale about a man called Tomas Lopez who shared his last pint of water with a stranger when they both were lost in the desert.

Tod tried to get the conversation back to what interested him.

"Mexicans are very good with women," he said.

"Better with horses," said the Indian. "I remember one time along the Brazos, I ..."

Tod tried again.

"They fought over Earle's girl, didn't they?"

"Not to hear him tell it," Calvin said. "He claims it was dough—claims the Mex robbed him while he was sleeping."

"The dirty, thievin' rat," said the Indian, spitting.

"He claims he's all washed up with that bitch," Calvin went on. "Yes, siree, that's his story, to hear him tell it."

Tod had enough.

"So long," he said.

"Glad to meet you," said the Indian.

"Don't take any wooden nickels," Calvin shouted after him.

Tod wondered if she had gone with Miguel. He thought it more likely that she would go back to work for Mrs. Jenning. But either way she would come out all right. Nothing

221

could hurt her. She was like a cork. No matter how rough the sea got, she would go dancing over the same waves that sank iron ships and tore away piers of reinforced concrete. He pictured her riding a tremendous sea. Wave after wave reared its ton on ton of solid water and crashed down only to have her spin gaily away.

When he arrived at Musso Frank's restaurant, he ordered a steak and a double Scotch. The drink came first and he sipped it with his inner eye still on the spinning cork.

It was a very pretty cork, gilt with a glittering fragment of mirror set in its top. The sea in which it danced was beautiful, green in the trough of the waves and silver at their tips. But for all their moondriven power, they could do no more than net the bright cork for a moment in a spume of intricate lace. Finally it was set down on a strange shore where a savage with pork-sausage fingers and a pimpled butt picked it up and hugged it to his sagging belly. Tod recognized the fortunate man; he was one of Mrs. Jenning's customers.

The waiter brought his order and paused with bent back for him to comment. In vain. Tod was far too busy to inspect the steak.

"Satisfactory, sir?" asked the waiter.

Tod waved him away with a gesture more often used on

flies. The waiter disappeared. Tod tried the same gesture on what he felt, but the driving itch refused to go. If only he had the courage to wait for her some night and hit her with a bottle and rape her.

He knew what it would be like lurking in the dark in a vacant lot, waiting for her. Whatever that bird was that sang at night in California would be bursting its heart in theatrical runs and quavers and the chill night air would smell of spice pink. She would drive up, turn the motor off, look up at the stars, so that her breasts reared, then toss her head and sigh. She would throw the ignition keys into her purse and snap it shut, then get out of the car. The long step she took would make her tight dress pull up so that an inch of glowing flesh would show above her black stocking. As he approached carefully, she would be pulling her dress down, smoothing it nicely over her hips.

"Faye, Faye, just a minute," he would call.

"Why, Tod, hello."

She would hold her hand out to him at the end of her long arm that swooped so gracefully to join her curving shoulder.

"You scared me!"

She would look like a deer on the edge of the road when a truck comes unexpectedly around a bend.

He could feel the cold bottle he held behind his back and the forward step he would take to bring ...

"Is there anything wrong with it, sir?"

The fly-like waiter had come back. Tod waved at him, but this time the man continued to hover.

"Perhaps you would like me to take it back, sir?"

"No, no."

"Thank you, sir."

But he didn't leave. He waited to make sure that the customer was really going to eat. Tod picked up his knife and cut a piece. Not until he had also put some boiled potato in his mouth did the man leave.

Tod tried to start the rape going again, but he couldn't feel the bottle as he raised it to strike. He had to give it up.

The waiter came back. Todd looked at the steak. It was a very good one, but he wasn't hungry any more.

"A check, please."

"No dessert, sir?"

"No, thank you, just a check."

"Check it is, sir," the man said brightly as he fumbled for his pad and pencil.

When Tod reached the street, he saw a dozen great violet shafts of light moving across the evening sky in wide crazy sweeps. Whenever one of the fiery columns reached the lowest point of its arc, it lit for a moment the rose-colored domes and delicate minarets of Kahn's Persian Palace Theatre. The purpose of this display was to signal the world premiere of a new picture.

Turning his back on the searchlights, he started in the opposite direction, toward Homer's place. Before he had gone very far, he saw a clock that read a quarter past six and changed his mind about going back just yet. He might as well let the poor fellow sleep for another hour and kill some time by looking at the crowds.

When still a block from the theatre, he saw an enormous electric sign that hung over the middle of the street. In letters ten feet high he read that—

"MR. KAHN A PLEASURE DOME DECREED"

Although it was still several hours before the celebrities would arrive, thousands of people had already gathered.

They stood facing the theatre with their backs toward the gutter in a thick line hundreds of feet long. A big squad of policemen was trying to keep a lane open between the front rank of the crowd and the façade of the theatre.

Tod entered the lane while the policeman guarding it was busy with a woman whose parcel had torn open, dropping oranges all over the place. Another policeman shouted for him to get the hell across the street, but he took a chance and kept going. They had enough to do without chasing him. He noticed how worried they looked and how careful they tried to be. If they had to arrest someone, they joked good-naturedly with the culprit, making light of it until they got him around the corner, then they whaled him with their clubs. Only so long as the man was actually part of the crowd did they have to be gentle.

Tod had walked only a short distance along the narrow lane when he began to get frightened. People shouted, commenting on his hat, his carriage, and his clothing. There was a continuous roar of catcalls, laughter and yells, pierced occasionally by a scream. The scream was usually followed by a sudden movement in the dense mass and part of it would surge forward wherever the police line was weakest. As soon as that part was rammed back, the bulge would pop out somewhere else.

The police force would have to be doubled when the stars started to arrive. At the sight of their heroes and heroines, the crowd would turn demoniac. Some little gesture, either too pleasing or too offensive, would start it moving and then nothing but machine guns would stop it. Individually the purpose of its members might simply to be to get a souvenir, but collectively it would grab and rend.

A young man with a portable microphone was describing the scene. His rapid, hysterical voice was like that of a revivalist preacher whipping his congregation toward the ecstasy of fits.

"What a crowd, folks! What a crowd! There must be ten thousand excited, screaming fans outside Kahn's Persian tonight. The police can't hold them. Here, listen to them roar."

He held the microphone out and those near it obligingly roared for him.

"Did you hear it? It's a bedlam, folks. A veritable bedlam! What excitement! Of all the premières I've attended, this is the most ... the most ... stupendous, folks. Can the police hold them? Can they? It doesn't look so, folks ..."

Another squad of police came charging up. The sergeant pleaded with the announcer to stand further back so the people couldn't hear him. His men threw themselves at the crowd. It allowed itself to be hustled and shoved out of habit and because it lacked an objective. It tolerated the police, just as a bull elephant does when he allows a small boy to drive him with a light stick.

Tod could see very few people who looked tough, nor could he see any working men. The crowd was made up of the lower middle classes, every other person one of his torchbearers.

Just as he came near the end of the lane, it closed in front of him with a heave, and he had to fight his way through. Someone knocked his hat off and when he stooped to pick it up, someone kicked him. He whirled around angrily and found himself surrounded by people who were laughing at him. He knew enough to laugh with them. The crowd became sympathetic. A stout woman slapped him on the back, while a man handed him his hat, first brushing it carefully with his sleeve. Still another man shouted for a way to be cleared.

By a great deal of pushing and squirming, always trying to look as though he were enjoying himself, Tod finally managed to break into the open. After rearranging his clothes, he went over to a parking lot and sat down on the low retaining wall that ran along the front of it.

New groups, whole families, kept arriving. He could see

a change come over them as soon as they had become part of the crowd. Until they reached the line, they looked diffident, almost furtive, but the moment they had become part of it, they turned arrogant and pugnacious. It was a mistake to think them harmless curiosity seekers. They were savage and bitter, especially the middle-aged and the old, and had been made so by boredom and disappointment.

All their lives they had slaved at some kind of dull, heavy labor, behind desks and counters, in the fields and at tedious machines of all sorts, saving their pennies and dreaming of the leisure that would be theirs when they had enough. Finally that day came. They could draw a weekly income of ten or fifteen dollars. Where else should they go but California, the land of sunshine and oranges?

Once there, they discover that sunshine isn't enough. They get tired of oranges, even of avocado pears and passion fruit. Nothing happens. They don't know what to do with their time. They haven't the mental equipment for leisure, the money nor the physical equipment for pleasure. Did they slave so long just to go to an occasional Iowa picnic? What else is there? They watch the waves come in at Venice. There wasn't any ocean where most of them came from, but after you've seen one wave, you've seen them all. The same is true of the airplanes at Glendale. If only a plane would crash once in a while so that they could watch the passengers being consumed in a "holocaust of flame," as the newspapers put it. But the planes never crash.

Their boredom becomes more and more terrible. They realize that they've been tricked and burn with resentment. Every day of their lives they read the newspapers and went to the movies. Both fed them on lynchings, murder, sex crimes, explosions, wrecks, love nests, fires, miracles, revolutions, wars. This daily diet made sophisticates of them. The sun is a joke. Oranges can't titillate their jaded palates. Nothing can ever be violent enough to make taut their slack minds and bodies. They have been cheated and betrayed. They have slaved and saved for nothing.

Tod stood up. During the ten minutes he had been sitting on the wall, the crowd had grown thirty feet and he was afraid that his escape might be cut off if he loitered much longer. He crossed to the other side of the street and started back.

He was trying to figure what to do if he were unable to wake Homer when, suddenly, he saw his head bobbing above the crowd. He hurried toward him. From his appearance, it was evident that there was something definitely wrong.

Homer walked more than ever like a badly made automaton and his features were set in a rigid, mechanical grin. He had his trousers on over his nightgown and part of it hung out of his open fly. In both of his hands were suitcases. With each step, he lurched to one side then the other, using the suitcases for balance weights.

Tod stopped directly in front of him, blocking his way.

"Where're you going?"

"Wayneville," he replied, using an extraordinary amount of jaw movement to get out this single word.

"That's fine. But you can't walk to the station from here. It's in Los Angeles."

Homer tried to get around him, but he caught his arm.

"We'll get a taxi. I'll go with you."

The cabs were all being routed around the block because of the preview. He explained this to Homer and tried to get him to walk to the corner.

"Come on, we're sure to get one on the next street."

Once Tod got him into a cab, he intended to tell the driver to go to the nearest hospital. But Homer wouldn't budge, no matter how hard he yanked and pleaded. People stopped to watch them, others turned their heads curiously. He decided to leave him and get a cab.

"I'll come right back," he said.

He couldn't tell from either Homer's eyes or expression

whether he heard, for they both were empty of everything, even annoyance. At the corner he looked around and saw that Homer had started to cross the street, moving blindly. Brakes screeched and twice he was almost run over, but he didn't swerve or hurry. He moved in a straight diagonal. When he reached the other curb, he tried to get on the sidewalk at a point where the crowd was very thick and was shoved violently back. He made another attempt and this time a policeman grabbed him by the back of the neck and hustled him to the end of the line. When the policeman let go of him, he kept on walking as though nothing had happened.

Tod tried to get over to him, but was unable to cross until the traffic lights changed. When he reached the other side, he found Homer sitting on a bench, fifty or sixty feet from the outskirts of the crowd.

He put his arm around Homer's shoulder and suggested that they walk a few blocks further. When Homer didn't answer, he reached over to pick up one of the valises. Homer held on to it.

"I'll carry it for you," he said, tugging gently.

"Thief!"

Before Homer could repeat the shout, he jumped away. It would be extremely embarrassing if Homer shouted thief in front of a cop. He thought of phoning for an ambulance. But then, after all, how could he be sure that Homer was crazy? He was sitting quietly on the bench, minding his own business.

Tod decided to wait, then try again to get him into a cab. The crowd was growing in size all the time, but it would be at least half an hour before it over-ran the bench. Before that happened, he would think of some plan. He moved a short distance away and stood with his back to a store window so that he could watch Homer without attracting attention.

About ten feet from where Homer was sitting grew a large eucalyptus tree and behind the trunk of the tree was a little boy. Tod saw him peer around it with great caution, then suddenly jerk his head back. A minute later he repeated the maneuver. At first Tod thought he was playing hide and seek, then noticed that he had a string in his hand which was attached to an old purse that lay in front of Homer's bench. Every once in a while the child would jerk the string, making the purse hop like a sluggish toad. Its torn lining hung from its iron mouth like a furry tongue and a few uncertain flies hovered over it.

Tod knew the game the child was playing. He used to play it himself when he was small. If Homer reached to pick up the purse, thinking there was money in it, he would yank it away and scream with laughter.

When Tod went over to the tree, he was surprised to discover that it was Adore Loomis, the kid who lived across the street from Homer. Tod tried to chase him, but he dodged around the tree, thumbing his nose. He gave up and went back to his original position. The moment he left, Adore got busy with his purse again. Homer wasn't paying any attention to the child, so Tod decided to let him alone.

Mrs. Loomis must be somewhere in the crowd, he thought. Tonight when she found Adore, she would give him a hiding. He had torn the pocket of his jacket and his Buster Brown collar was smeared with grease.

Adore had a nasty temper. The completeness with which Homer ignored both him and his pocketbook made him frantic. He gave up dancing it at the end of the string and approached the bench on tiptoes, making ferocious faces, yet ready to run at Homer's first move. He stopped when about four feet away and stuck his tongue out. Homer ignored him. He took another step forward and ran through a series of insulting gestures.

If Tod had known that the boy held a stone in his hand, he would have interfered. But he felt sure that Homer wouldn't hurt the child and was waiting to see if he wouldn't move because of his pestering. When Adore raised his arm, it was too late. The stone hit Homer in the face. The boy turned to flee, but tripped and fell. Before he could scramble away, Homer landed on his back with both feet, then jumped again.

Tod yelled for him to stop and tried to yank him away. He shoved Tod and went on using his heels. Tod hit him as hard as he could, first in the belly, then in the face. He ignored the blows and continued to stamp on the boy. Tod hit him again and again, then threw both arms around him and tried to pull him off. He couldn't budge him. He was like a stone column.

The next thing Tod knew, he was torn loose from Homer and sent to his knees by a blow in the back of the head that spun him sideways. The crowd in front of the theatre had charged. He was surrounded by churning legs and feet. He pulled himself erect by grabbing a man's coat, then let himself be carried along backwards in a long, curving swoop. He saw Homer rise above the mass for a moment, shoved against the sky, his jaw hanging as though he wanted to scream but couldn't. A hand reached up and caught him by his open mouth and pulled him forward and down.

There was another dizzy rush. Tod closed his eyes and fought to keep upright. He was jostled about in a hacking

235

cross surf of shoulders and backs, carried rapidly in one direction and then in the opposite. He kept pushing and hitting out at the people around him, trying to face in the direction he was going. Being carried backwards terrified him.

Using the eucalyptus tree as a landmark, he tried to work toward it by slipping sideways against the tide, pushing hard when carried away from it and riding the current when it moved toward his objective. He was within only a few feet of the tree when a sudden, driving rush carried him far past it. He struggled desperately for a moment, then gave up and let himself be swept along. He was the spearhead of a flying wedge when it collided with a mass going in the opposite direction. The impact turned him around. As the two forces ground against each other, he was turned again and again, like a grain between millstones. This didn't stop until he became part of the opposing force. The pressure continued to increase until he thought he must collapse. He was slowly pushed into the air. Although relief for his cracking ribs could be gotten by continuing to rise, he fought to keep his feet on the ground. Not being able to touch was an even more dreadful sensation than being carried backwards.

There was another rush, shorter this time, and he found himself in a dead spot where the pressure was less and equal. He became conscious of a terrible pain in his left leg, just above the ankle, and tried to work it into a more comfortable position. He couldn't turn his body, but managed to get his head around. A very skinny boy, wearing a Western Union cap, had his back wedged against his shoulder. The pain continued to grow and his whole leg as high as the groin throbbed. He finally got his left arm free and took the back of the boy's neck in his fingers. He twisted as hard as he could. The boy began to jump up and down in his clothes. He managed to straighten his elbow, by pushing at the back of the boy's head, and so turn half way around and free his leg. The pain didn't grow less.

There was another wild surge forward that ended in another dead spot. He now faced a young girl who was sobbing steadily. Her silk print dress had been torn down the front and her tiny brassiere hung from one strap. He tried by pressing back to give her room, but she moved with him every time he moved. Now and then, she would jerk violently and he wondered if she was going to have a fit. One of her thighs was between his legs. He struggled to get free of her, but she clung to him, moving with him and pressing against him.

She turned her head and said, "Stop, stop," to someone behind her.

He saw what the trouble was. An old man, wearing a Panama hat and horn-rimmed glasses, was hugging her. He had one of his hands inside her dress and was biting her neck.

Tod freed his right arm with a heave, reached over the girl and brought his fist down on the man's head. He couldn't hit very hard but managed to knock the man's hat off, also his glasses. The man tried to bury his face in the girl's shoulder, but Tod grabbed one of his ears and yanked. They started to move again. Tod held on to the ear as long as he could, hoping that it would come away in his hand. The girl managed to twist under his arm. A piece of her dress tore, but she was free of her attacker.

Another spasm passed through the mob and he was carried toward the curb. He fought toward a lamp-post, but he was swept by before he could grasp it. He saw another man catch the girl with the torn dress. She screamed for help. He tried to get to her, but was carried in the opposite direction. This rush also ended in a dead spot. Here his neighbors were all shorter than he was. He turned his head upward toward the sky and tried to pull some fresh air into his aching lungs, but it was all heavily tainted with sweat.

In this part of the mob no one was hysterical. In fact,

most of the people seemed to be enjoying themselves. Near him was a stout woman with a man pressing hard against her from in front. His chin was on her shoulder, and his arms were around her. She paid no attention to him and went on talking to the woman at her side.

"The first thing I knew," Tod heard her say, "there was a rush and I was in the middle."

"Yeah. Somebody hollered, 'Here comes Gary Cooper,' and then wham!"

"That ain't it," said a little man wearing a cloth cap and pullover sweater. "This is a riot you're in."

"Yeah," said a third woman, whose snaky gray hair was hanging over her face and shoulders. "A pervert attacked a child."

"He ought to be lynched."

Everybody agreed vehemently.

"I come from St. Louis," announced the stout woman, "and we had one of them pervert fellers in our neighborhood once. He ripped up a girl with a pair of scissors."

"He must have been crazy," said the man in the cap. "What kind of fun is that?"

Everybody laughed. The stout woman spoke to the man who was hugging her.

"Hey, you," she said. "I ain't no pillow."

The man smiled beatifically but didn't move. She laughed, making no effort to get out of his embrace.

"A fresh guy," she said.

The other woman laughed.

"Yeah," she said, "this is a regular free-for-all."

The man in the cap and sweater thought there was another laugh in his comment about the pervert.

"Ripping up a girl with scissors. That's the wrong tool."

He was right. They laughed even louder than the first time.

"You'd a done it different, eh, kid?" said a young man with a kidney-shaped head and waxed mustaches.

The two women laughed. This encouraged the man in the cap and he reached over and pinched the stout woman's friend. She squealed.

"Lay off that," she said good-naturedly.

"I was shoved," he said.

An ambulance siren screamed in the street. Its wailing moan started the crowd moving again and Tod was carried along in a slow, steady push. He closed his eyes and tried to protect his throbbing leg. This time, when the movement ended, he found himself with his back to the theatre wall. He kept his eyes closed and stood on his good leg. After what seemed like hours, the pack began to loosen and move again with a churning motion. It gathered momentum and rushed. He rode it until he was slammed against the base of an iron rail which fenced the driveway of the theatre from the street. He had the wind knocked out of him by the impact, but managed to cling to the rail. He held on desperately, fighting to keep from being sucked back. A woman caught him around the waist and tried to hang on. She was sobbing rhythmically. Tod felt his fingers slipping from the rail and kicked backwards as hard as he could. The woman let go.

Despite the agony in his leg, he was able to think clearly about his picture, "The Burning of Los Angeles." After his quarrel with Faye, he had worked on it continually to escape tormenting himself, and the way to it in his mind had become almost automatic.

As he stood on his good leg, clinging desperately to the iron rail, he could see all the rough charcoal strokes with which he had blocked it out on the big canvas. Across the top, parallel with the frame, he had drawn the burning city, a great bonfire of architectural styles, ranging from Egyptian to Cape Cod colonial. Through the center, winding from left to right, was a long hill street and down it, spilling into the middle foreground, came the mob carrying baseball bats and torches. For the faces of its members, he was using the innumerable sketches he had made of the people who come to California to die; the cultists of all sorts, economic as well as religious, the wave, airplane, funeral and preview watchers—all those poor devils who can only be stirred by the promise of miracles and then only to violence. A super "Dr. Know-All Pierce-All" had made the necessary promise and they were marching behind his banner in a great united front of screwballs and screwboxes to purify the land. No longer bored, they sang and danced joyously in the red light of the flames.

In the lower foreground, men and women fled wildly before the vanguard of the crusading mob. Among them were Faye, Harry, Homer, Claude and himself. Faye ran proudly, throwing her knees high. Harry stumbled along behind her, holding on to his beloved derby hat with both hands. Homer seemed to be falling out of the canvas, his face half-asleep, his big hands clawing the air in anguished pantomime. Claude turned his head as he ran to thumb his nose at his pursuers. Tod himself picked up a small stone to throw before continuing his flight.

He had almost forgotten both his leg and his predicament, and to make his escape still more complete he stood on a chair and worked at the flames in an upper corner of the canvas, modeling the tongues of fire so that they licked even more avidly at a corinthian column that held up the palmleaf roof of a nutburger stand.

He had finished one flame and was starting on another when he was brought back by someone shouting in his ear. He opened his eyes and saw a policeman trying to reach him from behind the rail to which he was clinging. He let go with his left hand and raised his arm. The policeman caught him by the wrist, but couldn't lift him. Tod was afraid to let go until another man came to aid the policeman and caught him by the back of his jacket. He let go of the rail and they hauled him up and over it.

When they saw that he couldn't stand, they let him down easily to the ground. He was in the theatre driveway. On the curb next to him sat a woman crying into her skirt. Along the wall were groups of other disheveled people. At the end of the driveway was an ambulance. A policeman asked him if he wanted to go to the hospital. He shook his head no. He then offered him a lift home. Tod had the presence of mind to give Claude's address.

He was carried through the exit to the back street and lifted into a police car. The siren began to scream and at first he thought he was making the noise himself. He felt his lips with his hands. They were clamped tight. He knew then it was the siren. For some reason this made him laugh and he began to imitate the siren as loud as he could.